Strength from Sorrow

ALSO BY YANG GUIJA

Gwimeogeori Sae
(The Deaf Bird)
1985

Babilon gangga-eso
(By the Rivers of Babylon)
1985

Wonmi-dong saramdeul
(The Neighbors in Wonmi District)
1987

Huimang
(Hope)
1991

Na-neun somang-handa nae-ge geumji-doen geoseul
(I Desire the Forbidden)
1992

Cheonnyeon-ui sarang
(Love for a Thousand Years)
1995

Mosun
(Contradicton)
1998

Yang Guija

Strength from Sorrow

Translated by Youngju Ryu

Cross-Cultural Communications
Merrick, New York
2005

**This book is published with the support of
the Korea Literature Translation Institute
in commemoration of Korea being the Guest of Honor
at the Frankfurt Book Fair 2005.**

The publisher is grateful to the KLTI for its support
and to the New York State Council on the Arts
and the National Endowment for the Arts
whose past seed grants, in part, have contributed
to making this publication possible.

Special thanks to Myunghee Kim
for her invaluable advice and assistance
in arranging for the publication rights.

Published in the United States by
Cross-Cultural Communications
239 Wynsum Avenue, Merrick, NY 11566-4725/U.S.A.
Tel: (516) 868-5635 / Fax: (516) 379-1901
E-mail: cccpoetry@aol.com
www.cross-culturalcommunications.com

ISBN 0-89304-739-2
ISBN 0-89304-740-6 (pbk.)

Photograph by Hwang Heonman

Art and Book Design by Tchouki
Hardcover binding by Frank Papp
Printed in Bulgaria

Contents

Mountain Flowers

The car slowed down noticeably just past Euijeongbu, where a road expansion project was under way. Bak, who was the driver, guide, and managing director of the agency, all in one, took the opportunity to light a cigarette. Bak looked youthful—he doubted that the young man was thirty yet—but his face was plastered with a layer of fatigue like dirt. Perhaps Bak's earlier comment that he now made this trip back and forth from Seoul at least two and as many as four times a day was still influencing him. He read immeasurable gloom in Bak's deep-set eyes reddened by the cigarette smoke. The freckles that were spreading like liver spots across his sun-greased face didn't bode too well, either.

The chilling thought that life and death were one and the same was constantly on his mind these days, now that he was frequently coming into contact with people who made a living selling plots of land for burying the dead. How many weeks had it been already? He tried to count in his head as he reached for his own pack of cigarettes. This was the fourth Sunday, which meant that a month had passed since he began this pilgrimage. As a working man, he could get away from the city only on Sundays. Still, he wanted to take his time looking. If it were up to him, he would have sacrificed his Sundays for months to come and combed all the different mountains. He found it impossible to snuff out the lingering thought that the perfect spot was waiting to be discovered somewhere that his feet hadn't yet reached. What fed that thought was his guilty conscience: The grave relocation had to be rushed, now that the city of Daegu was settled on the date. Heckled by the business called living, he had let his father lie in a public cemetery all these years.

The thought that his father's remains should be moved north was always in the back of his mind, like a callus. Daegu wasn't his family's home to begin with, and none of them lived there any- more It was just one of the places where his father had tried to build a foundation for living after coming down south all alone. So for fifteen years, his father had been lying in a place that had never held any meaning for him. He meant to have his father moved as soon as he had a bit of leeway, but there never was that leeway. He lived his life on a shoestring. After somehow getting through school and barely managing to land a job, he got married, and the only thing from that point on that increased steadily in his life was the number of people who depended on him. That bit of leeway he was looking for was always that much ahead in the future, and the future was anything but secure. Everyday was a mad dash to survive. While his harried life as a resident of Seoul was taking him from Sangdo-dong to Dapsimni, from Dapsimni to Gocheok-dong, and from Gocheok-dong to Gaebong-dong, his father endured fifteen long years, alone.

The date the city of Daegu settled on for the removal of the remains from the cemetery was a hairbreadth away. For some years, there had been talk of building a factory complex on the cemetery site, but he said to himself that the project was bound to be delayed for at least another couple of years. Then he received the notice that the construction date was set. Contrary to what he expected, he actually felt a sense of relief. Now he couldn't procrastinate any longer. He knew that it would be impossible to allow himself such a thing as leeway unless the authorities were on his back. When he started looking around for a new grave site, however, he felt the anxiety return. He hadn't realized that there were so many dead people in the world and so many more waiting to die. Cemeteries were full everywhere, and the available options were far from ideal.

The various cemetery managers that he talked to over the weeks told him that once the grave site is decided, the numerous procedures necessary for relocation would only take a day or two. The older the remains, the simpler the process would be; naturally, bones were easier to move than a half-decomposed body. A regular box, something the size of a milk crate, will do the job nicely, they said. It seemed that people in the business of burying the dead found everything a piece of cake. As in a factory production line, the whole process from death to interment was divided up into specific tasks, which made it possible for several "clients" to be "guided" to their final resting place in the course of a single day. Is anything difficult when there is money to be made? Nonetheless, the sight of death specialists treating the whole process with levity, spitting at will and cursing freely while handling the business of death as if it were mere pebbles to play jacks with, left a bad taste in his mouth. Everywhere he went, whether he met them in the city's backstreets or in cemeteries high up in the mountains, these experts had the same attitude. He didn't want to be difficult and to insist on his incomprehension. After all, what was the purpose of life if not to understand what seems incomprehensible? Still, he remembered how, during those moments in his life when he wanted to be anywhere but where he was, the possibility of dying would offer him consolation, wretched though it might be. The irreverent way these people worked wounded his heart for having ever drawn such consolation from death.

In that regard, Bak was a respectful individual. The head of the agency, who emphasized the excellent choice of land he would have since the agency's cemetery permit was only a few days old, had introduced Bak as his wife's younger brother. The two brothers-in-law were both younger than he. At first, he was disconcerted by the fact that such young people were handling death as a matter of daily routine, but he liked their straightforward and even-handed way of doing business. If it hadn't been for them, he would be on a bus to some place far outside the city looking for a broker who parcels out hillocks for a price. The search for something in or very near Seoul was pretty much over. Either the transportation was bad, or the plot wasn't any good. If both were acceptable, cost proved to be prohibitive.

Gangwon Province? Gyeonggi Province? He widened the search and hit the road every Sunday, following up on newspaper ads and introductions by friends. He visited a number of what they called "cemetery parks" as well. Even though these tended to be quite a ways from Seoul, the trip wasn't too strenuous because they usually provided their own transportation. A cemetery park was an upgraded version of a cemetery; instead of traditional round mounds that he associated with the word "grave," the souls of the dead were laid in orderly, sectioned plots. Spreading a mat and sitting down anywhere in the green, one could almost fool oneself that this was a pleasure outing. The season happened to be spring. New blades of green could be seen among the yellow grass. Pointy buds were like daubs of paint on every branch. He always took care not to step on the new sprouts. But right behind these buds, he saw heavy machinery in the process of lopping off the hill for the cemetery's expansion. The red dirt of the hill's inner flesh, exposed by the heavy machinery, made him feel awkward.

"After they expand the road between Euijeongbu and Pocheon, the transportation will be very good," Bak said, turning to look at him as they passed the sign that read, "Downtown Pocheon 4km." Little girls gathering mugwort leaves on the sunny side of the road waved their hands automatically at their car. Even though the car was quite a ways north of Seoul, forsythias by the walls were already in bloom and the blossoms were heavy with dust. It was always like that by the older national roads Dust-covered shopfronts and slate roofs of houses, identical in their shabbiness, flitted past at regular intervals outside the car window. And behind every village rose a mountain slope. The mountain, at least, looked fresh. A mountain was a mountain, especially in the season of budding leaves. For a moment, he wondered whether the buds would be covered in dust, too.

They passed through the downtown and got on the national road again. A blear-eyed dog barked distractedly as they made a left turn. "Prefecture of Changsu" read the sign about a hundred meters ahead. Bak finished the turn, then killed the ignition.

"You know that they make the most amazing *makkeoli* here."

Bak got out of the car and went into a small roadside store, then emerged with a bag containing a plastic bottle of milky *makkeoli* and what looked to be a bag of fish jerky or some such edible in his hand.

"It's all mountain roads from here. There'll be no stores around. This should taste even better up in the hills."

After a pause he asked, "Do you drink?"

"Of course. It's the drinking that gets me through some days."

He answered without thinking, and realized only afterwards how true it was. Days of near suffocation, snares that creep up on him everywhere in the city, family life that scrapes along like an old machine with loose screws. Alcohol lubricated human relations too, the maliciousness of which he thought he would never get used to. No matter how hard he worked, life was at a standstill, but the number of traps he had to be wary of increased everyday. Falling into one of these would turn all of his hard effort into dust. Success or good life had nothing to do with the orderly sequence of time. All that mattered was who had a better technique in avoiding the traps and neutralizing the landmines. He looked out at the verdure glued to the window on both sides of him. The car jerked along the unpaved road, shaking him along with the bottle of Pocheon *makkeoli*, and for no reason at all, he felt serene.

"You know, I'm thirty years old. Would you believe me if I said I've been driving for fifteen years?" Bak made the sound of falling pebbles as he laughed to himself. Thirty years old. That meant Bak was six years younger than he. What was he doing at thirty, he asked himself. Was he living in Dapsimni? If so, he was a newlywed then. He remembered his house in Dapsimni. The small kitchen had a low shelf spanning its entire width, and his mother and his young bride bumped their heads on it constantly. The old woman's bruises took a long time to go away and the young woman's disappeared quickly, but what remained the longest was the dull ache in his heart, the self-recrimination that he wasn't able to afford a more comfortable situation for his family. How did someone like Mr. Kim, the section chief at his company who loved to laugh at jokes, spend his thirtieth year? He suddenly wondered. What was it like for the people he stands next to everyday in subways or on buses? How about the countless souls laid up in tidy rows in all those cemetery parks....

Bak interrupted the chain of his thoughts. "I ran away from home at fifteen and started working as an assistant truck driver. Then I drove a truck of my own for many years and eventually started driving a hearse. I drove ambulances, too, for a while. Now I'm a graveyard guide. I guess one thing led to another. Transporting goods and transporting corpses aren't too different, if you really think about it. But moving corpses is easier on your body and kinder on your wallet."

That, apparently, was the reason why Bak's brother-in-law had jumped into the graveyard business. Unlike cemetery parks, Bak's company only asked him for the price of the land and maintenance fee for five years. Through his recently acquired experience, he was now a bit of an expert on the going price per square foot for burial plots. Where the land's development was restricted by the government, land prices were all the same. The difference was not in the value of the land but in what they called "facilities fees." Most cemetery parks charged fees that equaled or exceeded the per-square-foot price of the plot of land one bought. The money went into such things as paving the road leading into the park, arranging the graves, setting up the drainage system or building an embankment. Higher facilities fees meant that more artificial services were added, so that the natural beauty of the place became significantly reduced. Since Bak's company didn't charge any facilities fees, they were only selling the plot of land. In other words, the land in its natural state would receive the corpse.

Earlier that morning, at their first meeting, Bak and his brother-in-law explained to him repeatedly the advantages of the mountain in its natural state. They spoke at length about how much more comforting it is for the deceased to be buried in soil that allows natural draining, and about the superiority of natural embankments that old trees create. Why would anyone choose a place that piles one grave on top of another, they asked, if a mountain plot with loamy soil and an open vista in front were an option? To be sure, there were luxury highrises and low-income projects in graveyards as in apartments, but Pocheon Burial Ground, they said, was in a different league altogether. It was not an apartment at all, but a house with a big front yard.

The dead cannot choose their resting place, it was true. But what would his father have chosen? This was the question he asked himself whenever he went to look at a potential burial site. What would his father have done, a man who failed to become an urbanite even after repeated forays into different cities? His father used to say that it was only on account of him, his only son, that he had anything to fear in this world. He didn't remember his father saying that about his sisters. He realized only much later that this was not a declaration of fearlessness.

In fact, it was a declaration of precisely the opposite. His father shrank before the world and feared the people in it.

Listening to their explanation, he finally understood the reason why he hadn't been able to sign for a plot even after looking at so many different cemetery parks. It wasn't that he wanted to save a few bucks on facilities fees, maintenance fees, et cetera. He was willing to take out a loan, if it came to that. It was the artificiality of these cemetery parks which had made him hesitate, the clichéd layout that took the city's customs wholesale and imposed them on the dead. Even after delighting in the freshness of green leaves and nameless flowers that covered the grounds, something in him bucked at the sight of grave mounds standing at attention in immaculate rows. He seemed to hear a voice then. *This is not your father's place....*

At last, the first village of Changsu Prefecture shimmered silver in the distance. Bak drove past the entrance to the village and took a right onto an even narrower road, which winded along and barely admitted the slow ascent of a single car. The ground was muddy with the spring thaw, and the car crawled along at a snail's pace.

"We're in the middle of a construction here. We'll have the road widened at least a meter and leveled nicely by the harvest holidays. The ground is nice and solid, so you don't have to worry about getting your wheels stuck even when it rains."

Bak was right. The earth was fine and loamy like powdered rice. If the top layer were turned over, black and rich soil would be sure to surface.

The car climbed up the road almost to the top of the slope. Below them spread a valley and a gentle ridgeline; it seemed to him that the forest right outside the window would be soft to the touch, like a plush green fabric. The dusty air which never once left the tip of his nose for the nearly two hours they had been riding disappeared for the first time here in the mountains. In its place wafted the scent of a nameless plant and swept his mind clean. He had expected as much, but it was still astonishing to realize how different the mountain air was from the city's. The air here was different also from the air in the hills he climbed last week on neatly leveled roads. Looking at the bared flesh of red dirt and stumpy roadside trees covered in dust, he had felt absolutely nothing then.

True to his word that he has been driving for fifteen years, Bak handled the car masterfully. He knew the road like the back of his hand, and made the ride relatively smooth, avoiding all the bumps and depressions on the road. His confident driving shined all the more on the difficult mountain path. He seemed to realize it, too. Supple energy flowed through Bak's body.

Was such energy contagious? The greenery covering the far ridgeline cooled his weary eyes. He sat up with his hands clasped in front of him and imagined that the green outside was tinting his face, too. They rode along, absolutely elated. The pebbles shouted out from under the wheels, accompanying them with the softening rhythm of percussion instruments. And all the while, the mountain waited for them, silently.

The car stopped. They were almost at the top. Here and there, azaleas bloomed in bright, unassuming hues. Bak got out of the car and almost pranced down the pathless slope, and he followed the guide, ignoring the distressed toes squeezed inside his dress shoes. His pace was slower because he was trying not to step on budding sprouts. After a little while, they came to an open clearing. He saw dirt mounds not yet covered with grass—one, two, three. The sunny clearing, which faced south, was invisible from the road. He wondered how such a place could lodge hidden from view on a mountain slope.

"So here we are. You can use this plot right here. You see how the view is wide open in the front? It's a bit too big for one grave, but the price won't be a burden at all."

He walked over and stood on the spot Bak indicated. A cloud hung on a distant ridge. Below him spread a sea of trees. Not even a single peak obstructed the front view. Valleys lay unsullied below, drenched in sunlight, and the wind was as sweet as could be. Because the clearing faced south, the sun would shine on it from daybreak to sundown. From experience, he knew what a great blessing it was to be able to bask in sunlight.

In poor households, the useful sunlight through the south window was a lifesaver. Since rented units were usually in the rear or on the opposite side of the main complex, natural light was always a premium. His apartment now, which had finally made him a homeowner a few short years ago—faced east at a slant, and the sun only streamed in during the morning hours. Without the right amount of sun at right times of the day, his mother complained that she couldn't maintain her clay jars of pickles, not to mention dry vegetables or fish. His wife also prized sunlight. She scowled at the stout build of the neighboring houses that stood in the way of her sun and fretted about the dampness of the children's clothes. Spending all day locked up in an office, breathing in the putrid air and greed-streaked exhalations of his own and of others, he shared the women's feelings about sunlight. It warmed his heart to think that his father's final resting place would be on the sunny side of the hills.

"With the adjacent plot, this place comes to about five hundred and seventy square feet total. Your mother can also rest here when the time comes...."

He had been thinking precisely the same thing. How nice it would be if his father and mother could look out onto the vista below together! Free as a pair of birds, they can climb the peaks that undulate like seawaves in the distance and visit the home they left behind in the north. Will Father like it here? What would Mother say? As these thoughts coursed through his mind, the green of the untouched ridgeline grew more and more beautiful to behold.

"Let's sit down right here. We can't forget the *makkeoli*."

The plastic bag dangling from Bak's hand drew him out of his reverie. They plopped down on the grass and began drinking the region's famed *makkeoli*. It was simple yet savory, and too good to drink out of a small paper cup. Bak took care not to spill even a drop as he poured, and he received the cup with just as much care before emptying it with pleasure. As they drank, a nameless bird sang from afar and mountain flowers surrendered their gauzy petals to the wind.

"Isn't it strange? I come here several times everyday but I never get tired of it. My chest opens up when I sit here like this. When things get really irritating at the office, I wait, hoping for an excuse to come out here. A lot of people have come by to see the place but they are reluctant to buy it. I guess it's too far away for them."

He looked closely at Bak, realizing that the man's bronzed face was casting off its skin. With the warm spring sun raining down on them, Bak poured him another cup of *makkeoli*, and he saw that Bak's extended hand was covered with calluses. Fifteen years ago, his father entered the cold ground and a young man climbed onto the assistant seat of a truck and embarked on a life filled with hardship. That young man now sat next to him, shredding pieces of fish jerky. "I've tried this and that, but I confess this line of business suits me just fine," Bak remarked. "The dead don't talk. People pick on you and never stop their whining, but you do business for the dead and they leave you alone."

He thought Bak would press him to sign the contract, but he didn't. After setting the strips of fish jerky in front of him, Bak sat silently, gazing out into the distance. Then and there, he made up his mind to buy the entire five hundred and seventy square feet. With that decision made, he was able to drink the cups of *makkeoli* that Bak offered him in ease.

When was the last time he had *makkeoli?* He often got drunk in pubs on the way home from office, but only on beer or *soju*. Dragging himself home, he would be sodden with drink but he never felt like singing anymore. Some wise person once said that even if you were to soak your entire body in alcohol, you had to make sure to leave out three inches. Those three inches were the tongue, lest you reveal the hidden thoughts in your heart. Maybe that was the reason why there was something doleful about drunken revelry that stays within the proper bounds. Coming home with a red face, you washed your hands and feet before stumbling to bed, which left you with nothing but nausea. Everything one did to survive led to nausea in the end. When you lay there on your bed facing the wall, the future was as inscrutable as ever and you were saddened by your own body hanging limp like a withered tree.

"You couldn't have picked a better time. Cover the mound with grass and it will be the greenest ever. Plant a couple of trees around the grave, and they'll take root right away. In weather like this, put a stick in the ground and it will sprout leaves."

Bak's words made him think of his daughter, who once planted touch-me-not seeds and spent everyday in eager waiting for them to bud. There was a bit of green thumb in his family's genes. His mother was also given to bemoaning the fact that a perfectly good patch of land in front of the apartment building was left to lie idle.

In the depths of these mountains, with no one to tend them, azaleas in bloom gave a pleasant blush to the hills. He looked around in fresh appreciation, remembering that the azaleas is one of the few plants that flower before sprouting leaves. They were sitting right next to blooming azaleas. He plucked a blossom and popped it into his mouth. Bak did the same.

"You know, it's strange. You can't transplant azaleas. My wife loves flowers, so I transplanted a couple in my backyard; but they just withered away. I tried again a few times, but it was the same story. I guess they are mountain flowers meant only for the hills."

Was it really so? Now that he stopped to think about it, he didn't remember seeing azaleas on the streets. Rhododendrons, yes, but not azaleas. He had heard of forsythias by the walls, but azaleas by the walls had a strangely plaintive ring to it.

Flowers meant only for the hills. Flowers that can't take root anywhere but in the mountains. He walked up close to some azaleas. Five-petaled blossoms hung in clusters of two or three from the ends of the branches. As delicate as rice paper, the petals filled him with sadness, a touch of pity. They looked ready to shed sap-like tears at the tiniest sound, the smallest movement from him.

He reached out to touch a petal, then drew his hand back. An ant was wandering lost on the back of his hand. Carefully, he picked up the ant and put it down on the ground. It started crawling busily toward some unknown destination. He looked at the moving ant, then at the azaleas. They seemed to be looking fixedly back at him.

Bak filled the last cup to the brim and handed it to him. Bak was restraining himself from drinking since he knew that he had a long drive ahead of him, some of it through very windy roads. He, on the other hand, emptied the cup and took a long, slow look around the place where he would bring his father to rest, and later his mother. It was getting late in the afternoon, but the light was still falling evenly. The fine soil was neither too clayey nor too muddy, and among the weeds that had made their way through it, he could see wildflowers the size of his fingernails. In the faint trace of a wind that hovered around his head, he heard the mountain's soft, echo-like breathing.

It was past time to go, but he didn't hurry. He wanted to stay here as long as he could. Knowing that he'll have to return to the city soon and breathe its viscose dust again made that desire all the sharper. In silence, he stared at the flowers that dwell only in the mountains. Bak was sitting with his knees to his chest and looking at the ridgeline extending far into the distance. Bak then blurted out a question, out of the blue.

"Just great, isn't it?"

The Road to Cheonma Tomb

The child was sleeping so soundly, Jeong didn't have the heart to wake her. Shortly after the departure, a Chinese action movie had begun playing on the monitor, and she had insisted on keeping her earphones on through the violent and outrageous sequences that filled the screen from start to finish, drifting off to sleep only after the movie ended. Other passengers on the bus seemed to relish the nonstop succession of suspenseful moments, too: a warrior spewing blood as he fell to his death every five minutes, gangs closing in on the main character again and again. On the morning bus, not too many passengers were asleep. People champed hamburgers or popped pieces of tangerines into their mouths as they watched.

His wife was also asleep, her head against the window. She had every reason to be tired. After staying up late to pack for the trip, she had gotten up early to prepare breakfast. Still, all the way past Daejeon, she responded to every fleeting landscape with a face full of animation. At a rest stop in Chupungnyeong, she even talked him into taking repeated shots of her with their daughter striking the "ideal" pose—shoulders at a slight angle, lips arrested in the act of pronouncing "kimchee." To capture them in the view box, whole from head to foot, he had to stand at a considerable distance. He hated pictures that lopped off people's feet or lower body altogether. "I won't take a picture like that" was his position. His wife stopped him several times in the act, now to rub the

23

child's eyes, now to set her hair ribbon straight, now to sweep back her stray hairs, even though the little cruds around the child's eyes would not be visible from this distance.

They were past Waegwan when his wife finally closed her eyes. He was the only one who stayed awake to the end; he nudged his family awake when the driver's assistant picked up her mike. En route to the main terminal in Daegu, buses often made a brief stop at "West Daegu" for passengers' convenience. His family had to pay for this convenience by having to squint at the sudden onrush of light as they got off the bus at the corner of a busy intersection.

There was no need to think twice about what to do next. He had gone over the itinerary several times before leaving Seoul, and the first item of business was to take a taxi and rush over to Seongseo District 1 Office. He had thought that this would be simple enough. After more than a decade away from the city, he didn't expect to find Daegu unchanged, but he was confident that he would still have his bearings. He couldn't have been more wrong. With its gray buildings, labyrinthine network of signs, and speeding cars, Daegu was no different from the city they had left several hours ago. And it was proving just as difficult to flag down a cab. The child was sulky because she wasn't fully awake, and his wife kept on knitting her eyebrows against the spring sun. Hating himself for being so terrible at hailing cabs, he jumped into the traffic. The trip was just beginning, and it was already too much for him.

He wanted to be brave. This was the first long-distance trip he was taking with his wife and daughter, and this city had once been his home. Their faith in him would make them want to have faith in the city too, and he didn't want to spoil that faith. After flailing about some more with the heavy knapsack strapped across his shoulder, he finally managed to get his family into a navy blue taxicab driven by a man with a long mustache. Inside the moving vehicle, he daubed his sweaty forehead with a handkerchief. The back of his shirt was drenched with sweat as well, but he pretended it didn't bother him. I must be nervous, he thought.

Seongseo District 1 Office came into sight a few minutes after the car forked right from the road leading to the municipal cemetery. The taxi came to a halt by the narrow path to District Office. They took their time getting out of the car because the child had fallen asleep again, but the driver couldn't wait. His wife still leaned over the backseat trying to pick up the daughter's pink hat and nearly fell back when the car started moving without warning. He put his knapsack down and grabbed the front handle angrily, but the car slipped away like a sudsy bar of soap and sped out of his reach. All he could do to express his anger at the impatient driver was to glare at the disappearing car. He wished that the family trip could proceed a little, just a little more smoothly, as he walked toward District Office in silence. His wife scolded the child as she put the hat back on the child's head. See, didn't I tell you to get plenty of sleep on the bus....

District Office was a single-story structure made of wood. They went into the civil affairs office, and he put his knapsack down on the long wooden bench against the wall. He then went up to the window with a sign that said, "4. Miscellaneous." Although there were many windows, only two clerks were working, and five or six people stood in line ahead of him. When his turn came, the woman behind Window 4 peeked at him over her glasses and held her hand out, as if to say, "Gimme what you got." He gave her the entire envelope containing documents.

"What can I help you with?" she asked, without bothering to open the envelope.

"We moved our father's grave from the municipal cemetery...."

The woman peered at him again over her glasses.

"You're here for the compensation?"

He did not answer.

"Step aside and wait, please."

With expert skill, she stamped several different stamps on the front and back of the paper she had been fingering. A man went up to take the piece of paper splattered with stamps, left some change on the counter for the processing fee, and went on his way. Another man went up to the window and began telling his story in a pleading tone, holding a crumpled-up New Village cap in his hands. It was obvious that things took time to get done around here. He decided that he had more than enough time for a smoke and sat down on the bench to light up a cigarette.

Even though Seongseo District 1 was within the jurisdiction of Daegu, a city big enough to have an administration independent of provincial control, it was still a rural town consisting of not much more than rice paddies, vegetable fields, and hillocks. Eighteen years ago when the family was deciding where to bury his father, no one guessed that Seongseo would one day be incorporated into the city of Daegu. Early as it was, they did foresee that with the city expanding, cemeteries on its outskirts would soon have to be moved. To avoid the trouble of having to relocate the grave, they decided on a cemetery far away from the city on purpose. Seongseo was that faraway place. Several years ago, however, his mother came back from a visit to Daegu with a report of rumors that Seongseo may become the seat of a new factory complex. He was concerned at first, but forgot all about it when he heard of no new developments for the next couple of years. Then suddenly last fall, his younger sister contacted him urgently after a visit to the cemetery. She now lived in nearby Gumi with her husband, and visited the father's grave from time to time and tipped the groundskeeper whenever she did. The groundskeeper had told her that a public notice had gone out several times already regarding the grave relocation and families contacted individually at the telephone number on file. As for himself, he had not gone back once since leaving Daegu. Neither did his mother, though she visited her daughter in Gumi frequently enough. Caring for the grave of the dead was trouble wasted as far as she was concerned.

The clerk called out his name. She held in her hand the Declaration of Grave Relocation form, which he first obtained a month ago when his father's grave was dug up. At the bottom of the form was probably a line that read: "In pursuance with article 5, section 2 of provisions concerning burials and graves, I hereby certify that the above has been declared." At the time of disinterment, he had also received a few other forms that needed to be filled out before he could claim the compensation. The reason why he wasn't able to complete the whole process right then was because of the two photographs required by the provision regarding grave relocation: a photograph of the grave before the relocation and another of the hole in the ground after the remains have been removed. He had taken the pictures but couldn't wait around in Daegu for the film to develop. In Seoul, his family was waiting for him to arrive with the coffin. He didn't have a moment to waste since both the disinterment and the reinterment had to be completed that day.

"Did you bring the photographs?"

He handed her the photographs.

"You need two guarantors. Have them endorse the form and you can claim the money at County Office."

He had no idea that the process required two guarantors. He was beginning to get angry: The city was jerking him around. They hadn't consulted him about whether the grave should be moved. They certainly hadn't consulted him about how much the compensation should be. And now they wanted him to have not one, but two people vouch for him for the pitiful sum to which he was entitled.

"Is that really necessary?" Irritation crept into his voice, and the clerk reacted to it immediately.

"All they have to do is write in their resident registration numbers and stamp the form with their personal seals. Can't you get two people to do that for you?"

Coming up behind him unawares, his wife gazed over his shoulder at the guarantor form with a troubled look on her face.

"What do we do? It'd be a different story in Seoul, but how can we find people to vouch for us here?"

His wife, who knew intimately the limited nature of her husband's sphere of action, was the first to despair. Even if there were old acquaintances in Daegu whose contact information he could fish up somehow, he couldn't very well call them for the first time in many years and ask them to vouch for him out of the blue. She knew her husband was not the sort of man who could do that, especially for a tiny sum of money given as compensation for digging up his father's grave. She also knew that her husband would find it a hundred times easier to forgo the money altogether than to make an embarrassing request. The compensation was no more than hundred sixty thousand *won*.[1]

He decided to try his luck at County Office, come what may. With his dependents in tow, he trudged along some distance to a major intersection. It occurred to him that it might be even more difficult than before to hail a cab. Along the eight-lane boulevard, cars zipped by at speeds surely above a hundred kilometers per hour. His wife was looking noticeably crestfallen now that their attempt to claim the compensation had come to a creaking halt. His daughter also stood with slumped shoulders, getting a whiff of her mother's depressed mood. An empty cab was nowhere to be seen, and the sun was aflame like some live thing again, sapping even more energy from his family. He knew how

---

[1] Approximately a hundred fifty dollars.

disappointed his wife must be. Without the compensation, this trip was effectively over. All they could do was grab lunch somewhere and head back to Seoul. If claiming the money were the sole object, they wouldn't have come to this city at all, investing in the round trip bus fare and dragging their young daughter out of bed.

They left Seoul with only a handful of ten-thousand *won* bills in their possession, which was barely enough to cover three round-trip tickets from Seoul to Daegu. And yet, his wife had stayed up late into the night, packing excitedly in the name of a family trip, because the prospect of the hundred sixty thousand *won* that they were to receive created an anticipation of another, as yet unspecified destination. She deserved that anticipation, more than deserved it, in fact. The cost of moving his father's grave, including the transportation of the remains, came out to be more than two million *won* since they decided to take the opportunity to purchase the neighboring plot for his mother as well. He had two older sisters, but neither was in a financial position to contribute, so the entire burden came to rest upon him. The money for this came from the mutual loan club to which his wife belonged. It was her turn to take home the pot of two million *won,* and though she had been warbling incessantly for months about what she would do with the money, she tried hard to appear nonchalant as she relinquished it for his father's grave. There were extra expenses besides, so they were barely able to make ends meet. Then suddenly this opportunity had come. When he proposed that they take the compensation and go somewhere for a few days on a family vacation, his wife was overjoyed.

It was still spring, but one wouldn't have known it from the heat of the sun. Like all people setting out early, they were dressed warm enough for the morning chill, and now they had to sweat as they waited for the cab. They stood on a multilane boulevard as broad as a square where a field once had been. The last time he was here, it was in a van rented in Seoul, and he had been unable to locate the street leading to the cemetery. He circled around and around, failing to find a single landmark that his memory could latch onto. Though he had told himself a hundred times that the place would be transformed, he still believed that he would find something of the old landscape. He had forgotten the fact that "development" for outlying areas meant a complete overhaul from inside out, and the price he had to pay was the inconvenience of having to get

28

out of the car numerous times to ask passersby for directions.

Remembering this and that about the last time he was here, he forgot to pay attention to where they were. Now he realized that they were standing at a spot where it would be tricky to flag down a taxi. About fifty meters down the road, however, stood a couple of buildings and a factory. Taxis were sure to stop there to let off passengers, he thought. He grabbed his knapsack and began trudging down the unfamiliar street again, urging his wife and daughter along. The bag's straps dug into his shoulders. It was heavy, filled with the many things his wife deemed were necessary, even for a trip which would last two or three days at most. Last night, into the wee hours, she kept putting things in, taking them out, and putting them in all over again. Her hands were full, too. She was carrying a largish tote, a plastic bag containing snacks for their daughter, and a jacket.

When one is packing for a trip, laying out clothes to wear and thinking about what to bring, the weight of the bags remains an entirely forgivable matter. One rarely expects this weight to turn into a torturous burden. But happiness that is unmarred exists only in imagination.. Imagining this trip, his wife and daughter, too, must have believed that every step would leave behind a footprint of pleasure. Less than half a day into the trip, they were already worn-out, like defeated soldiers.

Defeated soldiers? The sudden thought made him force more spring into his walk. The head of a family with his dependents in tow needed to have more energy, more life than this. Defeated soldier—in all honesty, the description probably did apply to him, but not to his wife and certainly not to their daughter. If it hadn't been for the love he felt for the two of them, he would have quit the battlefield and given up on the futile struggle long ago.. Though he knew it was too late for excuses, he wanted to believe that his love for them may prove a shield behind which he might prepare at least an apology for truth. The fact that the scale of life did not always tip in the direction of truth was a small consolation, too.

He was right about the taxi. Before long, they were able to flag down an empty taxi coming out from the factory compound. The interior of the car was filled with a gentle fragrance emanating from a basket of quince placed behind the backseat.

"West County Office, please." The words were barely out of his mouth when his daughter said, "Daddy, we have to go to a restaurant.

Hanbyeol is hungry." The child hadn't had much of a breakfast.

"Your daughter's name is Hanbyeol?" The driver asked, showing interest in her name. His wife beamed with pride. The name had been her idea.

"Yes, Hanbyeol, Jeong Hanbyeol."

"Oh, I see. I thought for a second there that we might be of the same clan. You see, our last name is Han and my son's first name is Gang. Han Gang, the first son of the Han family, or Han Gang, the big river.[2] Nice, isn't it?"

His wife, who was fond of such names, didn't spare compliments. A boy named Hanbit and a girl named Hanbyeol—this had been her dream from the days when she was still a single woman.[3] A miscarriage six months into the pregnancy in that year known as 1980 shattered that dream. It took three long years for them to conceive again, and when he found out that she was pregnant, he decided to defer to her entirely in all matters regarding the child. No one knew better than he that he was solely to blame for the loss of their first child, who was to have been called Hanbit.

"Hanbyeol, wave goodbye to uncle."

The taxi driver waved to his daughter before driving off. In a much better mood now, Hanbyeol smiled back.

They were at the entrance to West County Office building when his wife pulled him back by the arm.

"I have a great idea. Why don't you call your sister in Seoul and find out what her resident registration number is?"

"What about the personal seal?"

"Over there. It won't cost much to have a wooden one engraved."

His wife whispered to him cheerfully as if she had hit upon an ingenious scheme.

"That way, we'll have our guarantors, no problem."

"You want me to have someone else's seal forged—twice?" He

---

[2] *Han Gang* is the name of the main river that flows through Seoul.

[3] "Han" means "one," but can also refer to the shortened form of "Hanguk" or Korea. "Hanbit"can thus mean "One Light" or "Light of Korea," and "Hanbyeol," "One Star" or "Star of Korea." Throughout the 1980s, it was a minor trend to give purely Korean names like these to newborns, rather than ascribe to the long-held convention of using Sino-Korean characters.

hadn't meant to sound harsh, but his voice was brusque. His wife closed her mouth, looking embarrassed.

The area by the entrance to the civil affairs office was done up like a waiting room. Next to the soda machine, there was even a plush couch, on which he now put down the knapsack that had been digging into his shoulder. His wife waited there with Hanbyeol, and he went up to the second floor by himself. The clerk, a man of sturdy build, looked over his papers and pushed the empty guarantor form back to him. He quickly jotted down the names of his brothers-in-law in Seoul and Gumi, and returned the form. The clerk was counting something while looking down at some kind of land registration map, and didn't look up at the form until he was done. Then he frowned. "You've got to be kidding me," said the expression on his face.

"Hey, look. Resident registration number here and personal seal there. Can't you read?"

The clerk's tone angered him in turn. He rummaged in his inside pocket and took out his press ID, which he proceeded to place on top of the map spread on the clerk's desk.

"I came all the way down from Seoul for this. I'll make sure to send you the guarantor documents by mail as soon as I get back."

Not wanting to see the sudden change in the clerk's demeanor, he focused his eyes on a distant spot on the wall. Therefore, he had no way of knowing what the clerk's face was like as he handed back the press ID and the guarantor form. And soon afterwards, he had a paper slip in his hand, stamped four or five times with the amount of compensation typed in coarse font.

"You can cash this receipt at the Kukmin Bank station on the first floor. Please send me the necessary document as soon as possible." The clerk tried with an effort to maintain a professional tone, but his voice contained a note of servility combined with indignation. "Hmph, as if the ID gives you some great power," the voice seemed to say. "But I'll just go ahead and give you what you want since I don't want any trouble." How could he explain in a few simple phrases how these things worked? The absolute absurdity of it all? He, too, had been on the receiving end of it much too often.

The press ID bore the name of his company's president as the issuer. This made Jeong the possessor of an ID that confirmed nothing more

31

and nothing less than the following: He was a journalist working for a company that has a national newspaper circulation. What it didn't say was that he himself was not a newspaper reporter, nor did he pretend deliberately to be one. If people assumed from the ID that he was and treated him as one, it was their fault for not looking carefully at his section name or not understanding the organizational structure of newspaper companies. For nearly ten years now, he had been working for a woman's magazine published by a company better known for its daily newspaper. Nevertheless, his ID was designed to convey power above and beyond what his actual status could command. Most of the time, presenting his ID was simply a matter of procedure, but he wasn't unaware of the effect it produced. Not that he had any particular desire to deny it, but on days like today, he had to admit that he was closer to "intentionally" capitalizing on that power. He had decided beforehand that it wouldn't hurt anyone for him to benefit from his ID. He also knew from extensive experience that this was the most effective way to deal with those on the bottommost rungs of the bureaucratic ladder. That didn't mean he felt good about it, but he wanted gentleness in all dealings.

Strictly speaking, his ID was void starting today. According to the letter of resignation he tendered to Kim, the managing editor of *Women's Living*, yesterday morning, he was resigning from his position for "personal reasons." With the submission of this letter, which had long been ready, Jeong was effectively bringing a chapter of his soul-searching to a close. Kim, whose eyesight was poor, squinted at the letter for a long time before relegating it to the third drawer of his desk, as if Jeong were out of his mind. It was well-known that the third drawer of Kim's desk was a kind of garbage collection center. Unpublishable articles, official notices of various kinds that did not need to be filed, and letters to the editor without much content found their way into the third drawer, where they served sentences of varying lengths before ending up in the incinerator. By placing his letter of resignation in this drawer, Kim was thus expressing the superior's concern and benevolence. Jeong did not try to press Kim to accept his resignation on the spot, either. His mind was already made up, and the formalities meant little to him.

Despite Kim's response, which was only natural, he meant to go home as soon as he was done with the number of pages assigned to him for this month. Since he was the most senior reporter at *Women's Living*, he didn't have that many pages to write. The April issue had come out only the day before yesterday, and his contributions for the next month's issue—a roundtable discussion and interviews that will depend on the results of the coming election—were not the type of articles that he could take care of at present. Aside from these, all he had to write was a short monthly piece on literature and art. Jeong didn't think he was being a chump, overly fastidious, for wanting to have the next month's articles ready before leaving the company. He was a strict person, most of all with himself. He couldn't rest easy otherwise.

Luckily, this was the slowest time of the month for the editorial staff. The next deadline was still far away and even the reporters with many assignments were enjoying the golden holiday from work. Close to the deadline, what with newly breaking stories, the staff had to pull all-nighters anyway. That was just the nature of monthly magazines. With most of his colleagues away on "assignments," he was able to pack his things in peace. He had been cleaning his desk out for several days, so he didn't have much to take home.

"Wait for me. I'll be back at the end of the day," Kim had said earlier that afternoon, tapping him on the shoulder before stepping out of the office. "Try not to do a number on me, you hear? I have a bad liver." How else could Kim react to a surprise resignation, Jeong thought. Kim was probably feeling guilty for picking on him last month for covering singer X's shotgun wedding with comedian Y so loosely. Or perhaps he was thinking of the incident involving the disappearance case. Kim had told Jeong to keep probing the ex-lover of the woman in question, but he had quietly turned the story over to Yu Illam. Kim let him know that he was none too pleased about that. A timid man at heart, Kim was given to fretting about things he said, after saying them. Jeong got up to leave. He had no intention of sticking around the office until Kim's return. Just then, Yu Illam sauntered in, holding a cup of coffee from the vending machine in his hand.

"Hey Illam, can I talk to you for a minute?" Jeong asked. They went into the small conference room. If Yu hadn't been carrying a cup already, they might have headed for the café downstairs.

"Are you really going to quit?" Yu asked.

Yu was still trying to dissuade him. Working shoulder to shoulder in the small office, they had become quite close over the years. Yu always knew what he was thinking, and right now he was the only one in the office to suspect what was going on, aside from Kim. Yu was a true gem of a journalist. No matter how shitty the story he was assigned, he had the knack of making every article that he handed over to the desk chockfull of interesting content. "Take my wife and give me Yu Illam" was the running joke at the editorial desk. Whether he was interviewing a singer, a sexy actress, or a taciturn baseball star, Yu brought back more scoop than what anybody had reason to expect. So was the quality of the articles he fashioned out of what he brought back. What's more, Yu didn't care whether the desk jazzed up his articles to make them spicier. Compared to Jeong, who couldn't bear to have a single punctuation changed once he was done with the article, Yu was a splendid women's magazine reporter.

"If you were the one quitting, all hell would break loose around here; but they can do without me just fine. I have complete faith in you. Well, let's not talk about this anymore. It's a done deal. There may be a lot of annoying little things that may come up after I leave. Will you do me a favor and take care of them as you see fit? I'll leave my seal with you."

He pushed his seal on his younger colleague, as Yu gulped down the rest of the coffee remaining in his cup.

"What do you think you're doing? Are you trying to demoralize people like me? Insult me?" Yu raised his voice. "This is a pathetic job, I know. But that doesn't mean you can chuck it away like it's nothing."

Yu was referring to the recklessness of his resignation. It made Jeong feel rotten. He knew that a nice guy like Yu wouldn't try to dissuade him from quitting if he were moving onto bigger and better things.

"You should have been a poet. You have something of a poet's rash pride. And I see these little signs of rebellion.... Come on, you are too hard on yourself. We're not even newspaper reporters, for Christ's sake! And even *they* rely on the system most of the time. You and I are the sheets of toilet paper that capitalism wipes its ass with. So how can we do anything?"

Once again, Yu was in the throes of what he himself was fond of calling "self-flagellation." It was a kind of catharsis. Dash a ball to the ground and it's bound to bounce back up. Grab a branch and rock yourself back and forth; the movement is easier to endure if you're the one doing the rocking.

"Try to be shameless sometimes," Yu said, it wasn't clear to whom.

"I'll give it a try, from now on."

"So you do have a plan," Yu brightened up immediately.

"What plan?"

"What else? A plan for putting food on the table for your wife and Hanbyeol."

Jeong didn't have a plan. Well, he did. It was an exceedingly simple plan, actually. To live again, to start a new life free of debt, free of oppression that remained in the depths of him as a tight clot of blood—this was his plan. He had a vague feeling that he could handle whatever might come afterwards, if only he could untangle that knot and bring proper closure to this chapter of his life.

"Let's go. It's kind of early, but we need a drink." Yu stood up.

"Let me take a rain check on that. I'll cash it in a few days. I think I might be coming down with something. I don't feel too good."

It was true. His body was about to give him an excuse for going home early.

He knew he had to tell his wife eventually, but he didn't know yet how long this "eventually" might turn out to be. The apartment where they lived was small, but at least it was theirs, and he figured in a vague sort of way that they should be able to get on for a while on his retirement pay. The Daegu idea occurred to him on his way home, just as he was turning onto his street. He had just been thinking that it might be wise to go away for a few days when the idea of a family vacation came to him in a flash. He began calculating how much such a vacation would cost, and necessity being the mother of invention, he remembered the unclaimed compensation for relocating his father's grave. He didn't think that his wife would object. According to the procedure decided upon by the city of Daegu, the claim had to be made in person. She had probably given up on the hundred sixty thousand *won* already, knowing how busy her husband was. But why put this money back into the government treasury? Why not take the hundred sixty thousand *won* and go on a short, inexpensive trip? For the time being, he could tell his

35

wife that he was taking a couple of days off from work. An unusual evening in an unfamiliar place might be just the setting he needs for softening the blow when he announces that he has quit his job. All the pieces fit together nicely in his brain. That was yesterday.

Seeing the guarantor form in his hand, his wife didn't try to hide her distress. "See, why didn't you listen to me about the seals?" He read reproach in her eyes.

"Keep it safe in your bag. I have to send it back to them from Seoul."

"You mean you got the money?"

His wife cheered up instantly. They went to the civil affairs office and looked for a Kukmin Bank station.

"We don't do that here. Please go to the regular branch right outside."

The bank teller pushed the slip back to him, though the clerk upstairs had told him that it could be cashed at the station. Jeong was angry but didn't want to bother going back upstairs to complain. One obstacle after another—it boggled his mind how much time and effort it took to claim a measly hundred sixty thousand *won*. It was already past three in the afternoon, and they hadn't even lunched yet. Lunch could wait, his wife argued. They should make sure to get the money before the bank closes. She started walking ahead. She was right. He wanted to end this wearisome quest once and for all, too. Hanbyeol didn't complain anymore that she was hungry. She had eaten the pound cake, chocolate, and other snacks left over from the bus ride.

They left the County Office and plodded along listlessly, looking around for the bank that was nowhere in sight, though it was supposed to be just down the road. He saw a young bootblack working under a tree and asked him where the bank was.

"You have to walk all the way down. Or take a bus. Two stops and the bus will let you off right in front of the bank."

"Right outside" according to the bank teller was two stops on the city bus. He strapped the knapsack on securely and started walking again. No one was to be trusted. He didn't want to take the bus and risk the chance of missing the stop. His wife and daughter followed him, dragging their feet.

Trudging along, he realized that he did recognize the street he was on, after all. It led to the reservoir they used to call Gamsaem Pond. Once, perhaps during his sophomore year in college, he had spent an entire summer there looking for carps. He was home from school and developing an active interest in fishing. "Gamsaem Pond ... What does Gamsaem mean?" he now wondered. Suddenly, the sensation of a carp struggling with all its weight to escape the hook came back to him. Holding the rod tightly in place, he used to feel as though the rod, the carp, and he were all one, like magnets stuck to one another. The summer ended, and he didn't return to Gamsaem Pond ever again. His father, who seemed would never breathe his last, finally passed away that autumn, and his mother took her youngest daughter and moved to Seoul immediately afterwards, as though she had been waiting for him to die. Since her older daughters were married and already living in Seoul and her son going to school there, she had no reason to remain in Daegu. The father had long been a noose as far as the rest of the family was concerned, and Daegu was simply a hollow in the ground where the noose had been laid. No one had any qualms about leaving him behind, alone in a public cemetery.

The man Jeong knew as his father, though he may have been a different man before Jeong was born, was someone who had never held a job and never shown an ounce of will to live. These were harsh and hateful things to say about one's father, he knew. But they were true; he hated his father. Jeong simply couldn't understand him. The first lesson in life that he and his sisters learned was to resign themselves to this incomprehension. Their mother was a woman tougher than weed, and she was the one who kept the family from scattering like the contents of a capsized ship. They did manage to survive, stuck together like glue, but it wasn't thanks to the man who should have been the head of the family. They had every right to blame the father, therefore, for making life a terrible, wearisome thing. It wasn't simply that the family's life would have been much more plentiful had the father tried just a little to do his part. It wasn't only that he resented his father for infusing his boyhood and adolescence with the acrid odor of inactivity, of a life cast away. While the father spent his days lying in his room or sitting out on the porch, the rest of the family had to thrash about in abject terror of poverty. The father didn't beat his wife or belt his children, but his utter idleness was violence too, of a different kind.

Born in 1912 in Jangdan, Gyeonggi Province, as the second son of impoverished peasants, Jeong's father led a life filled with twists and turns. His boyhood was spent in extreme privation, with the meager living his family was making from a small hillside plot ravaged daily by what they had to submit for the glory of the Japanese Empire. Full of youthful ambition at the age of twenty-five, he went over to Japan with his wife whom he had married the previous year. It was a time when landless peasants and day laborers from the cities were leaving Korea for Japan and Manchuria in droves. He and his wife got off the boat at Osaka and traveled on land, finally settling in Nagoya. They worked their fingers to the bone—he as a coolie in a forest reserve, she as a tenant farmer.

Whenever Jeong's mother reminisced about this life in Japan, something that resembled yearning crept into her voice. Listening to his mother's story, he thought he knew why. She was never again to see her husband the way he was in Japan. Your father was so good at his job, the owner of the reserve put in a lot of effort to get him exempted from the military, she would say proudly. But he couldn't even begin to imagine his father as a bare-chested lumberjack, felling trees more than an armful in girth.

Jeong's parents saved whatever they earned and sent it to the father's older brother back home every year at harvest time. The older brother was no spendthrift, either. He was careful with the money that represented the sweat of his brother's brow and bought plots of land with it. In Nagoya back then, she said, there was money to be made if you were willing to move your body. The young couple drove themselves hard, energized by the news from home, especially of the steady increase in their land holding. By 1945, when Korea was liberated from the Japanese colonial rule, they held a substantial amount of rice paddies and vegetable fields in their name.

She said she wasn't unhappy with her life in Nagoya. When the liberation came, she tried to persuade her husband to stay. Her argument was that they should stay in Japan and save up more money while they were still young to try to lay down a firmer financial foundation for their lives while the opportunity lasted. Their land back home wasn't going anywhere. But her husband was adamant about returning home immediately. His excuse, which wasn't really an excuse, was that he couldn't bear to stay in Japan when his land, the rich soil of his fields and paddies, was calling out to him. She finally agreed to go back when she saw other Koreans rushing home after the liberation. Now a family of four, though the two children would die soon after, they went back to Osaka and boarded a ship bound for home.

And the following year, on March 5, 1946, to be exact, land reform laws were proclaimed in North Korea. In name, anyway, these laws were based on the principle of giving the land to the tiller. Holdings by Korean owners exceeding five *jeongbo*,[4] in addition to land owned by Japanese individuals, corporations, and government agencies—were to be seized and distributed free of charge among tenant farmers. Since he wasn't a big enough landowner to suffer confiscation, at first, he stood back and watched. Even when he found out that his land had been handed over to the people's committee for management, he thought it a mere administrative measure. To become the rightful owner of this land, he had chopped down countless trees in rugged mountains on foreign soil, he told himself. Who could possibly take it from him? Trusting in common sense, however, turned out to be a fatal mistake.

Not long thereafter, he received notification that his land was now subject to permanent confiscation. The reason was that its owner was a "traitor to the people," a scoundrel who had worked for the Japanese to satisfy his personal greed. He was also criticized as lacking enthusiasm for the people's struggle since he had not been in Korea at the time of liberation. Beside himself with worry at the possibility of losing his land, he followed the people's committee around for a while, and finally came to grasp what he was up against. For those who could not adapt to the northern system, there was no choice but to leave. Taking his family, but leaving his land behind, Jeong's father came down south. It was the winter of 1946.

With the loss of his land, the father's life was utterly transformed. The family had grown in the meantime and he was now the father of three—two sons, aged six and four, and a daughter born the year of liberation—but their life was wretched. Moving from a place to place,

---

[4] One *jeongbo* is approximately equal to one hectare.

the couple barely eked out a living as farmhands. To make matters worse, their two sons died in the span of two months in the spring of 1948 when they were living in a hovel in Nonsan, Chungcheong Province and helping out at a ginseng farm. Fever claimed their sons' lives. After another daughter was born that winter, they moved farther down south and settled in a farming village near Masan where they stayed until the outbreak of the Korean War on June 25, 1950. With the news of the Allied Forces' northward march, the father decided to go back home and see about his land. But he never made it that far. Barely managing to save his life during an air raid, he came back deaf in one ear and with a limp in one leg. The limp wasn't severe, but the loss of hearing in one ear made him a taciturn, gloomy man for the rest of his life.

The father's life was effectively over at that point. During his absence, his wife had given birth to a son. She had endured the hardship of childbirth alone, expecting her husband to be as ecstatic as she that they now had a son again; but when he came home, he looked at the newborn and then looked away. Every time his mother told him this story, Jeong couldn't help thinking that the beginning of his life marked the end of his father's. From that point on, the livelihood of the entire family came to rest on the mother's shoulders. She gave birth to one more girl and raised three daughters and one son all by herself. The father didn't care about anything so long as he had his *makkeoli*[5] everyday. The image of him, sitting with a bowl of *makkeoli* in his hand, staring blankly as a bundle of twigs by the kitchen caught on fire, was branded in Jeong's mind.

From an early age, Jeong learned to hate his father from the bottom of his heart. Not even once did he see his father making money. What he did hear, until he was sick of it, was his father's drunken refrain, "I have lots of land over there, lots of land. All of that land is mine. They'll give it back to me one day, just you wait." "Lots of land over there" was one of the most hated phrases in all of his boyhood. And then he died, after plunging his family into a vortex of fear by being possessed of no other thought than "All of that land is mine." The family didn't suffer the slightest financial repercussion or emotional shock at his death. He had already been dead to them for a long time.

---

[5] Thick, milky wine made from rice.

40

It now appeared that the directions the young bootblack had given him were correct. When Jeong stopped a pedestrian to ask for directions again, he was told to keep going straight. Jeong's wife sighed. She was carrying Hanbyeol on her back. He felt that it might almost be better to give up on the compensation altogether, if this trip to the bank were not the very final step. So when the bank finally came into sight, Jeong was angry rather than relieved. He couldn't shake off the feeling that he had let someone play a practical joke on him. Even after he had the money in his hand, he felt as though he was being compensated for playing the fool. The feeling drained him so completely of energy that he couldn't begin to think of what to do next. "Let's get something to eat first," his wife suggested. "My legs need a break." He looked around for somewhere to go and spotted a small, home-style restaurant next to the bank.

It was late in the afternoon and the restaurant was empty. The first thing he did was to put his bag down and massage his numb shoulder. A woman came out of the kitchen, wiping her hands on the apron, and brought them cups of barley tea. A look of exasperation showed on his wife's face as she looked around the interior: five tables, a calendar, a clock, a television mounted up on the wall. Not exactly an ideal place for the first meal of our family vacation, her look seemed to say. Maybe the same thought occurred to Hanbyeol; she started talking about pork cutlets. Eating out meant fried pork cutlets to Hanbyeol and barbecued beef ribs to his wife. To Jeong, however, eating out was just eating out. It meant service to his family, if it meant anything at all. Resigning herself to the situation, his wife ordered two home-style rice sets with stew and placated their daughter with the promise of a pork cutlet dinner.

The money was in his pocket and he was having lunch at last, but he had spent too much energy running around to enjoy it. And the food was salty and tasteless. He had forgotten how terrible the food was in this city and realized that time had not made him any fonder of it. By the time he was done with half of his rice, which he ate with the stew that was bland and burning hot at the same time, he knew he hated this city. He hadn't known that a month ago when he was down here in a rented van.

In point of fact, he couldn't exactly say that he was here last time.

YANG GUIJA

He was in Seongseo Municipal Cemetery, not in the city of Daegu proper. He left Seoul at three in the morning, arrived in Seongseo shortly before eight, finished the disinterment two hours later, and headed back to Seoul, which left hardly any time to feel sentimental about returning to the city. But today was different. From the moment he got off the bus, the city had put him on guard. At every stage of the trip, he had a feeling that something disagreeable, some intolerable tension in the air was pushing him.

His mother, once she realized that the entire family might starve to death if she depended on her husband to do something, put an end to their itinerant life. She had to settle her family down somewhere; she had her precious son's schooling to worry about, too. Daegu happened to be where they settled, and Jeong started first grade the following year. He didn't remember harboring any particular feeling of dislike or disappointment toward the city growing up. His father monopolized such emotions so completely he didn't have any to spare.

"What do we do now? We have to decide where to go."

His wife seemed to share his feelings about the food. When she first sat down, she looked as though she was ready to wolf down the bowl of rice, but there was still a layer of rice at the bottom, and here she was, talking about their next destination. Their vacation was finally about to begin, but he didn't know where to go, either; they hadn't had a chance to sit down together and chat amiably about the pros and cons of different destinations. Donghwa Temple, Pagye Temple, Haein Temple—these were just about all he knew in terms of nearby tourist attractions. But Donghwa and Pagye were destinations for a day trip at best. When he suggested Haein Temple, his wife's response was lukewarm.

"What's there to see but the Great Tripitaka?"

Hearing the word "Tripitaka," the restaurant owner seated at the next table stopped peeling garlic and looked up.

"You folks plannin' to see some sights?"

"Yes. Do you have any recommendations?" His wife asked with alacrity.

"I say Bugok Hot Springs, if you ask me. Went there myself last winter, you know, around election time, and my skin was softer than a baby's for days. They do shows there, too; Bugok Hawaii is the name.

42

Ain't half bad. There are lots of buses leavin' for Bugok from Seongdang District."

His wife looked at him as if the idea appealed to her. Sensing his hesitation, however, the woman made another suggestion.

"What about Gyeongju? Closer than Bugok and a ton of things there to see. Lots of people who come to Daegu go to Gyeongju too, it being so famous and all. But never been there myself. Would you believe it, living so close and all."

The word Gyeongju brought images of tombs to Jeong's mind. First the tombs, then the glittering gold crowns and *hwarangs*[6] in armor. His wife seemed to be wavering between Bugok and Gyeongju, but Hanbyeol knew what she wanted. "Daddy, are we going to Bugok? Are we going to see a show?" The question was actually a suggestion. But in the context of his life as a whole, the idea of going to Bugok to take a bath struck him as being almost comical. Then again, the preconception he had about hot springs—that residues of greed floated on the water and the steam emanated an odor of corruption—was perhaps the most comical of all..

"Let's decide between Bugok and Gyeongju."

From the tone of her voice, he could tell that his wife was relieved that they now had concrete options to choose from. She wasn't her usual self; how should he put it, she was holding herself back. Perhaps because they were in an unfamiliar setting, it saddened him to see her trying to keep herself in check. . He decided to follow her wishes. If she wanted to go to the hot springs, he was going to soak himself in its steaming water and breathe its air of greed. Fortunately, his wife was slowly leaning towards Gyeongju. In the end, a hot spring wasn't exactly the most thrilling destination for a rare family vacation. People without much money tended to associate the word vacation with milling crowds, dazzling sun, and endless succession of tourist sights.

"It'll be educational for Hanbyeol to see Gyeongju. Let's go to Gyeongju."

His wife made up her mind at last. She laughed when Hanbyeol asked if they were going to see a show in Gyeongju.

---

[6] An elite corps in Silla which focused on spiritual cultivation and physical and military training.

"In Gyeongju, we'll see traces of how our ancestors lived a long time ago. This family trip, Hanbyeol, is Grandfather's special gift to us. You can see shows with people dancing and singing on television all the time, but a trip to Gyeongju is something really special. You'll remember it many, many years from now."

Hanbyeol did not fully understand the explanation. She asked what "Grandfather's gift" meant. "Grandfather's in his grave in Pocheon. How can he give me a gift when he's sleeping in the ground? What is the gift?"

"Grandfather's body may be sleeping in the ground, but his spirit is in heaven. He sent us money from above. He told mommy and daddy to take Hanbyeol somewhere nice with that money. That's why we are here today. Grandfather's always watching over you."

His wife's story was fast becoming a fairy tale, and a bitter one as far as he was concerned. A trip paid for by the grandfather for his granddaughter—he was amazed that she could make it sound so beautiful when, in point of fact, his father's capacity for love was destroyed the day his land was taken from him. How could such love cross heaven and earth and materialize many decades later before the granddaughter he had never known? His wife's story was far-fetched, even for a fairy tale, considering the absolute passivity of his father's life.

In any event, they decided that they should leave the city as soon as possible. He wanted to escape the feeling of oppression, confusion, and inexplicable resistance that the city was arousing in him. As for his wife, she was eager to start the "real vacation." Following the restaurant owner's advice, they decided to take a taxi to East Daegu Terminal and board one of the numerous buses bound for Gyeongju that would be lined up there. Jeong had been to Gyeongju before. In high school, he once cycled from Daegu to Gyeongju. He stopped to take a swig from his water bottle where he could see Nam Mountain in the distance, then turned around and cycled right back. Boys at that age had no desire to see tourist sights they already knew by heart from history books and travel catalogues. Jeong was no exception. As far as he was concerned, time for sightseeing would be better spent going to the morning market in his mother's stead and haggling over the box of Chinese cabbages or young radishes.

Jeong's wife, too, had been to Gyeongju before. She spoke of her class trip in junior high during which she spent one night in Busan and one night in Gyeongju. All she could remember about the trip, however, was laughing over the mustaches they had drawn on teachers' faces and being carried down Toham Mountain on her homeroom teacher's back because of a sudden stomachache. It wasn't surprising that these were the most memorable episodes. Class trips weren't about the setting at all, but about chatting the night away with your friends in some unfamiliar place.

Jeong had never had that experience, neither in junior high nor in high school. Not being able to go on class trips didn't pain him in the slightest. What did pain him was having to reject his homeroom teacher's generous offer to cover his expenses for the trip. He couldn't stand the feeling that he was being idle or relying on someone else's help. Even as a teenager, he didn't want to do anything that would make him even remotely resemble his father. He wanted to grow up fast and take the man's place as the head of the family to alleviate his mother's suffering. With fierceness that seemed nothing short of a miracle to him, his mother made the family's survival her responsibility, expecting nothing from her husband and showing no rancor toward him. The miracle did have its limits, however. He found out about that when the time came for him to apply to colleges. That was his first taste of despair.

They left Daegu behind them. They had spent only a few hours there, most of that time in taxis. They had bought nothing, ate nothing except for a bowl of rice at the end. On the bus to Gyeongju, he stared long and hard at the toll gate they were passing through as though he were leaving Daegu for the last time, never to return. A city that has always been at the center of power, Daegu exuded self-assurance to the point of arrogance. He recalled the strong attachment the city's residents had exhibited toward their vested interest during the December 16th election.[7] Providing a direct contrast to the numbers that another southern city had coughed up like blood,[8] this attachment remained the favorite

---

[7] Years of the democratization movement in South Korea, culminating in civilian protests of unprecedented size in June 1987, finally brought about the declaration of direct presidential elections which signaled the end of military dictatorships. The split in the opposition party, however, allowed the incumbent president and former military general Roh Tae-woo to regain office. Roh, as well as two military generals who preceded him as presidents, was a native of Daegu.

subject for analysis among the staff at *Women's Living* long after the elections were over. Yu Illam, for one, denounced it as proof that people of Daegu had never made the effort to find out about all the atrocities of the Fifth Republic.[9] Another staff member pointed out that election results were skewed for both cities and worried whether Koreans would ever be able to overcome primitive group psychology, of which regionalism was a prime example.

Though he had lived in Daegu for years, he didn't consider himself a Daegu person. In just the same way, he knew he wasn't a man of the present, even after working for years in a profession that should have given him an intimate understanding of the present. Something momentous was happening all around him, he knew; everyone sensed that they were living through history in the making.[10] What he sensed more sharply, however, was the shape of the new ruling structure lying in wait than the situation at hand. In retrospect, he saw that this was also an expression of his anxious desire to end his service to the system which had continued since 1980 in some way, shape or form. He feared that such service was becoming second nature to him and hardening into something that would soon be impossible to uproot. Even when other people were preoccupied with the behind-the-scenes stories of politics, which had suddenly grown more numerous than ever, Jeong spent his time trying to get his other self to imagine a different future in his mind. It was not easy to distinguish what he could do from what he couldn't, but one option he did not have was to sit back and do nothing. Who was he, really? He wanted to find out. If this indeed was a moment of transition in history, he wanted a genuine transition in his own life, too.

On the bus speeding toward Gyeongju, Hanbyeol fell asleep again.

---

[8] The city in reference is Gwangju, South Jeolla Province, where masses of civilians were killed by the military in May of 1980. A rival region to Gyeongsang Province, Jeolla has been persecuted generally under the regimes of Daegu-born presidents. Kim Dae-jung, a long time opposition leader and the seventh president of Korea, is the candidate from Jeolla Province alluded to here.

[9] The regime headed by Chun Doo-hwan, military general who came to power through a coup d'état. Throughout his presidency, Chun used his control of the military to squash political opposition, the most brutal example of which was the massacre of Kwangju's civilians by paratroopers in May of 1980.

[10] See note 7.

For the child, the trip probably meant no more than riding from place to place to place, but he knew that it wasn't so simple for his wife. Before arriving in Gyeongju, she wanted to know the full significance of the trip. The desire was only natural.

"I still can't believe we're taking this trip. It's one big riddle to me—I mean, it's so unlike you to suggest something like this. We've never taken a family vacation, you know. I didn't blame you when Hanbyeol was little. Taking a trip with a small child would be hard on me, too. But I started feeling bad about it a while ago. Looking at Hanbyeol's album made me feel worse. The best she has are pictures at the zoo, not a single vacation picture. Do you know what she told me the other day? Her kindergarten teacher told the class to draw the sea, and she was the only one who couldn't draw it. She told the teacher that she didn't know what the sea was like because she's never seen it with her own eyes. You know how she is. Hanbyeol thinks she has to touch it, feel it with her own hands, before she can know what anything is like. The teacher told her to draw it anyway, and Hanbyeol complained that she was a bad teacher...."

He stared at the stain on his wife's orange windbreaker. The words were on the tip of his tongue, but he couldn't say anything in the end. It wasn't the right time to tell her about his resignation. He reached over and held her hand in silence, unable to ignore the flush in her cheeks.

Knowing that Daegu was now far behind them made his breathing freer. The trip was only just beginning. They were heading toward Silla, a thousand years of history buried in the ground. As the bus raced on, he recounted that history to himself, from its beginning to its end in 935 with King Gyeongsun's surrender to Goryeo. That history was one of conquests—countless rebellions and suppressions, followed by taxation, military service, and corvée labor imposed on the defeated. In junior high or high school classes, this history was taught as a sequence that begins with a conquest, followed by unification, and stabilizes into a period of administrative rule. But he now wondered whether students shouldn't be taught to memorize and recite the chronology of destruction, violence, and humiliation instead. To Jeong, history was a process of ranking fear, regardless of whether the motive for inciting such fear could be justified. Gyeongju's case was no different.

A sudden fear gripped him. Maybe this whole thing was a trap set for him. He was taking his whole family and speeding toward the mouth of that trap. Why this destination and not any other? Someone must have engineered that choice. He regretted letting his guard down too soon and allowing himself to feel relief just because the two accomplice cities of Seoul and Daegu were now behind them. Then, as suddenly as the fear, came the realization that he was the one who had engineered this trip. Even so, he released his wife's hand. She was sitting back and looking at the scenery outside the window and now turned to look at his face.

"You're off again, somewhere I don't know," her face said. No doubt she was used to this. Whenever a sudden mood change came over him, she let him alone. She let whatever it was drift over him and flow away. "I may not understand everything that you're going through, but you still have my faith," she once told him.

He turned his eyes to the window again. Mounds of sod that farmers had left upturned to enhance the quality of next year's crop made him think of numerous cemetery parks that he had visited last month. To find a new resting place for his father's remains, he had ventured farther north every Sunday. If at all possible, he wanted to find a suitable place up north, closer to the border. When the relocation issue came up ... no, even before that when the thought of relocation would rise to the surface of his consciousness from time to time, the first thought that crossed his mind was always that the new grave should be somewhere up north.

He knew that his response to relocation must have come as a complete surprise to his wife. During all the years of their married life together, he had given her no indication that the one-time existence of a man he knew as his father had any impact on his life now. His siblings didn't bring him up in conversation, either, and the family conveniently decided not to commemorate any date associated with the father, using the mother's Christian faith as an excuse. So when the notification came that his remains had to be moved immediately, his wife broached the subject cautiously and volunteered to do the looking. "Since you're busy, I mean, if you're busy, should I look around for the new grave site?"

He knew what she meant, where she was coming from. But he shook his head. He didn't know if there were words that could make her understand what kind of shadow his father's life had cast on his own. Even as he set out every weekend in search of a suitable resting place for his father, with assiduousness that put his wife's considerate offer of help to shame, he couldn't give her any explanation for it. All he could do was mumble to himself, again and again, "How can I describe its effect on me when that shadow changes its shape and color every minute of the day?"

The bus slowed down and then began to crawl. Bumper-to-bumper traffic stretched ahead. From the front of the bus, a passenger reported that there had been an accident. Soon, the bus came to a complete standstill, bringing Hanbyeol out of sleep. Holding the half-awake child in her arms, his wife rubbed her daughter's cheeks with her own. Hanbyeol smiled.

The bus began to crawl forward again, and Jeong could see that one of the lanes was closed off. He saw a man waving a red flag and then the scene of the accident: a truck lying belly-up on the road and shards of glass bottles that the truck had been transporting strewn all around, pools of dark blood making a large map on the asphalt. Spotting the blood amid the sharp, sparkling glass fragments in the sun, he turned to block the window and shield Hanbyeol from the view. Then they passed a taxi, crumpled up like a used piece of tissue. Blood on the pavement was even more vivid in color. An accident of that magnitude usually claimed more than one life. Her curiosity piqued by all the gasps that filled the bus, Hanbyeol tried even harder to thrust her head out. Thankfully, the bus began to regain its speed, and he sat back from the window.

Outside, simple country scenes flitted past once more, in full innocence. He dropped his head, and saw his dust-covered shoes. Had he paid for them in full? he now wondered. It was a random thought but an important one. The shoes were custom-made, bought on a monthly installment plan. About two months ago, a man who professed to be an expert in hand-crafted shoes had come to their office and taken orders from him and a few other reporters whose shoes were getting old. The shoemaker measured their feet right then and there. The price was no cheaper than a major brand's, but his shoes had the advantage of being a novelty, especially refreshing to people who were fed up with standardized sizes and shapes. Not that the reporters were looking for particularly complicated designs. "No laces for me. Make them like his over there, but in dark brown," they would end up saying. Or, "What

I'm wearing right now is fine in terms of design, but make them really comfortable." When the shoes came, everyone welcomed them for the simple reason that human hands, not machines, had made them. Every month, Jeong took about ten thousand *won* out of his paycheck to pay the shoemaker; and if he wasn't all paid up, he needed to call Yu and let him know.

He had taken care of everything else, like his tab at a nearby pub or what he owed for the yogurt drink that he had delivered to his desk everyday. He made a list of potential problems that might arise at the office after his departure, and checked them off one by one. The task was far from simple. He was shocked to discover that even his body had become adjusted to the daily schedule of a white-collar worker. Perhaps it was silly of him to think that a list scribbled on a piece of paper would allow him to bring ten years of his life to a clean end. Only monetary transactions could be calculated with any sense of finality, and even there, as it turned out, he hadn't been thorough enough. His shoes were proof.

With all these efforts to leave no loose ends behind, Jeong was in fact binding himself with new ropes. He imposed silence on those things he really wanted to do, those he really should have done, by placing trivial things in the foreground. According to common wisdom, the first step toward quitting smoking was to declare to the world that you're quitting. Even if you didn't trust yourself to not smoke, the fact that you gave your word could help you abstain longer, if only for just another day.

The sense of peace he craved would be his in a heartbeat, if it were something that could be achieved by disciplining his desire, like quitting smoking. Extricating himself from the bonds of disgrace, however, was no simple matter. He still didn't know what it was that he had to say. Everyday he asked himself what the words were that he wanted to be held accountable for. It wasn't easy.

Even more difficult to endure was the feeling that oppressed him constantly that no matter what conclusion he reached—should he give up wrestling with reality? Yield unawares to yet another form of submission?—it was bound to be no more than the result of another compromise. This feeling first began to swell last summer. Shuttling between a popular singer's home and his record company in order to confirm the rumors regarding his divorce, Jeong would come across protesters. When he scuttled into the restroom of some building to avoid tear gas, he saw a crowd of students covering one another's eyes with plastic wrap. The proud wave that swept across the city—the red eyes, the heavy breathing, the crying out of slogans—awakened the fear that he thought he had forgotten. Past the rows of riot police, alien-like in their full gear, past the downtown shrouded in tear gas and flying stones, he walked to reach his office building that remained unchanged, as if it were oblivious to what was happening all around. He stood before the building's automatic doors, and for the few unbearable seconds before they slid open, he clutched at his chest and swayed as the pain exploded. The memory that he thought was nearly gone from his mind came back to him. He was standing before the automatic doors; he was being jostled down a staircase. It was June of 1980 again, as if the incident had taken place only yesterday.

Only yesterday. Though he was now sitting in Seat 11 of a bus bound for Gyeongju, he shook from a sudden chill. It was a sign that a certain memory of his was about to return: of a time when he was made to understand that there was nothing metaphoric about the expression "trembling like a leaf," that the convulsing muscles of his body had the value of a piece of meat on a butcher's chopping block.

There had been no omens that morning, no premonitions to prepare him for what was to come. The weather was lovely and clear as it usually is in the morning early in the summer, and all the grumbling from reporters facing the month's deadline was giving the office its proper air. He went into work as usual that day. The first thing he did at the office was to take off his shoes and put on his slippers, as was his habit. Next he took off his jacket and hung it over the back of his chair. A girl in a high school uniform with a dazzlingly white collar came to him and interrupted his routine. With the uniform and all, she was a refreshing sight. Someone's waiting for you downstairs in the café, she said. He realized that he didn't recognize her, though there were girls, mostly night-school students, hired as part-timers to run errands in every section office.

A writer is here to see you, she might have said. He didn't think anything of it. Such visits happened frequently enough when articles were due. He left the office and began climbing down the stairs toward the first floor. He saw two men standing on the landing. They walked up the steps toward him and asked him in a low voice, "Are you Jeong Yeongjun?"

He nodded.

"You need to come with us," said the one who appeared to be the older of the two.

"Where?" he asked gruffly, thinking that it was too early in the day for such shenanigans.

"Shut up and do what you're told, you shithead!" spat out the other man, who had two tiny slits for eyes, and clamped down on his lower lip. A vague understanding dawned upon him with the force of the unexpected cursing. *They're taking me in.* Before he could fully grasp the thought, the two men closed up on each side of him, all but grabbing his arms. *Start walking, you hear me?* The order was issued in a hushed voice. He was jostled down to the entrance on the first floor. He hoped against hope that some familiar face would appear and check their descent. Waiting for the automatic doors to slide open, he looked around frantically for someone to whom he could tell what was happening. One of the men elbowed him at his side. *Don't even think about pulling that shit.*

A black sedan was waiting for them right outside the front entrance. The older man climbed in first and he was hurled in afterwards like a piece of luggage. The slit-eyes got in after him. As soon as the car started to pull away, the slit-eyes jammed Jeong's head down so that his head was by his feet. *Don't lift your fuckin' head!*

He felt panic. The roughness of the men's language and movements did not bode well. As the car sped on, a thousand thoughts flitted through his mind. He tried to figure out why they were taking him into custody, but he really didn't have a clue. Staring at the gray floor mat and three pairs of shoes, he felt exasperated that he couldn't think clearly because of his panic, and tried to steel his heart against what may be in store. He didn't have enough time for that, either. The car stopped and he was dragged out. The men barked at him to keep his head down so he couldn't see much, but they appeared to be entering S Police Station. Jeong felt a modicum of relief that at least it wasn't to the notorious Seobinggo or Namsan "Office" that he was being taken. Groundless optimism reared its head: Maybe nothing will happen to him after all. But the men continued to create a climate of fear and intimidation after their arrival at the police station. Out of the public eye now, the men had no qualms about grabbing his arms. He was literally dragged up the stairs.

The interrogation room on the third floor was a large place with only three or four desks made of steel. When Jeong stepped inside, the men brusquely released his arms, which caused him to stumble. Two other men were already waiting for him. He spotted a chair in front of him and tried to make himself less prominent by sitting down. A shrill voice stopped him. *Look at this motherfucker! Who gave you the permission to sit?* Jeong froze. *He wants to be civilized.* Another voice taunted him. He fumbled about, not knowing which direction to look. The one who appeared to be the chief barked out an order.

"Take your clothes off!"

Jeong honestly didn't understand what he was being commanded to do. What did they want him to take off? Like the men around him, he was dressed in a T-shirt and pants. His jacket was back at his office.

"I said, take your clothes off!"

Jeong's cheek flared with the sudden slap. He didn't know which of the four men surrounding him had slapped him. He started to strip as fast as he could. He took off the T-shirt, which one of the men took from him and hung on a hook on the wall. Jeong's undershirt followed. When Jeong stopped, the chief ordered him to continue in a voice that was like a whiplash. Jeong undid his belt and a large hand snatched it away from him. He was now only in his briefs. He was so grateful that they didn't order him to take that off, too. His briefs kept him from a total humiliation. The date was June 16th and the weather was quite warm outside, but Jeong shivered from a chill. He didn't know what to do with his naked body—where to look, where to stand, where to place his hands. Fear swelled up to his throat from the bottom of his heart. He shivered uncontrollably.

"You know why you're here, don't you?" The chief asked. When he replied that he didn't, the leader actually grinned. The grin was so ill-suited to the situation that Jeong doubted his eyes.

"Climb up!"

Jeong hesitated. This order was even more incomprehensible than the earlier one. Climb? Climb up where? What did they want him to do? His incomprehension made him feel sorry for himself. They didn't wait but pushed him against the desk. They wanted him on top of it. After making him crouch on the desk, they took their time setting about their routine. Full understanding of the situation finally dawned on him. He had heard rumors of this. It was June of 1980, and rumors covered the city like a thick layer of fog, making him quiver with indignation. And now he was here, trembling with fear. He was about to be tortured, and he didn't know why.

Even after finding himself on top of the desk, a part of him still remained incredulous. He wasn't an expert in the subject by any means, but he knew that torture was a tactic employed to make someone confess. Even torture couldn't be as arbitrary as this, he thought. Shouldn't they start by asking him questions, like didn't you do such and such, where were you on such and such date, etc.? Could it be that they had screwed up the proper order of things? There was no time to protest. The men performed their job with expert ease. After tying his wrists together with a wet towel, they told him to bring his knees to his chest, inside his arms. Jeong had never taken that posture before, but he wasn't about to tell them that he couldn't do it. He tried as hard as he could to force his legs inside his bound arms, and one of the men gave him a hand. The posture made him fall backwards, his legs up in the air. It reminded him of the picture of a donkey tied to a pole that he had once seen in a children's book. The story of a father and a son who bound the donkey's four legs to a pole and carried the two ends of the pole on their shoulders; he couldn't remember its title. One of the men climbed up on the desk and sat astride him. The billy club in his hand was shiny from years of use. Jeong closed his eyes.

The club rained down on the soles of his feet at a merciless speed. If he had known that a pain like this would be inflicted on him, he would have bitten down on his tongue and swallowed his screams. But he was unprepared, and couldn't help screaming out again and again. The dull thwack of the club on his feet and the sound of his screams created an odd harmony, and he despised himself for screaming. If the blow missed his soles and landed on his toes instead, the pain was even more intense as though his bones were shattering into a thousand shards. But even more unbearable was the sight of the club swishing through the air the moment before landing on his feet. Imagining the dreadful pain to come suffocated him. After a while, he didn't know how long, another of the men took the club. All his screaming and writhing didn't seem to faze the men one bit. They were going in and out of the room, taking care of business as usual. An hour passed, maybe more. The one who had beat him earlier came back to relieve his colleague. Trying to endure the pain with everything he had made his tailbone ache. His entirely body was sticky with sweat. A moment was longer than eternity. The unbearable pain sharpened his senses and his mind.

Eventually, the beating ceased. Jeong heard the club hit the cement floor. Two men lifted him up and undid the towel binding his wrists. He was afraid. His arms were limp by his sides and his breath came in hoarse gasps as he looked around at the faces of the torturers. The chief wore a beige button-down shirt and was leaning against the desk on the far inside, and the two men who had been beating him by turns were sitting down on chairs and lighting their cigarettes. No one spoke to him. The men almost looked normal, like construction workers taking a cigarette break after a backbreaking job. They could have been digging or carrying bags of cement instead of beating another man senseless. *They'll start some sort of interrogation now. Please God, let this be it.* Abandoning his bloody soles to the ground, Jeong trembled with fear. No orders came, no questions. After about ten minutes, the chief simply said, "Let's have another round, boys."

Then the two men came to him and laid him back on the desk.

"Why are you doing this, why do you keep...?" The words of protest that escaped his body trailed off when one of the men fisted him in the stomach. Then they covered his face with a hand towel. Whitish fog clouded his vision. With his vision cut off, the weight of fear became even more unbearable. It assailed every inch of him, from the top of his head to the bloody soles of his feet. He couldn't stand the thought that he could die here at the hands of these men without knowing why. *No one knows that I'm here. Even if I die, I'll just be declared missing.* In despair the like of which he had never known, he cried out the names of his wife, his unborn child, his aged mother, his colleagues at work.

They bound his hands and feet. Someone sat on top of his thighs and ground them. All the while, the door kept opening and closing, and the beastlike howling from some other room down the corridor seeped in through the open door. Waiting for the frightful pain to begin again, his heart beat frantically and his entire body broke out in sticky sweat. Then it came. He felt water on his towel-covered face. He judged that they were pouring it from a kettle. Because the flow was constant, the torturer could aim it directly onto his nose. He thought he might be able to bear it, at least for the first few seconds. But soon, his breath gave out and heat flared up in his nostrils. He opened his mouth to control his breathing, but that made it even worse. The gurgling of water in his throat, a burning smell in his nostrils ... his breathing came in gasps as if it would cease altogether, but he couldn't even twist his body at will because it was tightly bound. Jeong didn't want to acknowledge it, but the feeling that he was slowly nearing the valley of death made him panic that much more. And yet, another part of him wanted to die. If death was the only way to stop this pain, he wanted to die from the bottom of his heart.

Jeong now realized that the beating was nothing compared to the water torture. As the wildly waving stream filled his nose and mouth, the water that he had not yet managed to swallow gurgled back up his nose and mouth. He had to twist his entire body and try with every fiber of his being to hold on to the breath that threatened to snap once and for all. He thought his heart would rip inside in chest, and sparks exploded in his brain. If he could only loosen these bonds and fly away to the sky, if he could only escape beyond the reach of the torturers, if only... if only someone could make this brutal stream of water stop, he felt that he would wage his loyalty to him for life like a faithful dog. He swore that he would.

How much more time had passed, he couldn't begin to guess. He had no strength left to move a finger. Over and over, he let go of his hold on consciousness, only to be forced to grab it again. He didn't know how he endured these moments in hell. Perhaps half a day had passed, but then again maybe it was less than five minutes. His twisted innards, his throat and nostrils on fire, and his straying mind gave up their hold on life, but just when he thought the shadow of death covered him like a white drape, he came back to life. The sound of water made him shudder and writhe all over again.

Did he come up on the other side of eternity? The wings of his mind snapped and he felt everything drain out of his limbs, when the stream of water on his towel-covered face finally stopped. He inhaled slowly. He breathed in and out, afraid that the freshness, the sweetness of these breaths would soon come to an end. Even though his body was drenched in sweat, he was so cold he couldn't stop shivering. He had no qualms about it now. He felt not even an iota of shame at the way his flesh convulsed. The men removed the towel from his face and untied his arms and legs.

"Here, why don't you sit back in this chair?" The chief spoke to Jeong in a gentle voice as he sat crouched on top the steel desk in his briefs. The smile on that face as he stood leaning against the desk with his arms crossed, and the gentleness of his voice moved Jeong to the point of tears. The man in a red shirt next to him laughed out loud, baring almost all of his white teeth, and said, "You're tougher than you look." It was as if they had all been involved in some friendly match. Grateful for a conversation that had a semblance of humanity to it, Jeong let his guard down, but his body wouldn't let him stay still. Shaking like a leaf in autumn wind, he crawled down from the desk like a wet mouse and sat down in a chair. He was given a pen and paper.

"Write down everything you've been up to since May of this year. And when I say everything, I mean *everything*." Jeong was grateful. At last, here was an order he could understand. He grabbed the paper ruled on both sides. If he had ever felt resentment or wounded pride, he didn't feel it now. Such human sentiments had disappeared a long time ago. How gracious of this man to tell him to use writing like the civilized citizen that he was, without beating him and making him swallow water! He held the pen between his numb fingers and squeezed out the last bit of energy he had left in his body to fill the paper with words.

It was now well into June, but the life of a reporter for a monthly magazine was organized in cycles that made everything relatively easy to remember. In the early part of May, he went to a village in the hills of Chungcheong Province to interview a woman recognized as an exemplary mother. For several days around the fifteenth, he was in the Banpo area of Seoul, busily collecting information on the scandalous affair between singer C and television actress J. He visited Cheongdam District several times to do a story on the actress O's life as a newlywed. His wife had complained of lower abdominal pain, and he accompanied her to the ob/gyn clinic. As he wrote out this part, he wondered whether the shock might not cause his wife to miscarry if she found out about this incident. The doctor had told them that she was at risk and stressed the utmost importance of having peace and quiet at all times. He then wrote about meetings with singers A and B and actors Y and Z. All of a sudden, something clicked in his brain.

One of his college friends had been taken into custody toward the end of May. For some time after the graduation, they hadn't seen much of each other, but now that he was in charge of the literature/theater page of *Women's Living*, they were meeting up quite often. Many people who were involved in the democratization movement in the 1970s were now in publishing or in theater, and his friend was one of those trying to write a play. Jeong kept abreast of what his friend was up to and heard that he had been arrested sometime at the end of May. Men had come to his home early one morning and taken him away in his pajamas. His wife was going all over the town trying to find out where her husband had been taken. He was concerned about his friend, of course, but he didn't worry too much since he knew that his friend was no longer involved in anything that would qualify as anti-government activity. The arrest was just based on his past record, Jeong said to himself, and adopted the attitude of an onlooker.

But now that he thought about it, he was almost certain that his friend had something to do with the reason why he was here now. He wondered whether making a reference to his friend in the statement would make them see that he was being completely honest, then decided that it would simply invite more problems should it turn out that his friend had nothing to do with his arrest. It was difficult enough to organize his thoughts and write them down on paper in some coherent fashion. His entire body felt like a soggy piece of cotton, and he was so cold that his teeth wouldn't stop chattering. It was a wonder that he could write at all, but then again, fear was an amazing thing. It turned him into an obedient dog.

When he was done writing, the leader read the statement and clucked his tongue. The sound stabbed his ears like a sharp needle. Shaking uncontrollably, Jeong waited for them to deal with him. There simply was nothing else to be done.

"The motherfucker thinks he's being funny, doesn't he? Television stars? Movie actresses? Hey, shithead, who told you to give me a rundown of your workday?" The chief snarled and slapped his face left and right with the paper containing his statement.

"So, you're a hard nut to crack. Well, boys, don't hold yourselves back. Kill him if you need to. Just make sure he cracks."

What was going to happen now? Jeong's heart skipped a beat. A new man and the red shirt walked toward him slowly with their stony gaze fixed on him. They were each holding a long, rectangular piece of wood the length of a small child. Instinctively, Jeong jumped to his feet and cowered in a corner. He couldn't face their gray stare as they neared him from both sides, dragging their feet like a pair of tarantulas. He balled up and covered his head with his arms when the first blow landed on his back. The wooden sticks rained down on him, ambushing his calves, shoulders, sides. He started running around the room, trying to escape the blows. It was better to be on the move. The swollen soles of his feet were numb, but he had no time to think about the pain. All he concentrated on was evading as many blows as possible. When the stick landed on the naked skin, blood splattered. If someone had told him this morning, when he was still a respectable thirty-something and a contributing member of society, that he would be running around in his briefs later that day, he wouldn't have believed it. And yet, here he was, being cornered like a pig by four men swinging wooden sticks at him. He was a pig, less than a pig, and they were all animals. Fear was much stronger than shame, though he did shudder with indignation that was much greater than fear at one point. But he couldn't think about anything for too long. All his attention had to be directed toward surviving. If one of those sticks were to land on his head while he was letting his thoughts about the indignity of the situation distract him, he would die on the spot. The torturers swung their sticks wildly as if they had the license to kill. Then Jeong felt a shooting pain and fell to the ground. The deadly thrashing finally ceased.

The men left their sticks leaning against one wall, and the one who seemed to be the youngest of the bunch helped him to his feet. Jeong was amazed that his body was still holding together. After all that, he could still walk. Sometimes fear produced superhuman strength. He probably would have walked even with both of his legs broken. He moved his wound-covered limbs and dressed all by himself. The young man guarding him held on to his belt and led him out of the interrogation room into another that was big and filled with rows of desks, much like his own office. Every employee of S Police Station must have a desk here, he thought.

They sat him in a chair in one corner. People in the room went about their business, without paying him any attention. No one seemed much interested in his wound-covered body. Shaking like a leaf, he drank the hot cup of coffee the young man brought him. It filled him with gratitude. *Do you feel cold?* The man asked him politely. Jeong didn't answer. He was sipping his coffee slowly to make every drop last. Then a tray of rice and some side dishes were brought in and placed before him. It seemed that even torture sessions observed the lunch break. The rice took his breath away. It choked him up to think that he was being fed for having been pummeled within an inch of his life. He eyed the hot bowl of soup hungrily, but he couldn't eat much because of his swollen throat. He lowered his head and tried to sit still, telling himself that he was having a nightmare and that all he had to do was wake up.

"You should eat. You'll need the strength." The friendly voice advised him again. He barely managed to suppress the impulse to throw himself at the man and sob his heart out in his arms. Jeong had never known that it would move him so to be treated like a human being. It was then that he learned that torturers have two faces which they kept strictly separate. During the torture, they curse you as if all they want to do is to eat you alive, and when the torture session ends, they return on cue to their smiling, polite selves.

When the lunch hour ended, the man took him back to the interrogation room. Once again, he was stripped down to his briefs. The shaking which had finally come under control during the break returned with a vengeance. The chief came back a moment later, and Jeong was allowed to sit in a chair. Then the questioning began. Jeong was ready to talk, the men seemed to think, now that he had been beaten within an inch of his life.

"We know you received money from X. How much?"

Jeong recognized the name as that of the leader of an opposition political party. He was dumbfounded. The question was so unexpected that he couldn't help but answer truthfully before he had had sufficient time to think. No, he didn't know him. He didn't know anybody in politics. The chief slapped him repeatedly. Blood gushed out from

Jeong's nose and splattered onto the chief's shirt. *Stinking liar, I know he gave you five million* won. When Jeong denied it, sticks rained down upon him as if they had been waiting for his reply. The men cornered him like a pig once again and pummeled him some more.

The chief then asked him, "A fellow named Bak Seonggeun, is he a friend of yours?"

So the question was here at last. Jeong decided at that point to give up. It was meaningless to resist any longer. From the very beginning, the torturers had all the keys, and they were going to wait until he volunteered to become the lock that fits the key they wanted to use. When Jeong acknowledged that Bak Seonggeun was indeed a friend of his, the leader demanded, "You received the money, right?"

He said, yes.

"There you go. How much? Two million?" The leader phrased the questions so that all he had to do was say yes. Jeong began to see the light at the end of the tunnel. Once he started acknowledging things, everything proceeded according to the scenario. The chief spun stories Jeong had never heard before and he said—yes, yes.

But they weren't going to let him off that easy. Jeong felt his breath catch in his throat when the chief asked him to name another organizational route. Who, what, how? He had to climb onto the steel desk again. The mouth of hell opened up and another round of water torture began. He wanted to faint the moment his hands and feet were tied. He now knew exactly what kind of terror awaited him, and he simply couldn't bear it. His teeth chattered. The torturers were machines. Before he knew it, an entire ocean started flowing into his nostrils again. Death flickered as he slipped in and out consciousness and made him thrash wildly. He couldn't breathe. His throat was swelling up, and it was going to rip to pieces. In the depth of his despair, a voice came. He didn't realize he was twisting and shouting at the top of his lungs. I'll talk … I'll talk … I'll talk….

The towel was removed from his face, and the leader drew near to him with a treacherous smile on his face. Jeong named names, he didn't know whose. Whatever name that came to his mind he gave. Once he was beaten twenty or thirty blows with the stick for naming too many names. He was in hell. His mind became a tangled knot, and he thought he would go crazy any moment. So this was how his friend had come to give his name, too. It was all too painfully clear.

Once he started crumbling apart, he wasn't sure about anything anymore. This couldn't be me, he thought. The loss of identity overcame him like a tidal wave. Because he wasn't himself anymore, fear grew that much greater, that much faster. Just the frown on the torturers' faces had him trembling. A tiny movement by one of men caused his heart to stop and his body to shrink back automatically.

The beating and the water torture went on all day. The first session had begun shortly before ten in the morning, and when everything was finally over, it was five in the afternoon. Jeong knew he hadn't dreamt it all, but wished all the more desperately that he had. How could this be real? A man gets up one day, goes to work by nine, and starts getting tortured. At noon, he has lunch, and at five, he's done. Just like a normal workday.

When the afternoon session was over, the red shirt had to help Jeong dress himself. His clothes scraped his skin as if they were made of razor blades, but they did help keep out the cold.

"Send him downstairs."

Following the chief's order, two men grabbed him by the arms and took him below. (Before that he had crawled on all fours to the bathroom. Hugging the filthy toilet bowl, he urinated and crawled back, again on all fours.)

The cell was in the basement. It was partitioned into two sections, and he lay down at one corner with the help of college students who were there before him. He felt as though his entire body would crumble apart. He couldn't localize any of the pain. A young Protestant pastor with an injured back was lying down on the bench. There were fifteen or so college students, and they did not appear to have severe injuries, at least at a first glance. From the other side of the partition came occasional moaning. Jeong spent the entire night in excruciating pain. The students helped him to the bathroom and put ointments on his wounds. They were mostly from Korea University, which was within S Station's jurisdiction, and told him that K, one of their professors, was in the next cell. Jeong found out that the young pastor, who had injured his back severely during a torture session, was receiving treatment on an outpatient basis. The young pastor went out for his treatment the next day and brought back a variety of medication. Jeong found them a great relief.

What little bit there was of his basic human pride left, which he thought had all but crumbled away, returned as he lay there in the cell. Its return made the pain mental as well as physical. Jeong did not have a moment's rest. That first night in the cell, he drew the blanket over his head and sobbed.

The torture and questioning continued the next day. This time he was told to write down everything that had happened to him since he was born. If they didn't like what he wrote, they pummeled him again. They also told him to write down how he had received the two million *won* from X. He listened carefully to their questions and wrote down what he thought they wanted to hear. Despite all his efforts to cooperate, they accused him of helping a certain individual on the wanted list hide out, and tortured him with water some more. Jeong didn't know what kind of relationship this particular individual had to Bak Seonggeun, but he was only a minor acquaintance to him and Jeong had no idea about his recent activities. The water torture was agonizing, but he couldn't say anything because he didn't have any concrete content to work with. The men, however, turned a deaf ear to his pleas. When they bound his arms and legs, he felt his breath catch in his throat. The feel of a towel over his face made him gag. He thought he would never forget the loathsome sound of water gurgling out of the teakettle. His throat on fire and his body convulsing, he floundered in the depths of hell and drifted in and out of consciousness.

Sometimes, as he tried desperately to stay afloat, snippets of conversation between the torturers would reach his ears. *My daughter got a second-place prize at a piano contest.... My eldest son does well in school but his health is poor. He'll be a high school senior soon, and I just don't know how he's going to survive the college examination hell.* Jeong wanted to hear more of their conversations, but couldn't help the death screams from escaping his mouth and drowning out their voices. When there was no more scream left in him, the acrid smell of something burning filled his nostrils. He shuddered, sprawled out by the side of men who went on talking about their children. A young pianist, a frail high school boy, a human being writhing at death's door. It gave him goosebumps. How could he ever forgive these fathers?

On the third day, they brought him face to face with Bak Seonggeun for the first time. His face distended like a balloon, Bak choked up when he saw him. *I'm sorry, man....* Jeong didn't hold any grudge against Bak. Well, he did. But not at that moment, no, not at that moment. One could tell at a glance that Bak, too, had been to hell and back. *Are you okay?* Jeong asked. There was nothing else for him to say.

He spent the entire third day writing out his statement. He wrote the same thing over and over again, and sometimes got his story mixed up. Fists and all manners of degrading curses flew at hjm then. The torturers knew that Jeong was just a peon, but that didn't make them slacken the reins one bit. Jeong even inserted some unsavory phrases into his statement voluntarily. When he returned to the cell that evening, the college students listened to his story, and told him that his sentence would be at least a year and half. Eighteen months. Oddly enough, he felt much calmer after finding out what his sentence would be. If he could do the time in jail without being tortured, he didn't care if the sentence were 180 months. One of the college students was released that night. Jeong wrote down his home and office numbers and asked the student to make some calls for him. The shock his wife would receive concerned him, but he felt that it would be better for her to know that he was in here rather than not know anything at all.

The next two days he spent in the cell without being called upstairs. On Saturday morning, a policeman came down and told him that he would be released in the afternoon. The unexpected news actually filled him with resentment rather than joy . Was it going to be over? Could they make a complete wreck of him and then wash their hands of him just like that?

On Saturday afternoon, he listened to a long speech given by a man who seemed to be one of the higher ups in rank. *At uncertain times like these, one should be all the more careful about one's actions and words. National security is a much more important and grave matter than you think....* Jeong had no other feeling than a heavy sense of injustice. Following the directions he was given, he wrote a note to the effect that he will go on with his life as though nothing has happened and endorsed the note with his fingerprint. *I will never divulge this matter to anyone. If I do, I will thereupon receive willingly any punishment that is deemed appropriate.* The red shirt whose job it was to hold the kettle during the water torture folded up the statement, put it in an envelope, and placed the envelope in a desk drawer. Then he returned the belt that he took

64

from Jeong on the first day. *Thank you for your hard work. Take good care of yourself.* The red shirt saw him to the front of the building and consoled him warmly. To the very end, Jeong did not look up at the red shirt's face. Once outside, he leaned against the wall and tried to calm his dizziness. Every time he took a step, a moan escaped through the gums of his teeth. He looked back at the building once last time. His mind was made up. He was never going to forgive any one of them, even if God did.

Jeong found out later that his release was arranged by his elder sister's husband. Among his brother-in-law's elementary school friends was a colonel who had just been transferred to a regiment in Seoul. Thus, it was a colonel's influence that had unbound him from eighteen months of incarceration. But the nightmare wasn't over yet. His wife greeted him, her complexion grown sallow in a matter of days. She couldn't hold back her outrage when she saw what had happened to his body, which looked as though it had been soaked in blue ink. She stayed strong for a few days and tried to nurse him. On the third day of his return, however, she collapsed. Their son was four months away from being born and the miscarriage was the price she paid for ignoring the doctor's orders to rest and avoid stress. Jeong's mother took over the role of nursing him. And thus the name "Hanbit" vanished into the void. Hanbyeol was the child that came to them after three subsequent years of waiting.

Several months after that, an even more abominable episode took place. Jeong ran into one of his torturers at a famous barbecue restaurant. It was a possibility he had feared: He thought he might one day run into the slit-eyes, the red shirt, the chief who had supervised the whole torture session, or one of the others. It turned out to be the chief. Jeong was with his wife. The leader was with his family—wife, daughter, and two sons. They were both on a family night out at a barbecue restaurant.

Of all the tables at the restaurant, the chief's was right next to his. At first they didn't recognize each other. Both he and the chief were seated on the left, so they could miss each other if they were not purposely trying to make eye contact. Jeong was trying to get his wife to eat. She was turning the pieces of meat over on the grill for him without eating them herself. Life had been dark and gloomy for them since his release, and the rare outing was an attempt to lift their spirits. *Their meat is supposed to be really tender. I want to see you stuff yourself. Don't just eat the burnt ones.* He was probably saying such things to his wife, when a voice from the next table paralyzed him.

"A man has to eat to have strength for the things he needs to do. You do well in school, but your health is terrible. How will you survive all the studying you have to do to get into college?"

The voice was familiar. So was the story. Tensing up instinctively, Jeong leaned back to look at the man behind the voice. He recognized him right away. The chief was dressed in expensive clothes, but there was no mistaking the eyes. The two of them half rose from their seats, pushed their chairs back and walked out to the aisle between the tables. The chief seemed very happy to see him, and extended his hand. Jeong met the chief's extended hand with his own.

"It's been a while. How are you?" The chief asked.

"Oh, yes, well, fine," he replied. After shaking hands, they each returned to their seat and rejoined their respective families.

"Who is that?" his wife asked in a tiny voice.

"He was in the business department, I think…," Jeong lied without batting an eye. His appetite was gone and his hands started shaking badly, still he made an effort to put on a calm face for his wife. But the chief was shameless enough to start a conversation with him.

"The meat's a bit on the tough side today, wouldn't you say?"

Jeong agreed hurriedly, wrapping a piece of meat in a leaf of Chinese lettuce. They then exchanged opinions on various other topics appropriate for the barbecue restaurant setting. When the chief said that an outing like this cost a lot of money because his was a family of big eaters, his fat wife laughed loudly. Jeong also asked questions from time to time, afraid that his wife would think it strange if all the conversation originated at the other table. *You've got such a pretty daughter. How old is she? Does she get good grades?* To the son with poor health, he asked where he went to school. This was the very son that the chief had been worrying about in the torture chamber, while Jeong lay there writhing with the pain of suffocation and the burning smell in his nose. There were still pimples on the boy's face. The boy seemed shy and innocent. He smiled bashfully.

The chief's family finished eating first. The chief came over to say goodbye.

"It was nice to meet you," he said to Jeong's wife, making her acquaintance just like that. "We'll be going now, but please enjoy the rest of your meal." The pimply son also bowed his head in greeting.

After the chief's family left the restaurant, Jeong almost crashed onto the table. Hadn't he vowed that he would never forgive them? From the way he acted, it sure seemed that he had, when even God couldn't have forgiven them yet. He was going crazy.

Had he really forgiven them, the gray-eyed torture specialists? On the bus to Gyeongju, Jeong asked himself again. For a long time after his return to normal life, he was plagued by physical symptoms. Standing before the automatic doors or climbing up the stairwell where the two men had waited form him that day made him turn white as a sheet. The torturers' faces would come back to him, and he broke out into a cold sweat as if he were having a nightmare from which he couldn't awake. True to the pledge on his release statement, he never told anyone the particulars of what had happened to him. That he was beaten a little, jerked around a little, was the extent of the explanation he gave to people. He was very cautious about his actions, too. No matter how trivial they were, he didn't take on any articles that had even a remote reference to political matters.

Living through the 1980s transformed him completely. He had been at the mercy of torture's vast power, experienced the omnipotence of violence firsthand. Everyday was an eternity, and eternity was hell. He endured that hell by peeking into movie stars' bedrooms and inquiring about baseball players' salaries. He wanted to believe that he might just be able to pass the time, if he locked himself up in that peculiar world of women's monthlies and blinded himself to the world outside. The fear before the automatic doors and the menace of the stairs instructed him to do that. When he heard stories of tortured people, he reminded himself of the oath of silence he had taken. He followed it so faithfully, he had to wonder sometimes whether what he had signed wasn't an oath of loyalty written in blood rather than a simple note. It was an idle thought. He knew that if an oath of loyalty, written in blood, had been what they wanted, he would have given it to them. Still, he didn't forget the torturers. He despised them. Even after the run-in with the chief's family at the barbecue restaurant, which made him realize how foolish this hatred was, he didn't forgive the torturers. He couldn't help but despise the era he was living in.

He suffered no additional arrests after that day. In time, memory dulled, then became lost. He still got up in the morning and went to bed at night, and spent the time in between filling the pages of a women's magazine. At times, he did wrestle with the thought that he was deceiving himself. His mind was never at ease and days without hope dragged on in tedium. It had to be a lie that his daily life went on as if nothing had changed, when he himself was an utterly changed man. Though he detested the system, he worked assiduously for the system; this unambiguous contradiction made him a depressed person, but it couldn't be helped. Of course there was a different path. He did ask himself from time to time why he wasn't on that path. There was now some distance between himself and the fear he had known, and whatever else he might be, he was no coward. But all he wanted was a gentle life, days lived in the absence of force. It was wretched to live with the knowledge that what he wanted would probably elude him for life.

Even when everyone was talking about reforming the constitution to allow direct presidential election to take place and petitions were circulating everywhere, Jeong did not believe that there was a future for him. The future was only for those who had countless torture specialists working for them. In an age of fear, how could sheets of paper with signatures on them possibly dethrone the absolute ruler? So when, on the thirteenth of April, 1987, the congress voted for a measure to keep the constitution unchanged, Jeong was neither surprised nor angry. His was the pessimism of the victim who had been the obedient lock for every one of the torturer's keys.

It was June of last year when he began to wonder whether there might be a future after all. Last June was the first June since his release that he hadn't come down with a terrible cold. The streets were wild. Groups of students and citizens stormed the riot police, and the police met them with equal force. Both sides seemed to be burning up with hatred of equal intensity. Instinctive fear assailed him, and Jeong felt that he would explode from the sense of crisis. Perhaps the easiest thing to do was to throw himself into the arrogant tide of citizens who had poured out onto the streets to demand democracy, their faces lit up with animation, with life. Once, he almost did.

Still, as tension mounted, both sides began to appear the same to him. For the price of spending June without falling sick, he had to look truth in the eye which he had tried desperately to keep stowed away in the depths of him. After nearly seven years, he couldn't run from the agonizing truth anymore: It was he who had once shouted that he would never forgive them, even if God did. The automatic doors left him swaying again, and hallucinations returned at the stairs' landing. What he couldn't forgive was no longer the torturers. It was the era of extremism that he was living in. This age had thrust him into that deep and murky cave of nihilism and made him defend himself with the quips of a skeptic. He couldn't forgive the age that had justified violence and made torturers of fathers.

On the other hand, he had to admit that he still despised the torturers to the point of madness, the laughter of the red shirt, the treacherous face of the leader, the humiliating command of the men. The hatred and rage came back alive after nearly seven years and possessed him completely. Perhaps it was this that urged his resignation. His letter of resignation stated that he was resigning for personal reasons, but the letter was no more than a mere formality. What he couldn't endure was the seven years that he had pawed the air in the swamp, the seven years of idleness in which he had faithfully kept every promise they had made him write in his release statement. While fully aware of the fact that a particular actor pandered to those in power, Jeong still wrote an article in praise of him. Jeong knew their conspiracies and still moved his pen along the paper to serve them. And now, he found himself in a snare. It wasn't the remorse for all those years he had served the system, but anger, an intense feeling of hostility that wouldn't let him go on as he had.

There must be a different way to live, he said to himself, as he struggled to create some order in his muddled brain. Then he tendered his resignation Though he wasn't sure about anything else, he knew that this resignation, at least, wasn't a mistake.

"Did you have a nice nap?" his wife asked. He had kept his eyes closed, and she had thought he was sleeping. "We're here. It's Gyeongju," his wife exclaimed softly.

Beyond the terminal, which was smaller and shabbier than he

expected it to be, he saw a series of traditional tile roofs. Even while taking their bags down from the overhead shelf, his wife couldn't take her eyes off the window. *From now on, we'll be treading on Silla soil.* She was getting a second wind, even after being hassled all day. In contrast, he felt as though his body weighed a ton. Just thinking about where and how they should travel in order to leave their footprints on Silla soil made him feel tired. The bus came to a stop, and he had to lead his family onward. Fortunately, there were enough taxis waiting at the terminal that he didn't have to worry about flagging one down. All of the taxis were waiting to drive passengers to Bulguk Temple.

At the mouth of Bulguk Temple was an entire compound of inns and motels. The taxi driver took them to a largish inn three stories high with the traditional tile roof. He gave the bag to the bellhop running out to greet them and stretched his shoulder. Walking up the three stories and then down the third-floor corridor, he did get a whiff of moldy smell he associated with inns in general; but their room was large and relatively clean. The accommodations were neither better nor worse than what one expected at the standard price the driver quoted for the inns in town. Hanbyeol, who had never been to an inn before, looked around in delight and peeked into the bathroom. Jeong saw a cockroach slipping into a crack between the wall and the folding screen standing against it. The suspicion that the room might be crawling with cockroaches became even stronger at the clammy feel of the floor and bedding, but he didn't say anything to his wife. Shouldn't he have been able to afford a stay at a tourist hotel for his family? The thought made him feel dejected.

"I guess they take class trips in spring too, nowadays," his wife said while looking out the window. Jeong walked up to the window and looked out at the compound. Tour buses with series numbers taped to the front window were unloading colorfully clad junior high school students. Every student had a bag in hand. Even at this distance, he could hear the sound of their chattering, though he could not make out the content of what they were saying. He looked around at the buildings. Every building sported the curvy lines and tiled roof of the traditional Korean house in clever ways. These tiles, new and mossless, on two- or three-story buildings struck him as strange.

After unpacking and calling the front ahead to request dinner downstairs, they decided to take a walk in the meanwhile. The room wasn't heated yet, so the air in the room was very chilly, and despite their fatigue, they didn't want to lie down and rest just yet. When they descended the steps, the manager of the inn came up to them and asked what their schedule would be for tomorrow.

"Actually, we haven't thought about it yet ...."

Before the words were out of his mouth, the manager suggested that they hire a taxi for the day.

"You start the day by watching the sun rise over Toham Mountain. Then you do a tour of Bulguk Temple and Seokkuram Grotto. After breakfast, you make the rounds of all the major spots: Bunhwang Temple, Daereung Tomb, Cheomseong Tower Observatory, the National Museum, Poseokcheong, and Geumgwan Tomb. This way, you'll have covered all the main sights in Gyeongju. This is the regular one-day route, and the flat fee is four hundred thousand *won*. It's hard to get a meter taxi to and from all of these places, and the cost will come out to be about the same anyway. Most tourists prefer to see Gyeongju this way. How do you feel?"

The price struck him as a bit on the high side, but the idea was attractive since he knew how difficult it would be for him to hail cabs. Back at home, his wife would have objected to the price, but here she agreed with a surprising readiness. As he was putting down the deposit, he felt rather regretful. He had the vague notion that sightseeing was supposed to be done with a 200:1 map open in your hand, where you marked off historical sights one by one as you made your way through the place. There was no room for imagination when you were racing from one sight to the next in a hired cab. Still, as the head of the family with a young daughter and a wife with delicate health, he couldn't ignore the advantages of taking the comfortable route. He also had to admit that a part of the relief he felt came from the fact that someone else was now going to make all the decisions.

When they returned to the room after the walk and the dinner at the restaurant downstairs, it was already past eight o'clock. They took turns washing their faces and feet, and by the time they were ready for bed, the nine o'clock news was on television. The story about New Village corruption that had first broken in March was still the top news, and there was a great deal of coverage on the national assembly elections as well. Jeong gazed blankly at the television screen. Watching the news in Gyeongju was no different from watching it in Seoul. What else did you expect? Silla news? He smiled bitterly to himself. Because of the strange new setting, Hanbyeol fidgeted a long time before finally drifting off to asleep. His wife also complained about how boring a night in Gyeongju was, but before long, her fatigue got the better of her and she was asleep. He called the front desk. *Yes, of course. We'll give you a morning call.* The manager was very courteous.

It was the same dream again. He was in that big room. Naked except for his briefs, he trembled uncontrollably. The one who had taken his clothes was nowhere to be seen, and the premonition of danger nearing him an inch by inch set his teeth chattering. From somewhere he could hear the clicking of hard-toed shoes on cement floor and the sound of dripping water. It was cold, so cold that he could die....

The telephone rang. The menacing sound of the footsteps retreated. He opened his eyes, but the room was still dark. Without turning the light on, he picked up the phone. Looking for the telephone receiver in the dark, he almost knocked down the kettle of water by his head; but he didn't care. He had to tend to the telephone first. The telephone ringing in the dark was ominous. He knew there was nothing ominous about it, that it was only a wake-up call; but it was still ominous. *Good morning, this is the front desk. The taxi will be here in fifteen minutes. Please get ready. I'll give you another call in ten minutes.* The voice on the other side of the line was courteous despite the early hour. By now the footsteps were completely gone. His wife turned on the light. Weren't you cold? Hanbyeol kept kicking the blanket off. They should have given us more heat..., his wife complained. She looked disheveled.

It was cold as they watched the sun rise over Toham Mountain. He shuddered as he watched clouds and the mist clear over East Sea. The moment the hot ball of fire crushed the horizon and sprang up, people exclaimed loudly, but he coughed. The taxi driver had them stand in a row for a photo against the backdrop of the rising sun.

He was cold at Bulguk Temple, too. They looked around the temple, surrounded by students on a field trip, and the chill morning air made his face smart. Hanbyeol and his wife also whined about the cold, but his wife insisted on a picture in front of every national treasure—Dabo and Seokka Stupas. He pressed the shutter while shaking. In order not to cut off the stupa or his wife's or daughter's legs, he had to keep walking back. His own picture was taken upon his wife's insistence. Then, in front of the dharma drum hung at the end of a long portico, he took a picture with Hanbyeol, and by the side of a bell in a belfry, he took a picture by himself. As he was getting his photograph taken, he heard one of the many tour guides give an explanation about the bell. "We ring this bell every morning and evening now, but it was originally rung to console the poor souls suffering in hell. The bell toll is supposed to ease sorrow and confer joy."

By the time they returned to the inn for breakfast, he had a runny nose and his head felt unpleasantly heavy. They satisfied their hunger with the same Silla set they had last night and returned to their room to pack. They had an hour before the taxi returned. As his wife put on her makeup, he stretched out on the bedding and smoked a cigarette. He was exhausted from fighting the cold: He had gone out into that dreadful cold again after struggling against it all night long. He was being aloof, and his wife was glum.

He hated himself for being unable to act more cheerful when it had taken so much effort to come on this trip in the first place. He was observing his every move carefully. He had the constant feeling that the ground was caving in under him, that he was trying all he could to stay afloat. Sometimes he would be startled by the feeling that his body had evaporated. Catching himself, he would look at his wife, and his wife looked away and pretended not to have noticed. His wife was observing him, too.

When they got in the taxi, he was puzzled to find that they had a new driver. He thought that hiring a taxi for the day meant that the same driver would guide them. The new driver, older than the one from the morning, had a kindly face and was chockfull of information about Silla's history. His manner of talking was experienced and smooth, even eloquent.

"As you know, there's no other capital in history that enjoyed as long a period of power as Gyeongju. Almost a thousand years. We would probably have to say that every pebble, every tree in this place is imbued with the breath of Silla people. Silla was the first unified kingdom in Korea and a powerful country and countless relics have been found all over Gyeongju."

His wife and Hanbyeol were listening attentively to the driver's explanation. It was the same old story: invasions on the Korean peninsula, the powerful conquering the weak, followed by years of prosperity. The sun was higher in the sky, and it was spring weather again. When they arrived at Bunhwang Temple, they didn't see a single tourist, perhaps on account of the early hour.

"Let me take your picture."

Jeong only paid for two adult tickets, but the driver walked through the entrance without hesitation. The family photograph was taken in front of the famous three-story stupa they had all seen many times in photographs. He thought the tour of Bunhwang Temple was over at that point, but the driver led them to a well on the other side of the stupa.

"We can't very well leave without tasting some Silla water."

According to the driver's explanation, three dragons believed to be guardians of the kingdom lived in the temple's well from ancient times. During the reign of King Wonseong, the thirty-eighth Silla monarch, an envoy from Tang China came to Bunhwang Temple and saw the dragons. Wanting to take the dragons with him back to China, the envoy schemed and cast a spell to turn the dragons into fish. Then he left on his way, taking the three fish with him. When he found out about this later, King Wonseong sent an army after the envoy and brought the fish back. They were returned to the well.

"That's the reason why this well is called the Well of Three Fish-Dragons. Taste the water. It's the same water that Silla people used to drink."

Using a red plastic ladle on top of the lid covering the well, they scooped some water from the well and took a sip, before posing for another photo in front of the well. Hanbyeol looked into the well and tried to find the fish.

The story about the well brought back memories of his father. Wherever he went, Jeong's father found fault with the taste of water. Either it was salty or it tasted like metal. No water could compare to the water that came from the well in the backyard of the house he had left behind in the north. For a man who exhibited little interest in life, Jeong's father could complain quite bitterly about the taste of water to the bitter end. But even Jeong's mother marveled about the taste of the water from that well.

"As your father would say, it was no ordinary well. Villagers with ailments would come to our house to drink a bucketful of the water. The well was so deep that even during droughts and floods, the water level remained constant."

But Jeong's mother didn't have time to indulge herself in such reminiscences. For Jeong, the well was just another reason to hate his father. At the crack of dawn, his father would sit up and gulp down the bowl of cold water at his head, and enveloped in the gray half-dark, grumble the familiar complaint. *Bah, this is sewer water; not fit for people to drink.* Jeong couldn't understand his father who made a fuss about the taste of water when there might be nothing to eat for dinner. Even though Jeong came to understand vaguely that his water and his land meant one and the same thing, he couldn't forgive his father for the terror of poverty that he bequeathed to them.

Five minutes each, which was the time it took to listen to the driver's short explanation and take a photo, was enough to look around Cheomseong Tower Observatory and Poseokcheong. At Poseokcheong, they dawdled slightly longer because of the squirrels that darted through the thick, old trees that surrounded the pond. The squirrels were big enough to be small pups, and frisked about freely without any fear of people. While his wife and Hanbyeol watched the squirrels' acrobatics, he sat on the grass near the entrance and enjoyed the warmth of the morning sun. The driver brought an old newspaper from the ticket booth. *Look! There are three of them. Mom, there are three squirrels.* It was clear that Hanbyeol was more interested in the squirrels than in both Cheomseong Tower and Poseokcheong combined. He opened up the newspaper, listening the child's squeals of laughter.

It was the morning paper from a week ago, dated March 24th. He thumbed through it cursorily. A four-column article on page ten caught his eyes. "Remains of Thousand Plus Japanese Conscripts to Return Home." Over the black gothic letters of the headline, there was a reddish stain, maybe from *kimchi*. Judging from the creases and the *kimchi* stain, he guessed that the paper had been used to wrap someone's lunchbox. Smelling *kimchi* all the while, Jeong read the article about 1,441 young Korean men conscripted into the Japanese army during the

Pacific War who had died on foreign soil. Their identities were finally confirmed, making it possible for their remains to return home.

"The number of Korean soldiers, comfort women, and coal miners conscripted by the Japanese who died on foreign soil from 1939 to 1945 is estimated to be over three hundred thousand. Many of them left behind a will as they prepared to die on foreign soil."

The article included one soldier's will in particular:

"Dear brother, if I should die on duty, and if the white box containing my bones should reach home, please bury me next to Father. I leave Mother in your care. The will of Private Shinyama Unshu,[11] 622th Company, Manchuria —Yongdu Village, 2700 Munin District, Okcheon County, Cheongju Prefecture, North Pyeongan Province, Korea."

Jeong lowered his head, after reading the will several times, including the Japanese name affixed to the end. *Bury me next to Father.*

His own father's remains brought from Seongseo were buried on the slope of a high mountain in Changsu District, Pocheon County, where one could imagine the distant horizon overlapping with the northern territory beyond the wide open sea of trees. If one jumped over a few mountain peaks, one might even see Hantan River flowing there. He had insisted on burying his father as north as possible, where the spring that fed father's well may even be in sight. He visited many places, but none appealed to him as much as Pocheon. Aside from the fact that it was close to the northern border, the quality of soil was excellent. At Seongseo when they disinterred the body, the workers expected to find just the bones. Everyone was surprised to find that the body hadn't disintegrated much over the years. Under the coffin, they found a large puddle, almost a pool, of water. *The land was no good.* All the workers clucked.

The corpse that had endured eighteen years intact was transferred into a new coffin. Transporting this coffin in a van to Seoul, Jeong

---

[11] Many Koreans adopted Japanese-style names under the Japanese policy of forced assimilation during the late colonial period. In the original text, the soldier's name is rendered in Chinese characters. It is impossible to determine definitively what the Japanese reading of these characters would have been. Shinyama Unshu is one probable reading.

stopped the car many times and straightened the shaking coffin. Heading north and farther north with his father lying in the coffin, he hoped from the bottom of his heart that the soil at the new site would turn out to be rich and fertile. He prayed that the change in the resting place would allow his father's soul to leave the body and fly, free as a bird, back to his land visible in the distance. Even though he still could not understand his father's wanderings, his frightful will to nothingness, he could now concede at least that his father, too, had been a victim. Father's idle life, just like the seven years Jeong had spent going through the motions, hadn't been intentional. Father's will, if he had left one, might have looked much like the one written by a soldier facing the end of his days in Manchuria or the Philippines. *Dear brother, if I should die on duty and if the white box containing my bones should reach home, please bury me next to Father.* A day will have to come when his father's bones will reach his home in the north. When that day comes, who will be the one carrying the white box?

As he gazed mindlessly at a tree's shadow flickering over the pond at Poseokcheong, the silvery notes of the child's laughter reached his ears. The clear, ringing sound was like that made on a xylophone, and it echoed through a thousand-year-old forest. He remembered his wife's words to the child. *This family trip, Hanbyeol, is Grandfather's special gift to us.* He looked at the child's round head bobbing up and down as she chased the squirrels around. Her hair as she wove in and out of the shadows shined as though studded with jewels.

After leaving Poseokcheong, they spent an hour in the National Museum, then headed for the Daereung Tomb Park.

"It takes time to look around Daereung Tomb. I'll pick you up at the front gate in an hour. It's really nice in there, lots of good spots to take photos. There's a lot to see in Cheonnma Tomb as well."

On the way to Daereung Tomb, the driver gave them pointers:

"The first thing you notice in Gyeongju is the huge mounds. They might look like grassy knolls at first. Daereung Tomb Park is over thirty-eight thousand square yards of flat land where there is a high concentration of these mounds, twenty mounds to be exact. Originally there were a hundred and eighty houses scattered all over the area but after the cleanup project in 1973, the entire area became a park. Including the mounds that have collapsed and flat tombs that are not readily visible, experts estimate that there must be hundreds of royal graves inside the Park, but we don't know who was buried where except for King Michu ...."

The explanation trailed off and the car came to a stop. They were at Daereung Tomb Park. The taxi went on its way after dropping them off in front of a brightly painted gate. He bought tickets, feeling the weight of the bag which didn't seem to have diminished one bit. It was a dazzlingly sunny spring day, but he was suffering from a headache. The headache had come on at the museum. Maybe it was just a headache that accompanies the onset of a cold. At least, that's what he wanted to believe. Feeling the pounding at his temples, Jeong went into the Daereung Tomb Park with his wife and daughter in tow. Since it was a Saturday, he thought the place might be milling with people, but the park was quiet, as though there were no one inside. He did hear the sound of footsteps and murmuring voices from afar, but the dense growth of pine trees at the entrance kept everything hidden from view. Entering the path that curved around the woods, Jeong realized that he was tapping his forehead with the palm of his hand.

He knew this headache intimately. It had intruded in his life before. For almost a year after he was released from his week-long stay at S Police Station, the pounding of a hammer at his temples followed him everywhere he went. Pain relievers didn't help. The doctors he went to see sent him on his way with the pat diagnosis of "nerves." The herbalist his friend recommended listened to his symptoms and prescribed ten-day's worth of tonics, which did help assuage the pain a bit; but the reason why the headache was so torturous was not only on account of the pain. With the pain, his mind fell habitually into a confused, delirious state. He hallucinated constantly, now seeing a warrior in a shining armor flashing his sword and now an executioner in red with glaring eyes pouncing on him. And there were so many other terrifying visions. The most frequent of these, one that filled his mind's eye on numerous occasions, was the vision of himself, stripped and crawling on all fours on the cement floor. All balled up, he looked like a beetle, and shuddered uncontrollably as a soiled shoe left an imprint on his cheeks. Sometimes he would hug the leg that bore the shoe and beg in a wretched voice. In time, the pain gradually diminished and so did the delirium. The tedious struggle with the headache lasted almost a year.

Today, he gritted his teeth through the headache. He had no desire whatsoever to repeat that devastating struggle. He adjusted the knapsack's strap on his shoulder and walked on with greater vigor. Massive knolls, round mounds arrayed in new green grass that had endured the winter, emerged before their eyes. The smooth and gentle slope of the ancient tomb had the power to comfort those who beheld it. He even felt the urge to throw himself on it and roll down its slope. The knapsack's weight was oppressive, its strap dug into his shoulder. He let it down and took a deep breath. His head still ached. They sat down on the grassy field between the mounds and rested for a while. Most of the mounds were covered only with grass, but some did have dense growth of trees on one side. Hanbyeol was delighted with the green grass. His wife, too, caressed the gentle curve of the tomb, her eyes filled with wonder. Not even a trace of wind disturbed the stillness that reigned in the park, and he had the sudden, other-worldly feeling that the three of them were alone in that broad expanse.

In the deep stillness of the park, looking at the blue sky and the mounds' gentle arcs, he ruminated about time. After a thousand years, even a history of swords and blood became an arc as gentle as that. Why should he reject that gentleness, too? Enveloped in the silence of ancient tombs, his heart was taking measure of the thickness of culture, the depth of all that sustained the humankind.

Divided in two, the interior of Cheonma Tomb was set up in such a way that people could enter and have a look around. Standing by the black, gaping mouth, he was scared for a moment to enter the dark passageway which gave him the feeling of being sucked into a wrinkle of time. His headache was getting worse, and he ran his fingers through his hair to press his skull. *Let's pay our respects with reverent hearts.* The message was engraved on a marble pillar, and several people stopped in front of it to put their hands together in reverence before making their way into the tomb.

"Daddy, let's go. Come on, hurry up." Hanbyeol's impatient urgings pushed him into the cave. He felt cold. Standing behind his wife and squeezing his child's hand, he shuddered.

Beyond the entryway, the interior of the grave was surprisingly bright. There were a surprising number of visitors milling inside. The sudden crowd that materialized before him made him feel that the solitary walk that had gotten him there was all a dream. Some people were looking into the display cases set up around the chamber's walls, and others were gathered in front of the wooden coffin placed in the far corner.

A number of senior citizens on a group tour were looking at a coffin that had once contained the remains of a king. The guide was a young woman wearing a light blue hat. He went to see the coffin while his wife and Hanbyeol looked at excavated items on display. The wooden coffin was the length of a fully grown man. Transparent glass was placed in front of it, barring visitors' access but allowing them to view the way the body had originally been placed. A crown and a belt of gold lay in their original positions as well. All around the coffin were rows of broken shards of earthenware. The soil, a bit of Silla's earth, that used to support the dead body was black as coal and powdery. The ancient king who had been laid to sleep along with over ten thousand pieces of relics, including the golden crown, golden belt and a long sword with the carving of a phoenix, was in that soil, having returned to earth as a handful of dust.

The guide leading the elderly group pointed to the black soil.

"Do you see that dirt? That's the very bottom of this mound. They didn't bury the corpse in the soil but placed a wooden coffin on level ground and built a wooden structure around it. Then they constructed a mound by piling water-smoothed stones, covering it with a layer of mud and planting grass on top. As you can see over there, the stones are the size of a human head. They would collapse when anyone tried to dig into the tomb from the outside, which made this tomb a very difficult job for graverobbers. That's why so many of the relics here remained intact over the years."

The elderly visitors nodded and let out little cries of amazement.

"Now let's go see those relics over there."

The visitors followed the guide over to the display cases. As if from habit, he tapped his forehead and looked at Silla's soil. Without warning, he recalled the desolate quiet of the strip of land where his father's been laid. For no particular reason that he could tell, loneliness washed over him.

He followed the elderly tourists and looked around the exhibits, too. His wife and Hanbyeol passed him by and went to a different display.

"Is the headache bad?" Noting the frown on his forehead, his wife asked him with a look of concern on her face. He nodded as Hanbyeol dragged his wife away.

One step from where rusty swords were on display was the painting of the *cheonma*, or the winged horse after which the tomb had been named. A white horse was standing on its hind legs at the base of a white birch tree, preparing to soar to the sky. Standing in front of that spirited winged horse, Jeong tapped his forehead again. The pain was relentless. He looked back at the black soil that had endured the passage of time along with the winged horse. His wife and Hanbyeol were standing there. He turned his head and looked back at the flying horse. Through the numbing ache in his head, he thought he heard its whinny.

He stared at the picture of the winged horse. The king was there by its side, having piled up hundreds of thousands of stones to bar the access of any animate being. Did this king need to dream, too? Did he dream of galloping through the world, urging his horse onward until everything became a part of his dominion? But why did he need a horse with wings? Did he see the end of his power?

Jeong asked himself again and again. The dream of a ruler who sealed up his tomb with hundreds of thousands of stones, of a king who couldn't relinquish power and glory even in death—what was that dream? He wanted to know. He shook his pounding head and focused on the painting of the winged horse. With his angry mane fluttering in the wind, the white horse was soaring up to the sky. Did kings have souls that dreamed of flight? Is that why they sought the sky, possessed by a sense of nothingness at the last horizon of earthly existence? What was the place they sought?

He felt thirsty. He wanted to see the winged horse take flight, shattering the hundreds of thousands, the tens of millions of stones that pressed down on his head. He wiped the few beads of sweat which had appeared on his forehead with his fingertips and stepped back from the painting. His throat was parched. He had a splitting headache. With the growing intensity of pain, he saw their faces. He heard their devious laughter, their voices. He looked into that fixed gray stare which remained calm and steady even during the clubbing, during the water-torture, during the senseless beating. He saw the face of his torturer at the barbecue restaurant, asking him how he had been since their last meeting, whether he thought the meat was a bit on the tough side today.... He shook his head. He had to ask himself why the nightmare possessed him again, here and now, at this place. He took a step closer toward the painting of the flying horse. *Can there be a new beginning for me? Can I start again?*

He rubbed his forehead against the glass. Its coolness gave him momentary relief, but the feeling of suffocation continued. From inside the glass pane, the white horse soared, rearing up on his hind legs and fluttering his mane in the wind. Just once more, couldn't he begin again just once more? The white horse springs to the sky from the last horizon of this world, carrying the rulers' dreams with him, but he wanted to live here and now, bonded to this earth to the very end. *On this land, just once more....*

In the end, he fled the cave like a fugitive, plucking his parched lips and shaking his splitting head. Outside, as he wiped away the cold sweat from his brow, his wife and Hanbyeol emerged from the dark passageway. The child was pouting, making no effort to hide her fatigue and boredom.

They started walking across the park again. Since she now knew how far it would be to the entrance, Hanbyeol continued to whine. *My legs hurt, Daddy, give me a piggyback ride.* He carried her on his back. His wife took the knapsack. They walked in between the gigantic mounds. The sun was blazing, and it was still quiet all around. To ease his headache, he frowned furiously. A bird's cry from somewhere made the child listen attentively, clinging tightly to his back.

With his hands supporting her bottom, he walked on in silence, looking only at the ground. Behind him, also in silence, his wife took one step after another. Their footsteps reverberated loudly. Looking up occasionally, he could see the haze from the heat undulate across the mound ahead. The sky was such a clean shade of blue that it hurt his eyes to look at it. They came to a wooded area. The exit from the park was just around the woods. He tightened his hold on the child. Her body was limp with fatigue, though she wasn't asleep.

Where the trees began, the road forked in two, and he saw a wooden signpost that he didn't remember seeing on the way in. *To Cheonma Tomb.* The neatly trimmed signpost was standing straight. He stopped in front of the sign. He looked carefully at each letter several times. *To Cheonma Tomb.* He read the words out loud.

He let the child down. She sulked, not wanting to leave her comfortable perch, but he pretended not to notice and took out the camera. His wife stood aside and watched them.

Standing in front of the signpost, the child's head came to just below the letters, *To Cheonma Tomb.* In the viewbox, the thirteen letters of that phrase were fully intact, and so was the face of his child which appeared right below. He adjusted the camera unhurriedly, taking his time to focus the distance and get the composition right. The child fidgeted. *Don't move, Hanbyeol. Yes, there's a good girl.* Looking at her through the lens, he soothed her. *Hold on just a bit longer, hold on.* Or was he trying to soothe his headache?

Behind the signpost were the woods. Seen through the lens, they were dark and obscure, but they made the signpost and Hanbyeol look all the more dazzling. He gazed at the picture intently—the darkness and the light, obscurity and radiance. He wanted to take a picture that is, above all else, whole. He wasn't going to cut off anything, neither the post holding up the sign, nor the child's legs. Hurting nothing, partial to nothing, keeping everything intact and whole.

The sun in her eyes made the child frown, but she managed to tweak a smile for him. Carefully, with all his heart, he pressed the shutter.

An Opportunist

The pharmacy was completely empty, save for the pharmacist sitting with a heater between his legs. The quiet struck Jeong as eerie, since the place had always required at least a five-minute wait whenever he stopped by on the way to and from work. The pharmacist got up lazily as if to take a stretch, then walked up to the counter and looked at Jeong silently. His expression seemed to say that he couldn't be bothered to open his mouth first, that he would wait quietly for the customer to speak. This expression caught Jeong by surprise, too. From what he had seen, the pharmacist's gift was his agility, an admirable ability to multi-task. "Try the medication for a day," he would say to one customer, then turn quickly to another and ask, "How can I help you?"

Flustered by the unexpected strangeness of it all, Jeong went through his symptoms haltingly. Hearing his own voice out loud, it struck him how vague and inadequate his descriptions were. Surely, he couldn't expect the pharmacist to make an accurate diagnosis based on such loose details? The thought deflated him. Recently, the useless expenditure of energy to find the words that would accurately capture his thoughts had become one of the most distressing aspect of his life. Every time he entered the labyrinth of words and groped his way out of it, he ended up abusing his nerves and detesting himself. The hackneyed quality, the dubiousness of words that actually resulted from these futile chases was quite appalling. In all likelihood, this thought that he was becoming more and more inarticulate had everything to do with the sense of inferiority he felt next to Son Mungil. He couldn't help feeling that way somehow, every time.

Luckily, when Jeong came to the end of his explanation, the pharmacist did not demand any supplementary information from him. The pharmacist was the model of efficiency.

"I think what you have is a cold, a cold of the throat, accompanied by muscle ache. You will have to take medication for two days."

"But I don't have any cold symptoms except for fever."

Jeong decided to doubt the pharmacist's diagnosis. Cold was the diagnosis he gave himself several days ago, and he had already tried cold medicine. It didn't do any good, of course.

"Some colds only cause headaches, and some muscle aches only affect arms and legs."

The expression on the pharmacist's face demanded that Jeong stop wasting his valuable time and decide whether to order a prescription or settle for an over-the-counter drug. Still, Jeong wanted to persist in his doubt a little bit longer.

"Well ... let me just try a day's worth. I have a hot flash every time I try to get some work done...."

He wasn't done talking, but the pharmacist was already in the dispensary. It was embarrassing to have to swallow the rest of what he had started to say, so he raised his voice deliberately.

"Even my eyes get red."

His head lowered, the pharmacist did not acknowledge that he heard anything. Suddenly, blood rushed to Jeong's face, and he could feel himself getting red. This was precisely the symptom he had been trying to explain. It began with a burning sensation in his cheeks. Then his face became flushed. Rarely did he suffer from this condition outside the office, but the symptom was about to make its appearance in the most timely fashion. Gingerly, he approached the mirror on the wall which was hung next to a baby formula poster. Perhaps it was all in his head, but his face really did look red to him. Holding his head high, careful not to chase the symptom away, Jeong drew the attention of the pharmacist walking out of the dispensary.

"It's flaring up again. Do you see how red my face is?"

The pharmacist's long white fingers approached Jeong's face and peeled back his eyelid. Momentarily, Jeong despaired, knowing that the fever wouldn't have reached his eyeballs yet. The white fingers made no attempt to be sensitive to his concern.

"Try this prescription for a day and come back. That'll be two thousand *won*."

Either Jeong had failed in making himself understood, or the pharmacist was stubbornly refusing to understand him. Faithlessly, Jeong handed over the money and received a paper envelope containing medicine that he doubted would work. He turned around to leave. Even before his hand was on the door, the pharmacist's goodbye was on his back, pushing him out of the shop. *Have a nice day.*

When Jeong returned to the office, he snipped open one of the three packets inside the envelope and emptied its powdery contents into his mouth. They filled his entire mouth, and he didn't like that one bit; but he was determined to give the prescription one solid day of trial at least. Even though he remained extremely doubtful, it was possible that the pharmacist had prescribed just the thing. The fact that he ran such a sizable pharmacy in the city must be a statement of some sort regarding his ability, Jeong thought. In his earlier visits to the pharmacy, Jeong had always bought over-the-counter drugs rather than the pharmacist's own prescription. He was leery of prescriptions in general. Thinking about what might be going on in that secret chamber they called the dispensary didn't reassure him at all. He wanted to verify everything with his own eyes. It was his opinion that prescriptions couldn't be trusted unless they could give him a satisfying explanation of why the dispensary needed to be closed off in the first place.

Jeong's red pen and the manuscript to be proofread were neatly placed side by side on his desk, but he found it difficult to start working. Except for the fact that Son Mungil and Bak Seongtae were not at their desks, the office's atmosphere was lively for a change. A couple of editors working on the traditional Korean fairy tales series were laughing over one of the tales. Though this couldn't be considered an extraordinary sight in a publishing office, he realized he hadn't encountered such a scene for a long time. At the office, Section One was in charge of children's books. It consisted of the section chief, assistant chief, which was the title automatically given to the most senior member of the team, second assistant chief, and a number of regular staff members. It was

Bak's opinion that these titles had to be the first to go. Positions like the chief and the assistant chief were products of a bureaucratic mindset, he said. One could tell what kind of man the company president was just from these titles.

The second assistant chief of Section One was a twenty-nine-year old woman who was still unmarried. Of a cheerful disposition, she was given to laughter, even over something as unfunny as the sight of leaves rolling on the ground. Though she was of an age to be called an "old miss," she had none of the nervous hysteria that people commonly associated with the unfortunate lot. She was laughing out loud when their eyes met.

"Mr. Jeong, Mrs. Jeong called earlier. She said you weren't feeling well?"

He shook the medicine envelope to show her. He didn't want to deal with other people making the gesture of inquiring about his condition, so he hurried away from the window and sat down at his desk. The fact that Son wasn't at his desk bothered him. *Ten o'clock today, Café Myeong.* The note that Son had tossed him in the morning was still there under the rubber pad on his desk. Son and Bak had slithered quietly out of the office before ten o'clock. As for himself, he left the office around ten past ten, and passed *Café Myeong* on his way to the pharmacy.

The manuscript he was proofreading these days was a collection of essays written by a woman poet. Though she was known as a poet, her essays were more popular than her poems. The company president was known to be sensitive to feminist issues, and it was a wonder that this set of essays had not dropped on his laps earlier. The president pretended to be worried about the fact that a collection like this didn't go very well with the company image, but everyone could see that he was actually quite excited about it. Compared to the twenty-volume series of fairy tales, the single-volume collection of essays was a minor editorial job; but from the moment he handed the manuscript over to them, the president pressured them about it in subtle ways.

The timeline and marketing plan for the essay collection had already been decided when the union was launched. The timing was a pure coincidence. The president declared that the profit from the sale of the essay collection would be spent entirely on improving the working conditions at the company, but the uncanny timing made his comment come across as a poor excuse that would have been better left unsaid. Moreover, his reaction to the unionization was surprisingly thin-skinned. For over a month now, the president was floundering, at a loss as to what to do. It seemed to Jeong that what the president found unbearable was not so much the actual burden that a labor union will place on him but the feeling of having been betrayed by his employees. How could they do this to me? he seemed to be asking himself.

Jeong understood why the president might be feeling this way. Theirs was a small company with nineteen employees in all, fourteen in Sections One and Two combined, and five in the business department. The president had been in the habit of using the expression, "our twenty-member family" to refer to the company. It was clear that he felt a sense of pride in considering himself one with the nineteen. Like the heads of many small-to-medium businesses, he emphasized family atmosphere at the workplace. On the anniversary of the company's founding, all the employees were invited to his house for an annual celebration, in addition to which there were company hiking trips every spring and autumn. He was fastidious about paying the employees on time and didn't pinch pennies about bonuses when he was in the mood. Jeong started working at the company in September of 1987 when "the solidarity of all workers nationwide" was beginning to be a fashionable slogan. The president's opinion on this issue was the following:

"The real problem is the distrust piled high between the employer and the employed. What the employers need is a paradigm shift, a completely new way of thinking about management. Total transparency is the way to go."

A year or so passed without any major problems. During that problem-free year, the president made sure to state his opinions about labor conflicts that raged on in other publishing companies. He firmly believed that there had to be a clearly identifiable cause behind every labor conflict or movement to unionize. He was right, of course. But his downfall was his inability to see that there could be something universal about this cause, and that this universality might come to enfold his employees in its grasp as well.

As soon as Jeong lifted his pen to start working, his face began to tingle again.

... My bags packed, I stood in front of the mirror. *Yes, I have to go away. I can't let myself be buried like this in daily routine, I can't sink into the swamp of trivialities.* The woman in the mirror was smiling with an effort. After seven years of loneliness, however, the smile was wounded and brittle like a shard of glass. Like a patient who has been diagnosed with a terminal illness, I let go of everything and embarked on a trip. This wanderlust that returned every year with the loneliness of an autumn day was a chronic disease. I set out in search of unfamiliar time....

A typo that had eluded several prior readings jumped out of the page. The same complaints, the same studied posture of a lonely woman filled every page. And his symptoms were returning. His throat felt like a pillar of blazing fire and his face began to throb with heat. Slowly at first, particles of blood gathered like swarming ants, but soon hot blood was coursing through his veins. He held his face in his hands, and his hands burned with the heat. He didn't have to look in the mirror to know that his eyes were burning, too. He tried pulling his head back and tapping his forehead as though he had a nosebleed. The fever did not subside. It was a matter of time before he got the rabbit eyes again and the face of a drunkard to go with them.

He sprang to his feet. Then regretted it, for any sudden or drastic change in the body's orientation could exacerbate the heat already concentrated in his face. He couldn't judge whether the medication was actually going to work or not, since not enough time had passed. Just stepping out to the corridor alleviated the condition considerably, but he preferred to hurry down the stairs and go out of the building altogether. There was no better palliative for his condition that the cold winter wind. Breathing in the outside air two or three times invariably calmed the fever, and it only took five minutes or so for his face to return to its normal yellowish tinge. Unfortunately, the reverse was also true.

In the beginning, such pyrexic episodes occurred only two or three times a day. He didn't worry too much about it, of course, and thought in a vague sort of way that it will go away soon. The office climate was tense because of the unionization issue, and there were a lot of additional things to take care because they were approaching the end of the year. He thought at first that the hot flash must be due to fatigue or an onset of cold and took a few capsules of cold medicine. After almost a week, his condition was no better. It was strange also that his face only got red when he sat down at his desk in the office. The moment he threw his work aside and came out of the office, the redness faded as though the whole thing had been some episode of the make-believe. Like a sleuth, he tried to deduce what the cause of this condition might be. If the condition were due to the high temperature in the office, his face had to grow red at the restaurant where he usually lunched since the restaurant maintained a temperature that was even higher. But he didn't once have his feverish episode, even when he was sitting right next to the heater. He was not inclined to redness genetically, either. He didn't get red when he drank, nor did he blush when he was embarrassed or found himself in a scrape. The exact opposite was true, as a matter of fact: He was likely to go pale in such circumstances. For decades he had lived with a face that didn't color at things that should have made it color, which earned him the nickname of "ice-man." And now, he was turning into a great ball of fire.

He found little sympathy at home from his wife. It was hard to convince her that he was sick. Ever since spending several nights out with other committee members of the labor union they were forming, he had been, if anything, more animated than usual. Carrying on private phone conversations late into night, coming home with books bearing strange titles, he was gradually becoming a man with a conviction in his wife's eyes. She wasn't obligated to show concern for his health as long as he didn't fail to empty his bowl of rice or get good night's sleep. *I do have a problem. It's just that I'm fine when I get home.* Her husband's comment did sometimes strike her as an indirect confession of love toward herself or of solidarity with the family unit. That was all.

As he paced back and forth on the street, he could sense that the fever was receding from his face at a remarkable speed. But what good was it when the heat would rush back as soon as he sat down to work? The condition was getting worse, and it was becoming impractical to rush out of the office every time. How much time would it take for the medicine to kick in? He looked at his watch. Not even thirty minutes had passed since he took the medicine. He resolved to wait at least an hour, then thought of Café Myeong, naturally.

Until the president provided a separate office for the labor union, the committee had decided to hold its meetings in Café Myeong. Most of the membership forms were in, and it had already been three days since the district office had issued the confirmation of registration. The days were over when union leaders had to remain undercover and keep their place of contact secret. The president also knew that since a few days ago Son and other executive committee members had been meeting regularly at Café Myeong during work hours. It was Son's opinion that they had to have the union office before entering into collective bargaining. The president's opinion, on the other hand, was that such formal demands were not in keeping with the reality of a small company like theirs. The president had no idea about the surprises that were waiting for him at the collective-bargaining table.

The reason why the committee designated Café Myeong as the interim office was because it had a large space partitioned off at the far end of the café, perfect for sitting around together as a group and having a discussion. Complete confidentiality couldn't be guaranteed, but individual training of union members or executive committee meetings could be conducted without much inconvenience. One of the committee members once joked that in lieu of an office inside their office building, the president should just pay the rent for this space. The comment caused a roar of laughter.

Jeong was surprised to find that Son was not at the café. Bak and Kim Gyeongsuk, however, were sitting opposite each other. Kim, who belonged to Section One, was one of the two committee secretaries. Jeong was the other. Kim was to serve as a representative of the company's seven women employees. Unlike Assistant Chief Cha, who was friendly but a bit of a coward, Kim was smart and tough, and thus a logical choice for the secretary position. Cha was assigned to the position of treasurer, which didn't require her to be in the vanguard, so to speak. Son was the chair of the committee and Bak the general secretary. Thus, Son, Bak, Kim, and Jeong comprised the executive committee. The two section chiefs were considered as part of the management, and the chief of the business department was also excluded from union membership since he was the president's brother-in-law on top of everything else. Of the "twenty-member family," therefore, sixteen employees were considered candidates for joining the union, and of this sixteen, two still had not submitted their membership forms. Consent from fourteen out of sixteen employees was more than enough to start a labor union, but Son was still urging Bak to persuade the remaining two to join. He argued that for a company their size, there mustn't be a single employee left as a non-union member. Jeong tried telling Son that such logic was no different from the family-style thinking that the president was so fond of employing; after continued activity of the union, additional enrollment would naturally follow. Son disagreed with him.

"That's not true. Once the union is established, the very logic of how to conduct the union affairs changes depending on whether or not there is universal enrollment. In collective bargaining, too, there's nothing as effective as a unanimous decision. It's easy enough to say that two or three nonmembers don't make much of a difference, but the president may decide that the work can be done only with nonmembers in the event that action needs to be taken. Do you think subcontracting is only for factories? You know that part-timers and freelancers are dime a dozen in our field. What's more critical is that the virus a minority element of skeptics can spread should not be ignored. Such a virus is very contagious and very destructive. It may be different for a company with hundreds of employees, but for a small union like ours, one hundred percent membership is a powerful weapon. Remember that."

Bak and Kim seemed to be discussing that problem, too. One of the two employees refusing to become a member was a woman in Section One. She was hired in the first place through personal acquaintance with the president; moreover, she was supporting her widowed mother and two younger siblings on her small salary. Kim reported that the woman had vowed never to be an impediment to union activity even if she remained a non-member on record. Bak was none too pleased.

"What kind of position is that? That's pure casuistry. She won't become a union member, but she won't be an impediment to union activity? Hmph, I think I've heard that one before."

Bak had a habit of linking everything to politics. The reference he was making at the moment was the current president's position that he will accomplish the task of democratization without arresting the former president for the crimes he committed during his dictatorship.[1] Or he could be picking on the recent declaration by the Democratic Party, one

---

[1] The "current president" referred to here is Roh Tae-Woo who succeeded Chun Doo-Hwan as the president of South Korea.

of the two opposition parties, that the party will now pursue policy-making independently but still walk the same path on issues that require solidarity among opposition parties. Bak was Son's right-hand man, but Bak had his own set of unshakable convictions which he carried over from his college days. He had been a self-proclaimed Marxist in the past, and he drew upon a wide range of radical revolutionary thought which he had swallowed in bulk in his youth. Since he had swallowed them in bulk, it was hard to predict when he would spew out the fiery flames again.

"Jeong, why don't you try to convince the other one?"

The "other one" was an employee in Section Two nicknamed Kant. Jeong had already tried to persuade him to join the union, without much success. Kant was scrawny, with thick eyeglasses, and looked as though he wanted nothing more from life than to live with his nose buried in books. To him, a labor union was just like a soccer game: It was an absurdity. Being a philosopher, Kant responded to Jeong's arguments by philosophizing.

"Where will you go in the end? To socialism? To a paradise where one "ism" gives birth to another "ism" and yet another "ism"? Well, let me ponder on that some more."

Kant's comments typically ended with the sentence, "Let me ponder on that some more." This was how he earned his nickname in the first place. One could not expect a definite "yea" or "nay" to issue from Kant's lips before he had time to engage in thorough contemplation and deep study. The process was bound to take a long time, however, and this roused Bak's temper.

"A person like that represents the biggest obstacle to our cause. Can contemplation divorced from ideology ever bring results?"

Jeong did not respond. Bak wasn't looking for a response anyway, but Jeong's silence wasn't one of agreement. In fact, he wanted to refute Bak. But it was not easy to wrap his thoughts up in a slipshod way and express them in words. If only he had something to grab onto—a crisp phrase, a few sharp words even—he felt that he would be able to unravel his tangled thoughts. Nothing like that presented itself; without an anchor, the vague feeling just ebbed away. The lingering regret that there must be a more precise way of verbalizing his thoughts had the effect of shutting his mouth. In the very beginning, when a labor union was still a beautiful idea that they discussed among themselves in secret, Jeong hadn't been this way at all. Only after the beautiful idea became a reality did he find himself lost in a labyrinth of words, a never-ending chase that eroded his confidence.

Jeong decided to talk to Kim instead.

"Didn't the president call you this morning?"

Kim nodded. "He didn't say anything about the union. He just wanted some changes made to the ad for the essay. We started with 7.5 centimeters, but now he wants to try 15 centimeters. I guess he means to overwhelm the market with a media blitz from the beginning."

Fifteen centimeters for a single volume was quite substantial as advertisements went. That morning the president had called him to his office through the intercom. He didn't have much to say other than that Jeong should pay extra careful attention to proofreading the essay collection. As Jeong was leaving the office, the president asked him to tell Kim to come to his office.

"We have to get an office. Meeting like this in a café makes it seem, well ... Yeah, we might be charged with negligence and there's a possibility that this will give the president an excuse to pick on us." This had been a concern of Jeong's for some time now. He felt uneasy and worried that they might all be marked as idlers whiling the workday away. But Bak refuted him immediately.

"In our collective demands, it says that the time we spend on union matters is to be considered time spent working. This is in addition to the provision of office space. The president is responsible not just for the space but for maintenance and various supplies the union might need. In other words, the money for the coffee we're drinking now has to come out of the president's pockets."

After drinking the rest of the coffee that the president was supposed to pay for, Bak lowered his voice. "Mr. Jeong, is the hot flash getting any better? We need you in tip-top shape. Once we get our office, which we have to do soon, there are so many things that have to be done. Son told me that you're going to take care of the news bulletin. He went out to get copies of news bulletins from other company unions to have them ready for you as reference. The first issue will be out in a few days, he said. He's going to meet the president this afternoon...."

The waitress came to take Jeong's order. He ordered ginger tea.

Kim then took off. It was almost lunch time. Bak got up, too, just when Jeong was thinking that he might as well have lunch, and really focus on the proofreading in the afternoon. Bak said that he had a lunch appointment.

"I'm having lunch with a newspaper reporter. Actually, he works for your old company."

After Bak left, Jeong took a sip of the hot ginger tea and thought about his old home. As workplaces went, the magazine that he used to work for was like a birthplace to him. He left the magazine right after June 10, 1987.[2] The decision to submit the resignation came from his desire to do something in the face of the monumental change that was occurring at the national level. In his personal life, as well, he wanted to draw a line that would allow him to say, yes, the movement left an indelible mark on me too. If he told Bak about that desire now, what would Bak say? Bak was sure to make his opinion without mincing words. How would Bak incorporate into ideology that foolish but earnest desire to start a new life in some way?

Jeong returned to publishing that very autumn. A few months was all it took for him to come back to where he had always been—the neighborhood of wordsmiths. Experience as a journalist for a women's magazine reporter counted toward publishing, too. At first, what Jeong wanted was a job that differed a little more, a work that would allow him to use his muscles and brain at the same time, but he was poorly equipped for anything other than reporting and editing. It was only natural that kids who grew up looking at the sea became fishermen. Kids who grew up imbibing the earth's energy became farmers. This job, which required little more than proofreading skills, was perfect for a pale-faced wretch who had spent his life poring over letters.

As expected, the medicine the pharmacist prescribed for him had no effect. Jeong wasn't disappointed. He didn't believe his red face was a simple condition that could be controlled by a few packets of powder so mechanically prescribed. After leaving Café Myeong, he spent the rest of his workday shuttling back and forth between the office and the street like a hamster spinning a wheel. Still, he did manage to

---

[2] The date of massive civilian rally nationwide that had the effect of forcing the regime of Roh Tae-Woo to approve a constitutional reform which would guarantee direct presidential election.

get some work done; the manuscript to be proofread remaining on his desk at the end of the day had slightly fewer number of pages in it.

Even though they didn't exchange many words, Son was at his desk for most of the afternoon. Toward the end of the workday, Son stopped by Jeong's desk and told him that he would like the executive committee to meet after work. One of the fruits the employees had reaped from forming a union was that they now knew exactly when this "after work" would be. They now ended their work at the end of the "workday," as if it were second nature to them. It had been a bit awkward at first, but they got used to it quickly, and now getting up from their desks at the appointed time was even a matter of pride. The president didn't betray much emotion regarding this. Inwardly, though, he was sure to be realizing what the strict enforcement of daily working hours meant for the management. Protecting something as basic as the workers' right to go home at six was proving to be a task that required endless patience from him.

They could take, for example, this matter of the essay collection. If it were up to the president, the volume would already be on display at bookstores. As before, he would have asked his employees to pull a few all-nighters even if that meant giving everyone overtime pay at the rate specified by the union. The book had to go into second printing before the start of the new semester in order to sell the projected number. Son had foreseen such a scenario and personally secured the consent of every union member on those parts of the collective agreement that dealt with the number of hours in workday and the rate of overtime pay.

The president, however, seemed to be taking extra care not to give the impression that he was on pins and needles about the essay collection. Perhaps it was a kind of obstinacy, a strange sort of pride, that made him think that he couldn't let on that he was holding a weak hand from the get-go. But it was clear that his back was against the wall. He knew that Son and Bak were not able to work much on the essay collection on account of all the union business they had to attend to. Even though Section Two had stopped working on all other projects and was devoting itself entirely to proofreading the essay collection, the project was not moving along speedily enough. And though the president had not noticed it yet, Jeong was lagging these days because of his strange condition. Had the president known that, he would probably have set everyone in

Section One to work on the essay collection, too. The reason why he had not done that yet was probably because he didn't want to have to deal with possible glitches that may arise when proofreading got divided up among too many people. Besides, Section Two was much better than Section One at tasks like dividing the contents into chapters and putting appropriate headings on each. Son had sensed all this and argued that it would be much more effective to start collective bargaining while the president remained impatient about the essay project.

The executive committee met "after work" in the backroom of some restaurant in one of the back alleys behind the office building.

"To Mr. Jeong's timely cold and fatigue!"

When the drinks were brought in, Son made a preposterous toast to Jeong's red face. It was time to be hungry, and everyone emptied the cups at top speed, except Jeong. He wet his tongue, but restrained from drinking. Alcohol couldn't be good for his condition, he thought.

The main issues discussed at the meeting were the publication of the newsletter and the various procedures regarding collective bargaining. Though it was a executive committee meeting in name, three men did most of the talking, with Kim Gyeongsuk chiming in only occasionally. One had to admit, however, that Kim had become noticeably firmer since taking on committee responsibilities and was more than pulling her own weight these days. But it was Son who reigned supreme. On any given issue, Son's position was both unambiguous and unshakable. He had a way of speaking that was neither hasty nor extreme, and what distinguished him from Bak was that his views never wavered from the beginning to the end. Even when they were drafting the initial version of the union's position in the collective bargaining, the difference between the two men became palpable. Bak wasn't terribly concerned about whether the collective agreement will be signed or not. He believed that they should be talking about strong action instead; for example, how to engage in a sit-in or a hunger strike. On the other hand, it was obvious that Son wanted to get the agreement signed if at all possible. They should be ready to engage in the kind of action that Bak advocated, but only in contingency situations.

"My opinion is that a labor union is not a site for head-on collision. The president thinks the same way. It's easy to pit the president as an enemy to be overthrown, but would that really be the right perspective to adopt? We need to establish our position clearly vis-à-vis the management. This is precisely the reason why the newsletter has to go out before collective bargaining begins. We have to get the president to become an avid reader of the newsletter like the union members and give him a chance to consolidate his position, too."

Son passed the cup to Jeong. Just when Jeong was wondering why Son didn't bring up the subject of the office space, when Bak broached the topic.

"The president wants us to put up a partition in the business department office and use that space for union matters. Don't you think that's a tad bit suspicious? How can we keep our confidentiality there? Everyone knows that the head of the business department is on management's side. I mean, it'd be a different story if he gave us the conference room next to his office ..."

The tenor of these discussions let Jeong know that Son had met with the president in the afternoon and made some progress regarding the office. It seemed that all the other committee members knew about this already. He felt embarrassed. He wondered whether he missed this new development during his endless shuttling in and out of the office. He felt hurt that he was the only one who wasn't told about this before.

"It'll be difficult to find a suitable union space in our building unless we move to a different building altogether. We all know how expensive the rent is, and we can't keep insisting on the conference room, when so many important meetings are held there. That's why I'm thinking about resolving the issue by putting up the partition and sharing the space with the business department. We don't know the president's intent in making this offer, but he says that the company will take care of the additional cost of putting up a sound-proof wall. Even if he decides to install a wiretap, what have we got to fear? Oh, by the way, we decided to make do with the office fixtures in the company storage." Son explained about the agreement regarding the office space.

Jeong couldn't help marveling once again at Son's ability to push things forward. As for himself, he had spent the entire day struggling with the heat rising to his head. Exhausted with dealing with that one thing, he was crumpled up now like a piece of used tissue, and he was pitiful even to himself. He supposed he should go to the hospital tomorrow. It was painful to acknowledge that he was becoming an incompetent. If it weren't for these symptoms that assailed him out of the blue, Jeong felt that he would be running around busily and getting things done, more busily than Son. At least he wanted to believe that. He was, or at least his head was, filled with the desire to run, to soar. He knew what it meant to live with his wings clipped; over the past several years, he had had plenty of life in a cage. It was only recently that he discovered that his wings still worked. "I can fly, I'm flying"—the mantra he repeated to himself was like a fresh breeze in the closed room of his life. Looking back, he couldn't understand why it had taken him so long to come to this point, why he had taken such a roundabout path.

As soon as he got home after filling his stomach with appetizers served with the drinks, he opened the last packet of medicine. His wife was finally alarmed, noting that his face had burnt black with fever. And so it was. His face was red while feverish and became black after it cooled down. Tossing the crumpled packet into the trash can, confirming that it had indeed landed squarely inside, Jeong felt a heavy sense fatigue binding his body like a tightrope. "I'll go to sleep early. It may get better tomorrow. There's no need to be downcast about it," consoling himself with these words, he drifted off to asleep.

He had a lot of dreams that night. He dreamt so much that he felt he hadn't slept at all. The feeling dampened his spirits. When he got to the office, his face started to sting even before he had time to spread the manuscript out on his desk. The three packets of prescription medicine turned out to be perfectly ineffectual. That morning, his wife had given him the insurance ID and repeatedly told him to go to the general hospital. But Jeong had a different idea. He went to see the head of the business department, a man who could be said to have achieved enlightenment in matters regarding physical health—the myriad ailments one could fall prey to, the range of therapy and medicine options available, and which hospitals were good for what. A list of conditions he had suffered in the past or was suffering now would take more than a page. He was fond of haranguing his colleagues from time to time for their laziness in tending to their health, and especially fond of dropping names of physicians and pathologists in various hospitals in Seoul with whom he was maintaining friendly relations. A staff member once characterized the business section chief's profession not as the distribution and circulation of published materials, but as a go-between between workers and hospitals, a man whose goal in life was to elevate this relationship to the level of circulation. Jeong thought he would ask him for a reference regarding good internalists in the area. As soon as he saw Jeong, however, he started giving Jeong an earful about all the bones he had to pick with the labor union.

"Mr. Jeong, what in the world do you mean to do by setting up an office? Quite honestly, I am not pleased with this sharing the room idea. First of all, I hate noise and disorderliness more than anything, and if the labor union comes in, with all their loud slogans, I might have a nervous breakdown. Besides. I know I've said this many times before, but what is there to complain about our boss? Let's be honest about it how nice of a boss he is. I don't see the purpose of this union. He pays well and treats everyone warmly like part of the family. I mean, doesn't he worry himself to death everyday wanting to do right by the employees? No one can accuse me of trying to take his side just because he's my brother-in-law. Nothing could be further from the truth. I really can't understand why we need a labor union in our company in the first place."

The business section chief shook his head. Jeong wished he were Son at that moment. Son would have a clear answer.

"That view of yours reflects mistaken notions about labor unions. It's the same logic that the dominant class has instilled in us stealthily for so long. If the task of labor unions is simply to counter the capitalist class through direct struggle or concern themselves with the question of pay raise or work hours, there's no need to form labor unions at all. Goals like these can be achieved in the name of any other group. But labor unions do not exist for the sake of individual profit. Unions build up our faith in a liberated society. We've only now begun to organize. We are not organizing in order to combat the president. We are proclaiming that together, the workers are a force that can combat the very relations of production in our society. We seek to overturn the institutions that allow human beings to bind and exploit other human beings."

Son would have responded in this way. Of course, since the business section chief was not a union member and had never participated in member training that Son conducted, he had no way of knowing that. Son, though he never voiced Marx's magnificent exclamation that labor unions are schools for socialism, subscribed to this thesis implicitly.

Son dreamed of the transition to a society where the working class would be liberated upon the premise of fundamental equality. Jeong shared most of Son's views. There were many times when it seemed clear to him that what Son expounded was the only prescription that would assuage the society's devastating ills. Jeong believed that social forces were dynamic whether changes were visible or not. Like Son, he believed that capitalism was polluted water that needed to be purified.

What he couldn't readily side with was Son's optimism. Jeong couldn't dispel a nagging doubt about a paradise where, to borrow Kant's words, "isms" give birth to more "isms." The doubt grew stronger when he considered the changes that socialist countries around the world were beginning to adopt. Can a perfect community ever exist? Did he believe that humanity was absolutely sublime? Wasn't loathsome violence that oppresses the individual going to bind us in the end?

Jeong liked Son, even loved him at times, but that didn't alleviate his doubt when he was left alone. Sometimes, his affection for Son made him want to throw himself blindly into Son's logic. But oblivious to that desire, Jeong's wings were scheming a preposterous flight in a different direction. He couldn't understand these conflicting urges within himself. The result was that he was robbed of all eloquence as he tried to respond to the business section chief's barrage of questions.

"The labor union's not trying to fight the president. We are fighting for hope ... so to speak ... hope for the labor ..."

His stuttering response was immediately squashed.

"Hope? Don't you mean to say sacrifice? The president's sacrifice, to be precise. Now, *that* sounds pretty good to me."

Discussing this topic with the business section chief any longer would make Jeong's wings flap uncontrollably. He couldn't risk breaking his fragile wings by exchanging words with a man who romanticized the past and refused to come out of his hard shell. Jeong changed the subject abruptly. With alacrity, the business section chief began a lecture about diseases in general.

"Hold on. I'll call ahead for you. You just tell them I sent you when you get there. Physicians who used to be the chief internal medicine specialist in a general hospital are usually really good. They buy these machines that cost ten million without batting an eye. The equipment is sometimes better in their private clinics than in the major hospitals. Six o'clock? Okay, I'll tell them that you'll get there around six. It's not very far. Take a cab and you'll be at Mapo Bridge in less than twenty minutes. Leave the office at five-thirty and you'll be in plenty of time."

Jeong came out of the room, telling the business section chief that he'll stop by again before heading out to the clinic, when he ran into Lee Jaecheol. Lee worked in the business department and was a very active member of the union. His great virtue was that he was affable, and these days, he was known as No Jaecheong, partly on account of that affability.[3] The nickname had stuck after the launching meeting of the union, when Lee's responsibility had been to call out, "I second that motion." For the launching meeting, they had to schedule every detail in advance in the interest of time. Lee was designated as the "seconder of motions" for the similarity his name bore to the phrase "I second that motion." He rendered distinguished service by reciting the phrase magnificently three or four times during the meeting. Lee didn't have a mean bone in his body. Even when his colleagues teased him by dragging his name out, "Mr. No Jaecheong—!" he laughed goodheartedly.

"I'm on my way back from an acupuncture treatment. I think I must have sprained by back last time when I was loading the books at the factory. I'm trying to get by with acupuncture since there's someone I know who does it really well...."

Jeong heard the word acupuncture and felt his interest piqued. The place Lee recommended was not a formally licensed clinic, but run by an old man in the backroom of a regular house. The business depended entirely on word of mouth, and the old man offered acupuncture and moxa cauterization only. Fantastic rumors had spread about him; his cauterization technique was reputed to have healed quite a few patients suffering from incurable diseases.

"One of my wife's relatives swears by him. My wife goes there for anything and everything, too. Who knows? Eastern medicine may be better for a condition like yours. Try this place first before going to an internalist. Hold on, I'll tell you where it is."

Lee drew a detailed map on the back of his business card.

---

[3] "No" is short for "nodong" which means "labor" in Korean. "Jeacheong," a play on the man's given name of "Jaecheol," means to request again or to second a motion. No Jaecheong, which is a perfectly plausible Korean name, means in this context to second the motion put forth by the labor union.

Jeong set out with this map in hand, knowing that he wouldn't get any work done anyway even if he stayed at the office. The old man's house was in Segeomjeong area.

"Follow the stream and you'll see a small multi-family house complex, go in farther and there'll be old traditional-style houses...."

Walking along, reading the map Lee had given him out loud, Jeong found himself smiling at the absurdity of it all. At the moment, his body was perfectly fine. There wasn't a single tiny thing wrong with it. Since he was no longer a patient the moment he left the office, no more needed to be said in the clean wind of this neighborhood. Was this an affliction of the mind? He started thinking about his condition systematically, exploring possibilities beyond a fatigue-induced cold or fever. Was he suffering from psychosomatic symptoms? Was he depressed? Perhaps he'd grown sick and tired of life as a white-collar worker. Or maybe this line of work didn't suit his personality, especially when he had to pore over something like that darned essay collection. Perhaps all that sentimental crap strung together with words like loneliness, wind, travel, love, star was nauseating him.

The diagnosis of the old man in a shabby room who wore his soiled *hanbok*[4] proudly—like a sage who shuns worldly comforts—took Jeong completely by surprise.

"Your heart's bad. You're getting by now, but you'd better be careful as you get older. You have problems with blood pressure, too. And your liver's a bit swollen. Everything's less than satisfactory, in fact. You lack vitality overall."

In the minute it took for him to feel Jeong's pulse, the old man managed to find out about problems of the heart and liver, and about his frayed nerves on top of that. Jeong had waited for half an hour to be seen, and there were four patients waiting after him. The old man was taciturn, and he spoke in terse, epigrammatic way as if one mustn't dole out wisdom too freely. Jeong waited for further instructions, but the old man only told him to "try some acupuncture."

"It will be painful tonight. And the day after the acupuncture treatment, you'll suffer from muscle ache and other cold symptoms. Let's do three or four days of acupuncture, and try the moxa after the

---

[4] Traditional Korean clothes.

106

blood vessels have been cleared."

Jeong liked the old man's restrained way of talking and behaving. After getting acupuncture on his stomach, back, nape, etc., he did feel refreshed for the first time in a long while. He imagined that there was a major unclogging going on somewhere in his body. The smell of incense and moxa that filled the room soothed him, and the old man's infrequent words were comforting, too.

By the time Jeong returned to the office and set back to work, it was almost lunch time. Was it okay for him to take so much time off from work? He did feel a pang of guilt, but he had no desire to work through the lunch hour. The executive committee was supposed to have lunch together. He knew that Kant and Miss Yun, the two employees who had not joined the union yet, were going to be invited to this lunch as well. Over food, Son was planning to concentrate on persuading the two to join. Jeong's opinion was that if they wanted union members' wishes to be acknowledged, they had to respect the wishes of non-union members as well; but this view was always dismissed by Son. Jeong seemed to be the only member of the executive committee that subscribed to the view that things had a way of taking place naturally over time. There were bound to be new members as well as new dropouts as days go by.

The lunch at the back-alley restaurant consisted of the usual simple fare—rice, soup made with dried radish leaves, and a few steamed vegetable dishes. The appeal of the restaurant was that its lunch sets were clean and economical, even though it also offered expensive raw fish or hotpot dishes to go along with alcohol.

Kim came in last with Miss Yun, and the small room was full with four men and two women. The waitress was highly efficient; as soon as she confirmed that the guests had all arrived, she brought out the side dishes. The robust aroma of soup suffused the room and turned the awkward atmosphere into a convivial one. As a conversation topic that was light though not trivial, Son brought up the issue of South Korean fishermen's opposition to importing North Korean pollacks. The discussion then turned to importing North Korean cigarettes and liquor. Son was deliberately trying to steer the conversation away from anything too heavy.

"With so many of these changes happening on the commercial front, there must be a lot of people who consider reunification a done deal. I overheard someone say on the subway yesterday that reunification is no longer something we need to have demonstrations about. Something else I heard on the subway: Bottle the fresh valley water of Baektu Mountain and sell it to South Koreans. Anyway, the attitude of the powers that be is that they are going to allow this kind of sideward movement to take place as much as people demand, but they'll be ready to squash any kind of genuine attempt to make changes that matter. All these little happenings are just red herrings. What the reactionaries want is to ensure that the one important step in the forward direction is never taken."

Bak, who was gulping down the bowl of soup in his hands, followed up on Son's comment by giving it a severe twist.

"They are thoroughly anti-reunification on the inside, but they go around saying Baektu this and Geumgang[5] that with every breath. They're worse than trash."

The word "trash" that Bak spat out so flippantly between gulps of dried radish leaves soup grated Jeong's ears. Bak always betrayed signs of violence. But whenever Jeong found himself noting these signs, he heard another voice within himself challenge whether he wasn't being an extremist himself when he thought of Bak as an extremist. Interactions with Bak always ended up turning Jeong into a pessimist. The common past that bound them together, the barbarity of violence that they had all suffered—Bak understood these as inevitabilities, but Jeong saw them as despair. *Worse than trash.* Would anyone be safe from that accusation? Where was the guarantee? Jeong felt suffocated.

"Isn't it problematic to think that way? I mean, does anyone really believe the rhetoric of the radicals that all social conflicts are going to disappear miraculously upon reunification? That strikes me as irrational, if anything." Kant responded out of the blue. He appeared at ease regarding his present situation. On the other hand, Miss Yun of Section One, the unmarried head of her household, was noticeably tense. There was so little rice on her spoon that you could almost count the number of grains, and though she mechanically extended her chopsticks to the plate of salted sea lettuce in front of her, she looked as though all she

---

[5] As two most famed mountains in North Korea, Baektu and Geumgang have long served as a shorthand encapsulating the desire for reunification.

wanted to do was to get through this torture called lunch somehow. Yun's widowed mother had sold fruit on the street to send her eldest daughter to college. After graduation, however, Yun couldn't find a job for more than a year. From her drawn-out experience with poverty, she had developed an inexpressible terror of not making ends meet, and she was extremely nervous about getting fired. Without the several hundred thousand *won* she brought home every month, her family would be out on the street that very day, and her resistance to joining the labor union was more than understandable. Surrounded by colleagues who pressured her nonetheless, Yun was shouldering that heavy burden alone. It wouldn't have surprised Jeong if the grains of rice she ate were turning into sand in her mouth.

Jeong kept stealing glances at Miss Yun's small hands and face, her green sweater. Every time Son or Bak opened his mouth, she cowered even more. She seemed to pull back in fright even at innocuous comments like, "You won't find better *dongchimi*[6] than this," or "This is no winter weather." There was one other person who seemed to be aware of how tense Yun was. Son had taken note of the fact that she remained slumped. Son was a warm-hearted man. He filled her cup with water and pushed the plate of seasoned arc shells toward her. Yun was in no state of mind to notice Son's kindness, however. She kept her eyes fixed on her bowl of rice and the dish of sea lettuce, seeing nothing else.

"By the way, are you still pondering?"

After pouring water into the bowl of rice he had emptied, Son asked Kant in a casual tone. Since Jeong was sitting right next to Kant, Son's gaze fell on him, too, and his eyes seemed to contain indirect reproof that grouped the two of them together.

"What is there to ponder about really...? It just takes me time to evaluate the executive committee's line, that's all."

Jeong could understand what Kant was driving at. Kant was someone who could more than accept unionization in the context of the struggle for human rights against the one-sided exploitation and oppression that laborers had suffered until now. The right to collective action was protected by the nation's constitution, at least in theory. The

---

[6] Chopped radishes pickled in salt water.

thirst for a society in which one could expand, albeit slowly, the search for a meaningful life was all the greater for Kant, as it was for Jeong, for the fact that they had never experienced it. Until now, politics—and political parties—had operated as a process of exhorting ordinary citizens temporarily so that they could be compelled in the end to come under the shadow of the politicians. By the time the people had wised up to the fact that the temporary goodwill the politicians had shown was a pure falsehood, power was so consolidated in the politicians' hands that dissent was no longer permitted.

"Beyond the basic common-sense fact that labor unions act as solid support for the workers ...."

Predictably, it was Bak who cut Kant off. Son pressed Bak's knee under the table to stop him. But there was no stopping Bak now that he had spurted out the first half of what he wanted to say.

"We're in a fix now because of all this theory without praxis, the petty bourgeois disposition of doing nothing but engaging in deathly contemplation. Anyone who says revolution of the people is the extreme leftist position is an intellectual to you, right? Why don't you leave off thinking for a change and try verifying whether your ideas will work in the real world?"

The pressure Son was exerting on his knee was getting stronger, and Bak stopped, but only for a moment. The target of his furor was now Yun.

"Do you know who exasperates me even more? People who get scared before examining all the facts concretely. In their cowardliness, they just cling to old truisms: Support for North Korea means war, Western countries are all good no matter what. Well, let me add another *idée fixe* to that. The notion that joining a labor union means getting fired."

"There's proof that the president was moved when he found out that Miss Yun didn't join the union," Kim blurted out in Yun's defense, but swallowed the rest of her words. She now lowered her head in embarrassment. Everyone in the room knew that the proof she was referring to was the gift certificate for a pair of shoes that the president had given Yun two days ago.

Son smiled. "If you have a gift certificate for shoes, go ahead and get yourself a new pair of shoes. I would. It's only natural. What Bak is giving us is the general theory of activism and shouldn't be taken as an attack on any one particular individual. As you know, Mr. Jeong, there's no need to feel discomfort about the union we've formed. It's the popular kind that workers are organizing everywhere else. If anything, we should feel guilty that we didn't form it earlier."

There was a reason why Son had singled him out and asked for his assent. Before starting the labor union, Son and Jeong had met frequently and exchanged many views. Privately, Son was a supporter of revolution. The reason why Son was putting in energy into the labor union was also because he believed that the working class needed to be elevated to the status of aggressive, revolutionary fighters, and that they were capable of being thus elevated. He emphasized mass struggle so much in the practical business of running the labor union because he held that revolution proceeded rationally in stages. Son was someone who knew very well that nothing could be achieved organically if the leaders overlooked the desires of the masses. He was one of those rare revolutionaries who possessed an open mind and paid close attention to the need to think rationally and respect individual differences. It was because Jeong trusted these virtues of Son's that he could believe himself to be at ease, caught though he was in the net Son had cast.

Bak was not in a conciliatory mood, however. He insisted on having his say.

"It amounts to the same thing. We need to critique the mindset that a gift certificate makes one indebted to the president, so that joining the union is now out of question. Really, what is Miss Yun is afraid of? Losing her job? And why is she afraid of that? Because she subscribes to the sort of class consciousness that says she's a college graduate and should at least have an office job. She fears that she'll fall to the bottom of the social ladder. What she wants to underscore is that she's not a common laborer. We have to critique that view, the view that she's not a laborer even though it's the product of her labor that puts food on her family's table, the view that you have to peddle little things on the street or work at the factory to be considered a laborer...."

Yun put her head on the table and burst into tears. Jeong didn't know what to do. He didn't expect Yun to crumble so easily. He thought Yun was brave. After all, not joining the union in their office required courage, too. The same thought seemed to be crossing Bak's mind. He rubbed his face awkwardly and smiled out of embarrassment. One person was crying, another was smiling, and the rest were silent. Son opened his mouth as if to say something, then closed it again. Jeong had never seen him struggle for words. It was Jeong who finally opened his mouth.

"The one certain thing is that no one is opposed to having a labor union. Miss Yun, too. It's not that she opposes the union, but because of, shall we say, personal reasons, she made the choice to … That's right, wasn't it the most basic of our beliefs that everyone should be free to make his or her own choice … The oppressive atmosphere in here … and the use of the violence of language … It's simply a shame."

"Mr. Jeong is right. Universal membership is my firm conviction but I don't mean to force anyone. Well, I hope that you'll all understand that Bak was just motivated by true desire to come together and work in solidarity," Son said.

The lunch meeting ended. Kim made the last comment in an attempt to be sympathetic to Yun, and underscored how difficult Yun's position was now that the president believed he had gotten her decisive pledge not to join.

On the way back to the office, Kant sidled up to him and asked, "Don't you think Son's optimism, so to speak, and the kind of organizer's view I have that the progress of humanity may be slow, but it's bound to happen over time, spring from the same thing?"

"Maybe. But this age we are living through requires someone like Son more, I think …"

"Which side are you on, then? I've thought hard about it … but I can't figure you out."

"Me?"

Presented with Kant's question, Jeong suddenly felt his face flare up. He stopped in his tracks and rubbed his face. He didn't think he could respond to that question while walking. *Who am I? Which side am I on?* His brain was emptied of all words. After scrambling for a long while, he managed to grab onto a few.

"It's like this. You fly toward reform, and then, how should I put it, you turn toward gradual improvement through negotiation. An approach like that, I believe, is criticized in the labor movement. I think they call that a compound approach. Me ... I'm probably ... a compounder."

A compounder. Jeong was a little bit of Kant and a little bit of Son, even Bak sometimes, and definitely Yun at others. He decided that he was a compounder; he finally walked into the office as a compounder. Before sitting down at his desk, Kant offered up another observation.

"You know, it's ironic to think that among all of us, Miss Yun is really the one who needs the protection a labor union can offer. The union can apply pressure on her behalf against unfair personnel decisions, should a problem like that arise. I guess she's not in a situation to be able to see this though."

The next morning, Jeong realized—with keen disappointment—that nothing was wrong with his body. The old man had said in no uncertain terms that he would have symptoms of muscle ache and fatigue severe enough to make it difficult for him to sit up. But he opened his eyes that morning earlier than usual and had breakfast as usual, not afflicted by any unusual symptoms. The entire afternoon the day before, he had endured his red face by brainwashing himself that the acupuncture treatment he had received might finally do the trick. Now that the old man's prognosis had not come true, Jeong felt out of sorts. The thought of spending another day with a red face and muddled head was horrific enough to make his head swim. His wife had been skeptical about acupuncture from the beginning. She was of the belief that the sooner he gets a thorough physical, the sooner he would have the medically accurate name for his condition. Since yesterday, she was pestering him to take a couple of sick days and go to her brother, and internal medicine specialist who had his practice in a different city. She said that he was being so laid back about the whole thing because he found the pain and the inconvenience bearable. He had nothing to say.

He set out early and visited the old acupuncturist. He didn't want to have to take more personal time off from work; he also wanted to get there before there were a lot of patients. Doubt was strong in his mind, but he decided to give the acupuncturist one more day to work his magic. The old man responded gruffly to his comment that there was absolutely no difference in his physical condition, neither relief nor additional pain.

"Did you really expect that you'd be cured after a single session? If it was so easy, why would anyone worry?"

The old man inserted the needles in various places he had poked yesterday and told him to stay still for a while. He left and came back ten minutes later to take out the needles. In the meantime, he had changed into a gray sweater and wide-legged suit pants. The sight of him so differently dressed shocked Jeong. On the spot, Jeong concluded that the old man was a quack, as if the shabby wrinkled *hanbok* had been the sole guarantee of the efficacy of the old man's acupuncture and moxa cauterization treatment. Dressed not in a *hanbok* but in street clothes that any country bumpkin peddler might wear, the old man took the money from him hurriedly. Jeong monitored the old man's every move with suspicion.

"You're lucky that you came early today. I have somewhere important to go this morning."

Jeong requested that he would like to get the cauterization treatment, too, but was summarily dismissed.

"I told you it won't do any good to do cauterization now because your pulse has to open up first."

This old man has a rock in his ear. I've wasted time for nothing. I should have gone to the internal medicine specialist the business section chief recommended.

Jeong gritted his teeth through the entire morning, watching the letters dance in the manuscript he was supposed to proofread. He didn't have the presence of mind to register the context. All he could do was to verify the printed symbols.

He didn't manage to spot any typos. The second round of proofreading was always tougher than the first; there weren't many typos to spot, so proofreading became reading, and in the process of reading one ran the danger of overlooking the typos. An essay collection like this was especially tough for him to read over. The manuscript was filled with expressions that struck him as strange, and words that made no sense to him, so that he had to double check everything to make sure that his incomprehension wasn't a result of an error on the writer's part. Try as he might, he couldn't follow the flow of the writer's emotions. He approached the text as if it were a riddle and hoped that there would be enough in it for him to marvel over when he finally solved the riddle. Could this manuscript be the cause of my condition? He suddenly wondered. Unable to bear any longer the heat his red face emitted, he closed the manuscript. Looking over at Kant, he saw that Kant was working hard, twirling his pen with exquisite skill. He went to the bathroom and came back with a wet handkerchief which he used to soak up the heat from his face. Helplessly, he opened up the manuscript again.

... The silence of the night makes us sad sometimes. We've been thrown alone into the universe which envelopes us like the great sea. Pain licks my entire body as it passes through it. At times like this, a cup of coffee is a friend that consoles me. Its fragrance calms my nerves and makes it possible for me to endure. Drinking that cup of coffee ensconced in the rocking chair in the living room, I plunge into a conversation with the darkness ...

Drinking that cup of coffee ensconced in the rocking chair in the living room? Jeong daubed his nape with the handkerchief which was already lukewarm. His eyes were dry and throbbing as if they would start twitching any second. Pushing the manuscript aside, he opened one of the labor union newsletters that he was supposed to use as reference. At once, a phrase jumped out and stabbed his throbbing eyes.

... *They want to see you at the office.* But when you come out, they take you, not to the office but to one of the dorms or to the old warehouse behind the infirmary. For four to six hours, you're then subjected to appeasement and intimidation tactics as they demand that you drop out from the labor union. How in the world can such a thing happen ...

How in the world can such a thing happen? That last question was premised on faith in humanity. He repeated that question to himself over and over. He told himself that people were capable of embracing a new hope even after living through the darkest of times and the harshest of treatments. But was it really like that? Could it be like that? Could a society in which every human being fulfills his hope ever become a reality? If revolution were necessary, institutions needed to be targeted for sure, but wasn't it more urgent to accomplish a revolution of the human character as such? He realized that he was being vague again. After all those heated discussions about revolution and the liberation of labor, the only thing he was sure about was that he aspired toward non-oppression. No matter how wide you spread your wings, you couldn't fly if you went against the wind. Had he really flown in the last weeks? Did he even try spreading his wings? Holding his head up straight as if it were some object foreign to his body, he slid toward the bathroom in order to rewet his handkerchief.

Before heading home, Jeong went to see Son. Son was understanding about Jeong's inability to attend the executive committee meeting. Son said that at the meeting they were going to put the finishing touches on the first draft of the union demands and hold a plenary session to get the whole thing approved before entering into collective bargaining. He also said that the construction of the partition in the office was scheduled to start tomorrow. In his heart of hearts, Jeong detected a wish that Son would think that it was strictly on account of his strange physical condition that he was going to be on the sidelines as important union matters were being decided. Why did he wish this? What was the nature of this desire? He couldn't understand himself.

"Please try to have the newsletter ready for distribution at the plenary session. I'll write a piece called 'Our Attitude' or some such thing to include in it. Think of a few more pieces we can do and let's talk about them tomorrow. The newsletter doesn't have to be very long, of course, and letter-size paper should be fine, I think. The general secretary will pick out the basic points from the first draft of our demands, so let's have that included, too."

Bak came in just then. A handyman who was to start work tomorrow was with him. Bak saw that Jeong was dressed to go home and didn't try to hide his displeasure. "Mr. Jeong, you're skipping out again?" he asked.

Even while Jeong waited for his turn at the clinic, Bak's words rang through his head. Did he want the kind of understanding he

116

sought from Son also from Bak? If so, whose sympathy did he want
more? He thought constantly about that question. It was a childish
question no matter how he looked at it, and he couldn't understand
why it mattered to him so.

"Your blood pressure is normal. Please have a seat over here."

The nurse finished taking his blood pressure and took him to the
doctor, who appeared to be around forty years old. He had a pale,
neat-looking face.

"At the office ... umm, I work for a publishing company... umm,
my face burns every time I look at the printed page ... it's really
unbearable, you know, even my eyes get red ... it's been quite a while
since this started happening," Jeong stammered.

The doctor waited for him to finish and had him lie down on the
examination table. What made the whole process so unbearable for
Jeong—whether he was at the pharmacy, or the backroom of the
acupuncturist, and now in the examination room here—was the
slightness of the reaction the specialists showed to his words. The
slight reaction, the indication that they're trying to hide what they
really thought, made Jeong suspect them right away. No, it could be
that his suspicion came first. Maybe he suspected them of not taking
his words seriously or of trying to hide their derision, because he
couldn't deal with them otherwise.

The doctor tapped his belly a few times with his stethoscope. He
then sat down at his desk and started scribbling. Jeong knew that he
would soon be banished to the next room for his shots if he didn't say
something to interrupt the process.

"What kind of disease do you think this is? My blood pressure's
normal ... and nothing is outwardly wrong with me right now."

"You have a lazy circulation. Stress tends to be the cause of such
conditions. You'll be fine in two or three days if you get enough rest
while continuing the treatment. We'll give you a shot to help you.
Miss Oh, where is the chart for the next patient? Please see that this
gentleman receives appropriate care."

But Jeong felt that he couldn't be banished just like this. He had
to say something.

"What do you mean stress? Does everyone who feels stress
respond this way? Good God, how sick and tired I am of all this!"

He did take the medicine prescribed at the clinic, precisely thirty minutes after meals just as he was directed. He had already decided not to trust the internal medicine specialist that the business section chief had introduced to him. All the injection managed to do was to calm him down a little. From prescription drug to acupuncture, and back again to intravenous shot and drugs. Where was he going to go now? Watching the nine o'clock news, he really wanted to cry. Though he knew that he was neither simple nor optimistic enough to believe that something could cure him overnight, he wanted to be a simpleton and an optimist at times like this. He wanted something that could give him that kind of blind faith.

The reason why he didn't trust the doctor was simple. The doctor hadn't shown any interest in him. If the doctor had decided that Jeong was suffering from stress, after listening to his story and paying close attention to the particulars of his situation and emotional state, Jeong might have taken faith in the doctor's diagnosis. But it seemed that there were a number of standard diseases and ready-made prescriptions that formed a grid in the doctor's head. His reputation as an expert was based on how well he placed the individual patients in this grid. The stethoscope only transmitted the sounds the doctor wanted to hear.

In the end, Jeong gave into his wife's pestering and decided to call his brother-in-law. There, at least, his rambling story would get a full hearing. He was going to tell his brother-in-law of all his symptoms, down to the last inglorious detail.

"I don't want to say I told you so, but didn't I tell you to go to him? True he's my brother, but that doesn't mean he's not a good doctor. You know, he's quite famous and really well-respected in his city. Just call him. I don't know that a phone call will do, but what have you got to lose?"

Jeong got through to his brother-in-law right away. After exchanging a series of greetings typical between in-laws—endlessly generous and good-willed, but still in keeping with all the formalities— he began to explain about his red face. Even over the phone, he could tell that his brother-in-law was listening to him attentively. Every now and then, his brother-in-law double checked his symptoms, and asked more questions to clarify what he wasn't sure about.

Jeong described his red face at length. Well, at least, he tried to.

His words came haltingly because he couldn't find the exactly right expression to describe his symptoms. Was the only way to describe a red face by resorting to the imagery of a drunkard? He stammered, trying to find a more fitting expression. Red eyes, red like rabbit eyes. Couldn't there be a better simile? He groped for a way out of his confusion, the mesh of threads all tangled up in his head. If it weren't his brother-in-law he was talking to, he might have given up in the middle. Despite the fact that he was an editor himself, he was being every editor's nightmare: long-winded sentences without any specificity were spurting out of his mouth. He found himself repeating words like fever, redness, flushed face over and over again. At long last, his brother-in-law delivered his opinion.

"From what I gather, and there have been several clinical reports recently of such patients, your condition is a kind of an allergic reaction to air. It's a condition most common in winter among people who work in office buildings of big cities like Seoul, and the cause is interior air pollution brought on by heating. You might say that your body is reacting against the air in your office. In other words, the air doesn't agree with you. It's the air."

Then his brother-in-law gave his prescription. Writing down the name of the medicine on a memo pad, Jeong sighed. Did he have to take medication again and wait for it to take effect? His brother-in-law seemed quite confident about his medical opinion, but Jeong still couldn't shake off his doubt. Why did this condition erupt now, all of a sudden? He had been fine all along. And why was he the only one suffering from it when everyone else seemed to be fine? He couldn't trust the diagnosis.

"Take it three times a day, half a pill at a time. It's a round tablet so you'll have to cut it in half. You'll feel the difference in one day. Don't forget to take it three times, half a pill at a time. And don't stop taking it just because you feel better. There's no need for another physical examination. I'm telling you, it's allergy."

The next day, he stopped by the pharmacy. He handed the pharmacist the memo, without saying anything. The pharmacist seemed to have forgotten him. Handing Jeong the medicine, he said, "Try it, but if it doesn't work, you should get a prescription. Actually, my recommendation would be that you start with a prescription."

In front of their office building, he caught up with Kant. The office was on the third floor, but they headed toward the stairs. He felt claustrophobic in elevators, and Kant always preferred to walk up the stairs. He called it "jogging to work."

"Mr. Secretary, I would like a membership application."

Jeong was absorbed in thought about his new medicine, and didn't hear Kant.

"I've thought it through, and it does seem to me that a labor union can be a breakwater of sorts."

Kant smiled at him. The two eyes inside the glasses, however, did not appear to be very merry.

Son and Bak didn't seem to be around the office. Jeong broke one of the new pills in half, swallowed it, and sat down at his desk to work. He felt that he might finally get to the end of the manuscript today. Well, he had to. Of course, as soon as he sat down, blood bubbled up and coursed to his face. He prayed that the tiny little pill, half a pill to be exact, would spread through his veins swiftly and block the blood from surging up to his face. Though he was full of doubt, he was also full of faith about the treatment. He had been the same way with the pharmacist's prescription drug and the acupuncture treatment. Ever so gingerly, he tried to immerse himself in work.

Son came in about half an hour later. He passed his desk, holding a notice regarding the plenary meeting. Half way to his desk, he stopped abruptly and turned around.

"No Jaecheong wants out. It seems that our president is no pushover after all. He turned No Jaecheong into Sa Jaecheong[7] while we were out to lunch."

The expression on Son's face at that moment could definitely be characterized as steely. With that expression, he probably meant to reprimand the man who was once the seconder of the union's motions and now served as the seconder of the president's motions. But Jeong didn't care too much about the whole sordid story. What he cared about was Son's unbreakable solidity, his steeliness. He envied that about Son. Did life serve up moments of doubt to everyone, or only to him? How long was he going to have to walk the path of ambiguity,

[7] Since "Sa" stands for the management, "Sa Jaecheong" would mean, "I second the management's motion."

120

unable to blind his eyes to what he didn't want to see....

Jeong didn't respond to Son's words. Nothing would come out of his mouth at that moment, not even the news that Kant had finally ended his thinking and made up his mind in the union's favor. All he could do was look at his hands in awkward silence.

Suddenly, he remembered his brother-in-law's words. *Your body is reacting against the air in your office. In short, the air doesn't agree with you.* The remembrance made it hard for him to breathe normally. Maybe it really was the office air. If so, could half a pill stop this disagreeable air from interfering with his body's needs? Once again, he grew doubtful. *The air doesn't agree with me? Really...? Could the air really be the sole reason...?*

The Hidden Flower

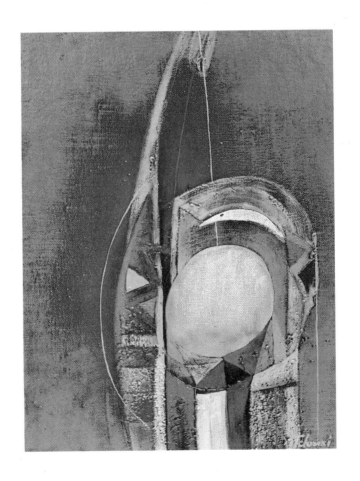

1.

He was at Guisin Temple. I met him at Guisin Temple, for the first time in fifteen years. Naturally, I didn't recognize him at first, unable to undo the fifteen years that had passed at a single glance. If he hadn't recognized me, the fact that this chance encounter ever took place would have gone unconfirmed. We would have brushed past each other, neither one of us able to draw back the thick curtain of time to admit the light of memory. I might have stood around for a while, gazing up at a lanky poplar tree with all its leaves of tender green directed toward the sky, and caressed a wilting azalea petal or two before turning back.

In which case, there would be no story to tell. I would have missed out once and for all on the opportunity to record a giant's voice. Taking a trip, hoping against hope, and coming back with nothing but a sense of futility—how I would have hated myself then! The thought makes me shudder even now. Perhaps he knew all this, knew the reason why I had to go there in the first place, and was waiting there for me. If anyone had suggested that to me before, I might have laughed; I have no desire to do so now. It doesn't matter whether something like that can actually happen. What matters is your attitude, whether you can let yourself go ahead and say something that defies all sense. And so I say it. At Guisin Temple, I learned that it is possible to say such things.

The trip started with a regret. It assailed me the moment I was left alone in the crowded plaza outside Seoul Station, No, to be precise, I have to go further back, to the breakfast I rushed through to make the train on time that morning, to the sighs that escaped me the night before over all the trivial details that had to be arranged so that my absence wouldn't be felt. Perhaps, even that first day at the station when I first purchased the train ticket in a haze of doubt had to be entered on this page of regrets. Despite all that, I duly made my appearance at Seoul Station plaza that morning, in time to claim my prepaid seat on the train. The more susceptible you were to regrets, the less likely you were to give up in the middle. As the departure day approached, I couldn't think of a brilliant idea which would allow me to give up on this trip without feeling—regret. .

"You didn't forget your ticket, did you?"

My husband had only this to say when he dropped me off at the plaza. It didn't occur to him to say a comforting comment or two like, "Have a nice trip" or "Try to get a lot of rest." He just looked at me, as though he were worried about my severe forgetfulness, and turned the car around. I envied the sense of ease he seemed to have, his air of composure as he maneuvered the car through the traffic crowding the plaza and onto the streets bathed in the radiance of spring sunlight.

It seemed so unfair. Even though I was the one about to embark on a trip, I felt like the unlucky employee left behind with piles of troublesome tasks while everyone else was hurrying off to their vacations. So horribly unfair. The sense of injustice I felt at that moment was powerful enough to make me regret my whole life, let alone this trip. I wanted to throw away the label "writer" that dogged my name as if it encapsulated my entire being. If only I could do that and get back some other life that had drifted away from me long, long ago, I wouldn't have to stand all alone in the station plaza, feeling jealous of anyone who wasn't me.

There was a rock in my chest pressing down on me. Still, going on a trip wasn't the sort of thing I usually did to remove that rock. From day one, I wasn't the kind of writer who gets herself unstuck by leaving the routine of her daily life behind. Colleagues of mine habitually took trips for the sake of their writing either to get over the hump when the story wouldn't flow freely like thread from a well-wound spool or in search of new material. I worried about their feet dangling in the air. That the business of living came before the demands of writing had always been my view. If a writer needed to take a trip, then it was because her life demanded it. Suspending the routine of one's lived life and taking off for the sake of writing was a contradiction in terms, much like the saying that one lives in order to die. It struck me as a furtive but still undeniable piece of pretension. To be sure, there were writers who managed to craft whole stories from their trips, but I still believed that the demands of life took precedence. The novel was no more than an unexpected bonus, a lucky reward that came your way if you probed life with enough diligence.

But this wasn't one of those trips made absolutely necessary by life's many duties. That was probably the reason why the hesitation and regret proved so persistent. As far as writing was concerned, planning this trip and actually taking it was a big gamble. To throw away a full day or two just because the writing wasn't coming along, when there wasn't a minute to spare if I wanted to keep the deadline! If this trip guaranteed anything, it was only that I wouldn't be able to keep the deadline this month, either, like so many months before. One did not gamble on writing, no matter what the odds.

Because I had such deep misgivings about this trip, I couldn't feel much cheer as I sat by the window and gazed at the scenery outside. What depressed me even more was the thought that if this had been just a regular trip and not a desperate measure to overcome my block, I would be injecting much feeling into the wild confusion of azaleas, forsythias, and fresh green buds outside. The free and easy laughter of women across the aisle affected me strangely, too. They had swiveled the seats around and they were already preparing to eat, even though the train was less than five minutes out of Seoul Station. All of the women appeared to be around my age; I guessed that they were close neighbors. It was too late for breakfast and too early for lunch, but they laughed and chatted without restraint over their meal, each enjoying her rare escape from home. Stealing looks at the loudly laughing women, I leaned away from them, drawing up even closer to the window. No matter which way I looked, I didn't see a single passenger wearing an ambivalent expression like mine. Far from being ambivalent, their faces were clearly etched with whatever emotion they were feeling. All of the passengers were leaving the routine of their daily lives behind, for some clear purpose. Their certainty and confidence intimidated me.

If you are lost in a maze, you should retrace your steps and proceed slowly from where you first got lost. Was it wrong of me to think that I could get out of the maze by examining the start and finish of life with diligence, with earnestness? Wasn't it too early to despair that the era of unexpected bonuses was over? Sure, the signposts may be gone, but not the places where they used to stand. Why had I become so enervated, so quickly? Why the impatience, even in coping with this enervation?

A poet once said, suffering is the monthly rent you pay for living in this world. Endure that pain, suppress it, and a root or two were bound to sprout against the pressure. Did I still believe that? Maybe I was afraid that even that belief was subject to waste disposal now.

When you do something that is not in keeping with your character, all manner of doubts creep into your heart. They crept into mine, throwing even more weight to the rock already sitting in my chest, and making it all the more impossible to remove. There was nothing I could do. I couldn't even kill time by entering the world of letters since I didn't have any printed material on me. I had my reasons for not bringing any books on this trip. But even before the train reached Suwon, I was already berating myself for maltreating books. I had secretly counted on the train's big windows to frame endless country scenes and keep me engaged. Requesting the window seat that first day when I purchased the ticket, my voice had even been forceful for the first time in a long while. Almost as soon as the train pulled out of Seoul, however, I realized that the window placed my face in the direct path of the April sun. Sunlight was strong, no longer the gentle rays of early spring that caress you with their sweet warmth. The sun stung my face maddeningly and in less than five minutes, I was reaching for the soiled curtain. The window's betrayal immediately kindled my thirst for something to read, but to no avail. A hopeless fool who never has a back-up plan ready— that was me.

While waiting for the train to board, I had peeked into the small bookstore in one corner of a station pharmacy. It might be all right to bring something printed along, I was thinking, so long as it was something merely to look at rather than read. The words would hover before my eyes for a moment before flying away, leaving no permanent marks in my brain. But even there, it was the same story all over again: I couldn't decide what to get. Maybe it was out of irritation at myself for being unable to choose a few titles to toss into my bag that I decided to bring none at all. Had I been able to find something in books, I wouldn't have resorted to this trip in the first place.

All the same, I couldn't pass the small bookstore without looking in and wandering lost for a while in its forest of titles. Only after some browsing did I remember the resolution I reached at home. No books. Just then a grumbling comment my mother once made about me flashed in my mind. *She's born all goat. Goat-hour, goat-month, goat-year. She's gonna spend her whole life munchin' on paper.*

For three hours on the train, the only reading materials I came across were labels of various snacks in the Benevolence Society pushcart and advertisement for energy boosting beverages printed on the back of the seats. From the back of the white cover in which every headrest in the car was swathed, the advertisement copy in green ink read, "Feeling tired and sluggish? Drink this for a fresh burst of energy." Even as I shuddered at the tedium of the repeated content, I could not stop my eyes from clinging to those letters and constantly interpreting their meaning. Reading them over and over, I thought of an unhappy princess in some fairy tale cursed to dance on and on. Can someone, anyone, stop this dance, she cries. I dance while I eat, I dance while I sleep. Help me, please. Stop this dance.

I finally shut my eyes and leaned back against the headrest. I needed that energy booster; I was exhausted from reading and reading about it. For more than a month now, I had been suffering from constant fatigue, though I didn't try any such energy boosters, of course. This fatigue had no clear origin. I wasn't sure what I needed to seek relief from. It wasn't as though I worked my limbs all day, or moved my fingers across the keyboard assiduously, producing a page after page of manuscript. Since resolving firmly a month ago to write another short story before more time goes by, I spent my days in front of the word processor with my arms dangling by my sides. As the days of arm-dangling continued, fatigue began to pile up. Never had writing been so torturous from the start. The last story I published was "Strength from Sorrow," a piece dealing with the fierce struggle Korean Teachers' and Education Workers' Union waged in its inaugural year. Already, it had been three years since that story appeared in some literary quarterly. How could I have forgotten how to write in that time? Three years could be a long time but not long enough for that.

The problem was that the world had changed. The phrase "Even sorrow can be strength" could no longer move people. The world seemed empty all of a sudden. Following the world, a kind of dazed confusion fell upon my mind, too, where all the things I needed to write about used to clamor urgently. Trying to combat this pall, in recklessness of despair, I committed myself to submitting the short story manuscript I had been promising the publisher for a long time. The timing couldn't haven been worse.

The tidal wave generated by the great transformation of the Soviet Union and the collapse of the East European bloc threatened to engulf the presentiment of a new life in Korea and the search for a different society, such as it was. The sight of people from that part of the world pouring out of the airports with metallic suitcases in hand and unfamiliar gleam in their eyes to join the capitalist order left a bitter taste in my mouth. The words of a dead leader, that the socialist project had never once been realized, struck me with all the force of pessimism regardless of its significance. If morality was indeed an institutional device invented to allow people to live together, it appeared that morality wouldn't show its face around anywhere for a while. Was a mad dash all that was left for us to do? If so, if so ... I could never go beyond this "if so." No matter what anyone said, the short story had always been a form of confession for me. No matter what its content, the short story was a writer's confession, her prayer.

Though I desperately wanted to, it was too daunting a task to resume this interrupted prayer. I retreated from the word processor every time, my arms hanging limply by my sides. Even on those rare occasions when a sudden burst of confidence gave me the strength to sit in front of the machine, my fingers were paralyzed, even before they could type out the first sentence, with the feeling that this wasn't it. Fatigue started to build up. Days of utter confusion continued for an entire month, and I was unsure about everything save the fact that whatever it was I was writing wasn't "it." In the end, this uncharacteristic trip was yet another desperate attempt to silence that scream in my heart, "This isn't it!" To be more frank, the trip was the plot I devised out of the hope that I could go somewhere far away, bury that screaming thought, and come running back alone.

Was it possible? I didn't even have a clear idea what it was that I needed to bury in the ground. Or maybe I was afraid. What guarantee was there that I wouldn't bury something really important and come back with some utterly useless thing, making the confusion more complete than before? I could not bear to face the contradiction that persisted within me: In spite of all my whining, was I really willing to throw away everything? Could I abandon the greed that made me cling to something that I knew wasn't "it"? I couldn't put a period to any sentence with a peace of mind until I could settle that question.

I did not open my eyes until the train was almost at Iri. I wasn't sleeping, though. I was still in this world, only with my eyelids in between. Even though I knew I would be able to think much more clearly after taking a good nap, I found it difficult to fall asleep. Even the easiest of things weren't easy anymore once things started going awry. So I decided to forgive myself for submitting to the torture of sitting there for over two hours, feeling every little tremor of the moving train with a fully alert mind.

My head ached slightly as I opened my eyes when the train stopped at Iri. People who were waiting to get off were lined up in the aisle. They all had a bag in one hand; with their free hand, they were straightening out their rumpled clothes or ruffled hair. After they got off, new passengers boarded the train. Unlike their wilted and tired-looking counterparts, the new passengers' hair was neat and their spring outing clothes unwrinkled and bright. Their presence injected freshness to the heavy, stuffy air inside the train in no time. I drew the soiled curtain aside and looked out the window. The train was already pulling away. People and history were slowly moving backwards. Everything in the station retreated out of sight, and I looked at them disappear, my face plastered to the window. The safety coordinator in blue uniform appeared to be moving backwards though he was running toward the train. Magnolias in full bloom, the petals trembling perilously as if a mere sigh would be too much for them, grew distant without warning.

In contrast, forsythias on the station fence stood their ground proudly, though the clusters of yellow blossoms studded with sharp green leaves showed traces of decline. As the station grew distant, dog holes began to appear amid the forsythias on the fence. Dogs weren't the only creatures to make their way through these holes, though. I might have crawled through one of them a long time ago, one faraway day.

I opened my eyes wide and gazed out at the landscape by the rail tracks. The sun was still strong, but its rays no longer poured straight down on my face. And even if they were, I could no longer make my compromise with the soiled curtain. The road that now stretched outside the window had once been my gateway to the world. All the memories of a certain period in my life took place on or near that road. Memory came to life most vividly at the place of its birth. Having your mind and body occupy one place at two different times was a profound experience. I was here then and I am here now. How many ebbs, how many flows lie between these two points in time? How innumerable the occasions when the wave's sprays covered me! All those waves that broke at my feet, where did they end up? The middle-aged woman gazing out now— where would she end up? In the inexorable flow of time, I was making my way onward without knowing my way back. I rubbed my forehead against the window glass, and felt myself dissolving into the thin air like seafoam. Time was drawing me into its whorls. It was sucking me in and spitting me back out into the universe....

There was once a poet who left the city because he couldn't bear to be drawn in. I knew him from the time when he first became a recognizable name in the literary world. He once brought my daughter, who was then just learning to speak, a parakeet doll with a recorder in its belly. I played with it, too, sometimes. So did the poet whenever he visited us. Opening and closing its beak, the green parakeet echoed whatever you said, but its limit was two words. If you said, "I love you," it echoed "I love" and swallowed up the rest. The poet and I came to focus on getting the parakeet to pronounce "you." This was no easy task. Unless we spoke quickly, the machine swallowed up the word "you" and dispersed it to nothingness. But when we succeeded, through repeated pronunciation exercises, in saying "I love you" quickly enough, it still wasn't any good. Unless each syllable was enunciated clearly, the sound came out garbled. Echoed back as "avew" or "alew," "I love you" became a taunt rather than a declaration.

When the sentence became garbled and resulted in weird combinations of vowels and consonants, my daughter squealed with delight, but the poet looked despondent. One day, he declared his intention of taking the toy back to the store and exchanging it for some other parakeet. If all of the parakeets had the same problem, he said, he was going to go to the manufacturer in protest. A parakeet that could not be made to say "I love you" had no use whatsoever in his opinion.

In the end, only my daughter's fierce opposition prevented him from acting on his indignation. She wouldn't part with the green parakeet no matter what, and even slept holding it tight in her arms. She didn't mind the nonsense syllables that issued from its beak, probably because she didn't yet know the pain of being taunted. How could anyone expect a child to understand a poet's despair over broken words?

A bird that cannot be made to say "I love you" is not a bird, the poet said. A parakeet that sticks its tongue out in mockery at "I love you" is not a parakeet. The insignificant episode proved to me that this man was a born poet. Because I wasn't one, I did not think to exchange the parakeet or make a complaint to the manufacturer. Inside the parakeet's belly was a recorder small enough for even a child to hold. When I opened the zipper to change the battery, what I thought about was the machine's capacity, its ability to record only a short segment of a phrase. If the machine couldn't handle "I love you," I would be satisfied with shortening the declaration to "Love you." I was a novelist, after all, and I accepted in prosaic terms what remained an intolerable insult to the poet. He could not speak of "love" if he could not fully say "I" and "you."

That poet had left Seoul last year. He walked out of his job one day—which entailed putting syllables together to make lines out of them, and putting lines together to make a book—and left the city. We were no longer in touch, and I did not know his reasons for leaving. I guessed that he simply wanted to leave, that meaninglessness of life and lackluster poetry were oppressing him. Then one day, I heard the news that the poet was raising birds somewhere out in Gyeonggi Province. He was raising moorhens, in fact. Moorhens were birds that made their home by streams and ponds or in grassy summer fields. They were known for their long beaks and legs, and for their poor flying skills despite their wingspan which can reach up to ten centimeters. They cried *ttumbuk, ttumbuk* morning and evening. A moorhen wasn't a parakeet, but I thought it worth leaving Seoul for. The poet was right to leave Seoul. One couldn't make a moorhen cry in Seoul, after all.

When I heard the news, I slapped my thigh in wonder of admiration and said to myself that nothing suited the poet better. His moorhens would be sold as pets, and every morning and every night, their songs will be heard in homes around the city.... My admiration came to a sudden and merciless halt, however, with the discovery that my imagination had led me completely off-track. I was naïve.

The poet incubated moorhen eggs until they hatched and fed the little chicks diligently. When the birds grew nice and fleshy, he sold them, for food. In fancy hotel restaurants, the poet's moorhens graced the baroque-style tables, transformed into the most delectable of delicacies. While nicely dressed men and women were busy cutting up his moorhens with steak knives, the poet listened to their song, *ttumbuk, ttumbuk*, all by himself. There was no one else around to hear them. *Ttumbuk, ttumbuk*, sang the poet's moorhens morning and night. Or was it the moorhen's poet that cried, I love you...?

Songs of birds, people who feast on songbirds, moorhens that bring in profit, a poet who makes his living selling them. Every time I thought of the poet's life, these miscellaneous headings would flit through my head, making me shudder. It wasn't the despair I felt regarding the poet that made me shudder, but the wonder of it all, the sad and bizarre harmony of this monumental contradiction. The poet strode into the heart of his own poetry. How did he do that? I asked myself in utter bewilderment. Did he have a compass? What kind of compass? Didn't he get lost? Didn't he crumble apart?

Without a compass, the train ran its course and deposited me at my destination. Hearing the conductor announce Gimje, I suddenly remembered that I threw away the green parakeet not too long ago. My daughter had long outgrown it, and it was dirty and ugly to behold because it couldn't be washed on account of the electric wiring that connected its belly to its beak. Still, I kept it for years. In the name of spring cleaning, I finally brought myself to throw it away only this past spring. The raggedy parakeet that now couldn't repeat a single word because the battery inside its belly had long gone dead finally found its place in the dumpster. So the parakeet left us, never having succeeded in saying, "I love you," still holding in its belly a machine that must break that declaration in two. And now the poet was raising moorhens. Moorhens that sang morning and night, moorhens that got eaten morning and night.

I had so little with me that I felt embarrassed by the announcement requesting the passengers to make sure that they left nothing behind on board. I got off the train and trudged along the platform holding only a small bag and with no one to accompany me. Did I have my ticket with me? The sudden thought drove me into a panic. I had not made sure before getting off the train that I still had my ticket. I started scrambling through my bag and my pockets, certain that I must have dropped the ticket somewhere around my seat. The scenario was all too familiar. I could not trust myself. Whenever something new grabbed my attention, I completely forgot about what I had been doing just before. This lack of balance in my mind made me despair. The train was gone, and though my hands were rummaging through the bag and my pockets, their movement was less than confident. Without the ticket, I was sure to be accused of having jumped the turnstile. What could I say to defend myself from the charge? How would the stationmaster react if I told him that moorhens were responsible for all this? Would he know anything about moorhens in the first place?

And then I saw the train ticket dangling from my fingertips. Folded in two, it was nestled deep in my bag. The conclusion that I had dropped it somewhere in the train had been premature. All the same, I doubted and doubted again. I couldn't fully believe that my hasty conclusion was wide of the mark, that my belief was unfounded, that my train ticket was not lost.

2.

The trees by the national road leading from Gimje to Geumsan Temple were maples of considerable age. Last autumn, red carpet had covered the sky above this stretch of road. Leaves flaming red against the blue of the autumn sky, the spears of radiant golden light shining through—

at winter's end, the brilliant memory still colored the window of my mind.

The road that had been blazing red in the fall now formed a wave of fresh, bright green. Perhaps on account of this change in color scheme, the scenery that flitted past outside was very different from what I had cherished in my mind all through the winter. I had to ask the taxi driver twice to make sure that we were going the right way. I asked him clearly the first time, but the second time, I muttered out my misgivings in a barely audible whisper before resigning myself. It wouldn't be the first time my memory was betraying me anyway. Just because an image gets saved in one's mind didn't mean that it was permanently fixed, like an engraving in stone. From the moment it became saved, memory started moving of its own accord, so that the image frequently ended up looking quite different from how it had started. Too often, the attempt to match up the memory with reality injured one's feelings in the end. Nevertheless, people trusted their memory too much, and invested it with great meaning, clinging stubbornly to what they used to see rather than what they saw before them now. I wanted to rattle my brain and chase off the vision of maple trees in red. I wanted to shake it clean of all the haze and dust.

My trip to this part of the country last autumn was made with a group of friends. We were visiting a friend of ours who lived near Geumsan Temple. She was now living in the city of Jeonju, but was enjoying her life in the country then, and our visit had no other purpose than to leave Seoul behind for a breath of fresh country air. In keeping with this general goal, the trip was filled with nothing but pure relaxation. The time was late October, the cusp of the change in season, and there were enough tourists trying to catch the last of autumn foliage to give the whole trip a festive air. The train we took then left Seoul Station at around the same time as the one that I took this time and dropped us off at Gimje around the same hour. We took a taxi then, too. I was retracing my steps exactly. But half a year had made all the difference. Back then I was on this road with close friends, feeling cheerful if not merry, and now I was traveling alone, trying to keep my heart from sinking underwater. The choice of this destination probably had much to do with my longing for the carefree rest of that autumn trip. For months, I had sat in front of a machine, ceaselessly typing vowels and consonants, only to hit the delete button and make all the letters disappear without a trace. Then I would type a consonant into the screen again, and look around for a vowel to go with it. Wandering lost among the keys, I was possessed by the thought that I was falling apart. What I needed was a rest to restore things that had fallen apart. Burying myself in thé backseat of the speeding taxi, I looked out at the fresh new leaves on trees that had survived the winter.

I hadn't planned to repeat the exact course, but there wasn't an alternative, really. Just as I had done last autumn, I got off the taxi at the interchange where a large zelkova tree stood in the middle. Last time, our friend met us in front of that tree, but there was no one waiting for me this time. I thought of my friend's old house and her yard with trees: two quinces, one thick-set cherry, one sweet persimmon, and three black persimmons with branches that were bent like bows with the weight of all the small persimmons hanging on them. She sold that sun-drenched house with all those fruit trees and opened a pizzeria in Jeonju. She now lived in a rented apartment and smelled shredded cheese and sliced mushrooms all day instead of fragrant quince and fresh, sweet black persimmons. She said that she couldn't bear so much as a look in the direction of Geumsan Temple now for the thought of that lovely house that used to be hers. She would never know that I was dallying about in the area now.

Since I wouldn't be going back to the station and boarding the last train bound for Seoul, I went ahead and took a room in the inn where I had stayed last time. Actually, the logic of that sentence had to be turned around. The truth was that I headed for the inn out of the fear that if I didn't make a commitment to someone to spend the night here, I might go right back to the train station and hop on the last train to Seoul.

As I had expected, a quiet sense of peace came over me once I asked for the room. The sight of the innkeeper's back as she led me to the room, the absolute trust it showed in the sincerity of my request, was like a sign sealing my fate. Now the die was cast, and I couldn't take it back. With that, I forced myself to put a period to the endless hesitation that had assailed me regarding this trip. I followed the innkeeper up the stairs in silence like a child waiting for a new assignment after finally managing to finish her first.

The room was surprisingly clean. The window looked out onto the backyard. Cherry blossoms in full bloom created a flickering silhouette on the window, and the effect was like a painting. Last time, my room had been quite noisy since it faced the street. Though I hadn't minded the noise then, it was also true that my expectations, coming back to the same inn, weren't particularly high. Now that I had a quiet and clean room in which to spend the night, I felt much more cheerful. I decided to go out and have a late lunch. How long had it been since I last decided on something with this kind of certainty? I took my wallet out of the bag and left the inn, walking tall. In the front yard, there were also several cherry trees laden with weight of fully-open blossoms. Though it would have required wings to completely avoid stepping on the wild array of delicate petals strewn on the ground, I tried as best as I could to leave them unmarred.

The restaurants were all at the mini-mall. In addition to restaurants, the mini-mall also contained souvenir shops and bars that doubled as dance halls. Foliage season was still a ways off, but there were tour buses lined up in the parking lot. I asked the restaurant owner and was told that the cherry trees the Japanese planted during the colonial period made the cherry blossom season even more spectacular than the autumn foliage.

"Not that people need an excuse to go around looking for fun nowadays," she added as an afterthought.

I had nothing to say in response. I realized that I, too, must appear to her to be one of those people who didn't need an excuse to go around looking for fun. Even to myself, I couldn't fully admit that since the trip was an extension of my writing, I was here for work. I was one of those writers who still found it uncomfortable to accept the notion that fiction writing is a form of creative labor. Something in my heart always rebelled at the idea. Despite the stiffness in my shoulders and the ache in my back that had me rushing to the pharmacy for medicated pads, I couldn't call what I was doing labor without blushing with shame. I certainly wasn't on the side that elevated literature to the status of something absolute or mystical. Still, I was skeptical about whether this "labor," as back-breaking as it was, had ever properly served as "our daily bread" for all of us struggling to survive. I didn't dare call writing labor. I wasn't sure that I would ever be able to.

One advantage of classifying fiction-writing as a form of labor, however, was that it helped to prevent literature from closing itself off to the world. Open up and receive willingly, so the saying goes. Sometimes it seemed to me that this was the way literature could become a true companion to an era. But the phrase also struck me as a reproach to the tendency of writers to keep a part of themselves under wraps even as they sought to open up to the world. In the end, it was precisely the tension between these two demands which served as the source of the resistance I felt. Because I was closed, I learned a writer's disposition, and because I had to open up, I learned to doubt ceaselessly. So how could I call myself a laborer without blushing with shame? In face of the debt inherited from the last decade, how could anyone be free from shame regarding questions of class? In any act, so long as it was an act of creation, one committed an error the moment one ennobled it. Literature was something whose value was liable to fall, the more its weight was emphasized. Life, not literature, was what needed to be emphasized.

Probably because it was past lunch-hour, I was the only customer in the restaurant. The owner was trying to help her son with his homework and getting all worked up in the process.

She reprimanded him in a loud voice, "See what happens when you hang around the video arcades everyday? I haven't seen you do these worksheets on time, not once. What's the point of getting them delivered at home if you won't do them?"

The comment was a familiar one to me; I could have been back home in my neighborhood. The boy looked as though he might be in elementary school, perhaps in second grade. Swinging his feet and stealing frequent looks out the window, he made an unenthusiastic attempt to do his homework while paying only half a mind to his mother's scolding.

"I live here because I have to run a business, but really this neighborhood is not fit for raising a kid. All you see are people wanting to have fun. What can a kid learn from that? My kid's education is a mess," the store owner said as she filled my water cup.

' The mother of Mencius, the famed Chinese philosopher, is said to have moved countless times for the sake of her son's education. In Korea, there were many mothers who also believed this to be the secret of virtuous motherhood. But would a move to the eighth district of

Gangnam in Seoul, supposedly the best in the country, or anywhere else in the country for that matter, put an end to mothers' sighs? While paying for lunch, I peeked at the child's homework. He was working on a test sheet copied from a problem-solving book. The problem provided a list from which the child was supposed to pick flowers that bloom in spring and flowers that bloom in summer. He was waiting for his mother's directions.

"They always have all these weird flowers. Why do kids need to know this? Just tell them the names of the really common ones scattered all over the place, that's enough. I mean, this isn't supposed to be some sort of a riddle, is it?"

The woman broke into a smile in the middle of the comment, and I smiled, too. Thinking, learning, living, everything in fact, was a riddle—the thought made me feel calmer somehow. One couldn't continue to get mad at riddles. Maybe because this was the first good meal of the day, I felt much better leaving the restaurant than I did entering it. Didn't some wise person once say that an empty stomach brought on a depression? He had a point. A change of mood required energy, too. Without refueling, it would be difficult to crawl out of depression. Depression was like a well.

Guisin Temple was around ten minutes away by car and thirty minutes on foot. A stroll to the temple and back would take rest of the day. There would be time for it in the morning, too, but I had nothing else to do. The other option would be to go see Geumsan Temple, but I had no desire to see its façade painted brightly like the traditional bride's dress. The truth was that Guisin Temple was the reason why I was here. The first thing I wanted to do upon arrival was to sit for a couple of hours in the complete silence of Guisin Temple. I couldn't help feeling that there might be something hidden there. When the thought of this reckless trip had first occurred to me, it was Guisin Temple that had hovered in the back of my mind. But I kept putting the trip off, afraid maybe that the sooner I make the trip, the sooner I would have to suffer disappointment. I couldn't be sure that the image of Guisin Temple stored in my memory would not betray me. Perhaps all that waiting had a purpose: I was preparing myself for the inevitable disappointment to come. Even after coming here, I could have gone directly to Guisin Temple from Gimje station. Or headed there after booking the room.

There were places near the temple where I could have lunched. I was dawdling on purpose, trying to hold on to something and keep it from exposure for as long as long as I could.

Last autumn, Guisin Temple had captivated me, starting from its name. The Temple of Divine Return, the place where gods find rest from their wanderings in eternity.

"Isn't it a great name?" my friend had asked. "The temple itself is really humble, but I take my son there from time to time. It's quiet and snug."

More than satisfied with the simple fact that we had gotten away from Seoul, we weren't planning to go out of our way to visit any famed scenic spots. So when the friend suggested Guisin Temple, we responded with alacrity; visiting Guisin Temple would add variety to our trip. Guisin Temple certainly did not have anything to offer in the way of tourist attractions to draw people from afar. In fact, there wasn't a single tourist on the premises. The temple had the kind of exterior that made it almost indistinguishable from an old house of some respectable family. Until one actually opened the door to the main hall and saw the gilded figure of the Buddha that had begun to lose its luster, one would not have known that it was a Buddhist temple at all.

But Guisin Temple was the kind of place that spoke volumes, if only you were willing to look with your heart, not your eyes. Though old and shabby with nothing to flaunt on the surface, Guisin Temple had everything, and it stayed with me the longest, defeating all the other, more glittering memories of that trip. The temple grounds was small and there wasn't a single stone stupa worth seeing, but even this had seemed to be a message to look with my heart and leave the place spiritually fulfilled. In my imagination, I saw a sign that read, "We do not welcome visitors who just want a quick look around." Guisin Temple was that kind of place.

Maybe fidelity to that imaginary sign was what had brought me back. Last time, I hadn't been able to do much more than pass through. For a long time afterwards, the feeling that I did not manage to fill my heart with what I needed at Guisin Temple stayed with me. As time went by and the once vivid images in my memory began to dull around the edges, that feeling solidified into the thought that I had left something really important there. It would disappear forever if I didn't hurry back and claim it before the expiration date. The thought now generated a sudden sense of urgency. I flagged down a cab that was about to make a left turn at the interchange.

The flowers that were blooming in the front yard last autumn—what were they called? Only the roots must remain now. How comforting those clusters were, generous and hearty rather than beautiful in a delicate sort of way. At the very end of autumn, they were still blooming in abundance, not even a petal showing signs of withering. Would the wind chime still be swinging under the eaves, singing with the voice of the wind?

I remembered the simple grace of the old wooden pillars, faded to brown without the trace of the once-bright paint, holding up the swinging wind chime and the weight of the blue sky. I thought also of the old persimmons left alone to ripen on that small hill behind the temple, how they would be sporting new buds now and watching the sunflowers open themselves up to the sky. Last autumn, one of us had picked up a bamboo stick from the ground and shaken a persimmon tree. It seemed that no human lips had touched the persimmons at the very top for decades, too high for mere groundlings. But persimmons that fell to the ground were our share. They were ripe to bursting and sweeter than words could describe. After returning to the city, I looked for persimmons like that for days, in vain.

The taste of those persimmons from half a year ago was on my lips when the cab pulled up by the path leading to the temple. As soon as I got off, the taxi driver spun the car around to flee the way he had came. I headed toward the temple, peeping over the walls at village homes. There was no sign of human life anywhere, but many dogs looked out at the sound of my footsteps. Leaning on twig gates, they fixed their wide-eyed stares at me, but slunk back furtively with their tails between their legs if I approached. A persimmon orchard stretched to the left of the road. If my memory was correct, I had to turn the corner and pass five or six houses on the right to be in sight of the temple. No part of the temple could be seen from the path. It revealed its profile to you only after you reached the end of the path and reoriented yourself. I walked up the path, smelling the fragrance of earth.

It was then that I heard a shriek. The shrill sound of a woman's voice nearly tore my eardrums and brought me out of my reverie. From the direction of Guisin Temple, I saw a woman sprinting toward me with all her might. No one except the dogs had greeted me since I got off the taxi, and the sight of the woman who materialized before my eyes was so astonishing that I wondered for a moment whether she might not be a phantom of my imagination. She could very well have been. She was running barefoot, her long skirt with bright peony patterns fluttering behind her, and her face beamed with a bright peony smile, too, despite the metallic screech that had issued from her mouth just a second ago.

The woman was as nimble as a wild hare and disappeared into one of the houses before I could blink. As she passed me, however, I saw once more the gleam of her white teeth between smiling lips. Before I could collect myself and wonder whether the blood-curdling scream that I had heard weren't just a figment of my imagination, I saw a man racing my way with the speed of a rolling rock. He wasn't screaming, but the movement of his rib cage, clearly visible under the white tank top covering his broad chest, was more intimidating than any scream. I tensed up and stood aside.

Unlike the woman, the man didn't race past me. Two or three steps from me, he stopped dead in his tracks and scanned me up and down with his big, bright eyes. I looked about me, almost instinctively. Then I heard the woman's sharp scream, warning him not to keep her waiting.

"What are you dawdling for? Come on, hurry up!"

She was standing behind me again, leaning against the wall of a house. The big peony prints on her skirt were red enough to make you dizzy.

"You stay right there, bitch!"

The man's ribcage arched like a bow, and he disappeared after her as if she were his prey. I couldn't see what he was doing to her, but from somewhere inside the house came that piercing scream again, immediately followed by peals of breathless laughter. In a daze, I stared at the gateless house into which the couple had disappeared.

The small commotion had the effect of hastening my steps toward Guisin Temple. But I was no longer in the mood to inspect in serenity whether the temple's atmosphere was the same as before. The couple had trampled mercilessly the foot that I had pushed forth into the recollection of the last trip. For a while, I actually did feel toe-breaking pain in my right foot when I stepped on dry yellow earth. That pain marked the start of my trip proper. Before the appearance of the man and the woman, the trip had simply been a reflection or an extension of the last. My heart hadn't trembled with a single new experience. If my toe did tingle once or twice, it was probably with pain resulting from pinching myself hard to see whether everything wasn't a dream.

Real experience continued to shatter the cherished images in my memory one after another, without even giving me a chance to catch my breath. When I finally arrived at my destination, the scene that unfolded before my eyes had me gasping. Guisin Temple wasn't there. Sure, there was a temple, but it wasn't the Guisin Temple I was looking for. What remained of it was a mere skeleton undergoing renovation. The temple grounds that I thought would be sunk in stillness was bustling with noise made by five or six workers, each with a dirty towel hanging from his waist and a half-smoked cigarette over his ear. Everything save a few big pillars had been stripped off of the two structures that faced each other across the small yard: The shrine for ancestral tablets and the main hall containing the Buddha-statue. Yellowish broadcloth was draped over the entire contents of the stripped structures, giving the whole scene an ominously funereal air.

Yellow as if faded, though it had not been exposed to the sun, the broadcloth was the kind from which funeral clothes were cut. Probably on its account, the temple seemed less a bonny place of rest but a dreary one to which aged gods drag their diseased bodies to breathe their last breath. The thought fit strangely well with several ladders placed around the two buildings. Was it the hem of the gods' robes that I saw ascending to the sky, the spirits doggedly climbing up the rungs of these ladders to the heavens? I finally turned my eyes to the roofs. Where countless blades of thin grass used to sprout, finding life in the cracks between tiles the color of despair, there was only the roofs' bare flesh shamelessly exposed. Horrified at the sight of the roof, I stopped in my tracks and retraced the few steps I had taken into the courtyard. Guisin Temple was so small that it took only a few steps to look around the whole place. Even though the workers on the grounds couldn't have failed to notice my presence, they went on mixing cement and sanding down wooden boards as if they didn't. I wished that one of them would ask me why I had come. This would at least give me a reason to linger in the yard. I dallied, unable to turn back but not knowing what I else to do.

After the initial disappointment of finding Guisin Temple in such a state of dismemberment, it occurred to me that where a mound of sand was piled up high under a jig might have been the exact spot where those clusters of flowers used to bloom, the nameless ones that were warm and comforting like an older sister's face. Those flowers had much to do with my inability to walk way from the place that had so betrayed my memory. I had to compare my memory of them to the real thing. Over the past half-year, those nameless autumn flowers that bloomed with sisterly generosity and offered comfort to visitors, had turned into the *udambara* of Buddhist lore in my mind. *Udambara* flowers were said to bloom only once every three thousand years. Their fragrance was so powerful that just a hint of it was supposed to chase away every tear, every worry. But the *udambara* were now buried under a grave of sand, gone without a trace. I stood there, looking fixedly at the soft mound of finely sifted sand as if my gaze could penetrate to its core and discover the flower hiding within.

Now there were only the persimmon trees left to see. If Guisin Temple's autumn flowers had become the *udambara* in my mind, the persimmon trees that covered the small hill behind the temple had turned into the *udambara*'s arboreal counterpart: the ever-fruiting tree of Buddhist legend, every branch of which continues to offer the most delectable fruit no matter how many you picked. To reach them, I had to walk between the workers and go behind the main hall. Of course, I knew I wouldn't find any fruits hanging from the trees now. Even a kid knew that persimmon trees didn't fruit in spring. I asked myself why I was climbing the hill then. The memory of tranquility that had held the temple in its bosom during my last visit flooded back. Yes, that was it. I hadn't found that tranquility yet. I wanted to soak my entire body in the radiance of that stillness, long enough to make everything in my body evaporate.

No one stopped me as I crossed the courtyard. Only a white-haired old woman stared at me quizzically over the low fence from one of the houses next to the temple; the workers still took no note of me as I stepped over and around the tools scattered on the ground. They worked in silence, maybe because they were in a temple. Even this silence seemed to be dictated by the power of the yellowish broadcloth in the naked building. I looked away, not wanting to see the broadcloth covering the Buddha figure and the tablets bearing names of the dead. As I climbed, I saw piles of new roof tiles and Styrofoam, next to pieces of wood that I supposed were what remained of the old building. It was obvious that the hill of ever-fruiting trees had been turned into a warehouse. I looked up at aged persimmon trees with fresh green leaves on every branch. Then I looked down at my feet where nameless wildflowers showed their white and yellow faces. Luckily, there was no more damage here. The materials for renovation stayed put where they were placed. Since I seemed to be the only moving creature in this warehouse of green, I hoped that I would finally be able to taste the tranquility I sought. I wanted to rest.

From where I parked myself, I had a clear view of the now naked roofs of Guisin Temple. The wind was warm and small critters whose names I didn't know were busily flying through the thicket. I wanted to lie down on the grass and nap for a while. If one of the workers hadn't shown up just then, I might have dropped my head between my knees and reminisced about the tranquility of Guisin Temple with my eyes closed. The worker came up the hill and started scrambling through a pile of old building materials. I thought at first that he would go back down as soon as he found what he was looking for. The white undershirt he was wearing seemed familiar, but I didn't recognize him as the man whom I met on the path to the temple. After scrambling through planks of varying lengths and widths, he looked straight at me.

"Yup, I thought you looked familiar. I know you, don't I?"

Though I knew that there was no one there, I looked behind to see if he could be addressing someone else. He wasn't. But I had no idea why he would be talking to me.

"Didn't you teach Korean at one time down in Osan? You remember Geogeum Island, don't you? Geogeum Island, just below Goheung."

Geogeum Island? I glowered at him, feeling as though my diary was being read aloud to the public. A town called Osan on Geogeum Island was where I spent my first year as a teacher. And like the man said, I had taught Korean. But who was this man? Only then did I realize that he was the one I saw chasing the wild-haired woman earlier.

146

But how did he know me?

"You know, I'm ... well, never mind. I'm not worth remembering. Let's just say I'm from Osan."

The man didn't try to hide the fact that he was glad to see me. He plopped down by my side and took out a cigarette. The tips of the fingers holding the cigarette were blunt. I realized that I had seen those fingers before, I saw the sea surging at those blunt fingertips. I blurted out his sister's name, Sukja. I didn't have a chance to doubt my memory.

"So you remember me, after all. Well, actually, anyone from Osan who says he doesn't know Kim Jonggu would be lying. In the end, that's why I left Osan, though."

He grinned, taking such a hard drag on his cigarette that his cheeks hollowed.

Kim Jonggu. I examined the man's face closely, dazed by the chance encounter with the past. The vivid lines of his eyebrows, the slightly squarish forehead, the long, deep furrow above his lip were all coming back to me. Despite the fifteen years that lay between us, I saw the surge of sea waves in his face again. Fifteen years ago, there had been a certain volatility to the roaring of those waves, but the sea engraved on his face now betrayed no signs of an impending storm, though it was still rough. I could see that he was a man of the sea that he had always been. "Man of the sea" wasn't necessarily the same thing as a "seafaring man," but someone whose life couldn't be anchored to any one place, a man who was destined to drift all over the world upon its waves.

"Aren't you curious how I managed to recognize you after all these years? I saw a couple of pictures of you recently. Sukja, I mean my little sister, keeps a scrapbook of all the magazine articles on you. She's still a packrat, she'll collect anything. She even took her notebooks from elementary school with her to the in-laws when she got married."

Kim Sukja. A girl who always sat in the back of the room and struggled to crane her thin neck to see me. With her little nephew strapped to her back, she used to work picking out baby shrimps and octopus from boiled anchovies. Whenever she saw me, she lowered her reddened face in embarrassment. Memories of Kim Jonggu came flooding back one after another, too. I counted the episodes I remembered about him and there were four in all, all of them surprisingly vivid still. Once the thread of memory began to unravel, so much emerged to the surface.

Memory did not disappear with the passage of time but only became tangled.

When I first met Kim Jonggu, I was his sister's homeroom teacher. The island's small junior high school was my first teaching post. The school had six classes in all, one for the girls and one for the boys in each grade, and at the foot of the schoolyard spread the deep blue sea. The wind that blew night and day battered all the doors of the teachers' dormitory. When the storms came, one had to stay locked inside for days in helpless gloom until the sea calmed down again. Even now, I couldn't clearly understand why the year I spent in the village surrounded on all four sides by the sea became one of depression and anxiety, when the sea was the very reason why I had gone there in the first place. But then again, was there any task more daunting than having to make sense of one's youth? The further one drew away from one's youth, the more its analysis was bound to fall wide of mark. It would be much easier to talk about Sukja's unexcused absences instead. After all, my memory of Kim Jonggu began with those experiences.

I was the Korean teacher for all grades and the homeroom teacher for eighth-grade girls. Since life in a remote island didn't exactly follow the academic calendar, all the girls in my class were mature for their grades, more mature than their years even. The ninth grade girls were sometimes wiser about the ways of the world than I was. They knew how to do so many more practical things than I did. If a snake crawled into the classroom, the girls chased it out. If I had to go to the next village for a home visit, one of the girls rowed me there. The children had responsibilities of full adults at home. At the peak of the anchovy season or when it was time for thrashing seaweed, the classrooms emptied out so much that it was difficult to carry on with the teaching. Sukja's unexcused absences, which began less than two months into the new semester, occurred for this reason, too. I asked other kids in the class to find out what was going on at her home and learned that she couldn't come to school because her brother was forcing her to stay at home and take care of the household. The kids described Sukja's brother as a "real tough guy," and the fishery science teacher who was a native of the village assessed him as a "brute who could easily have become a thug." According to this teacher, it was commendable of Kim Jonggu that he was now home, going through the motions at least of taking care of his aged mother and young sister. Kim Jonggu had come home the year before after many years of roaming the mainland. The news that his oldest brother was missing at sea had somehow reached him. I asked around about Sukja's home environment. When her brother returned last year, he had brought a woman with him who was in the last trimester of pregnancy. The woman fled back to the mainland as soon as she gave birth, and now Sukja had to take care of her motherless nephew on top of everything else. I started visiting Sukja at home, but the visits didn't do any good. Her mother, old, diseased, and exhausted after a life of struggling with hardships the world had thrown in her way, would only blink her rheumy eyes and repeat her line, "What could an old woman like me do? I just listen to what my son says." It didn't do any good to talk to Sukja, either. She turned bright as a beet whenever she saw me and could only rummage through the anchovies laid out to dry in the yard, not daring to lift her head. I decided I had no other choice but to go to the anchovy shed on the beach and talk directly to Sukja's brother.

Anchovies netted from the sea were boiled in a beachside shed first before being laid out to dry in the sun. On the pebbly beach on the eastern side of the village, there were several sheds with huge kettles in them. I asked Sukja to take me to her brother, and she pointed at a newer-looking shed among the bunch. A bare-chested man was standing in front of a steaming kettle heated by a log-fed blaze in the firebox. Sukja went ahead to tell him of my coming, and while waiting, I stood back and looked out at the sea. Kim Jonggu didn't make any haste on my account. He strode toward me leisurely across the beach only after he was done with what he had to do. I steeled myself, observing how Sukja's body shrank with every step as she followed her older brother a couple of paces behind.

"I knew you'd be trouble. Believe me, I understand. You don't have any experience, so you have to go by the book."

Kim Jonggu didn't beat around the bush and didn't waste time on shaking hands or exchanging pleasantries. He did not even bother to focus his big, bright eyes under the thick eyebrows on me. After spitting onto the pebbly ground, he went on speaking before I could respond.

"There are only two women in my house. One you see over there and the other crawls around on all fours because of her arthritis. You know how it is, you've been there yourself. So what more do you have to say?"

I didn't, in fact, have anything to say. This man with two knife scars on his face was doing a number on my pride as a teacher. If I had come with the thought of expressing a teacher's love for her student, her concern about the student's future, such thoughts beat a hasty retreat before this guardian. Kim Jonggu himself hammered his point home.

"I don't know why people forget this self-evident fact, but living, surviving comes before everything else. Compared to that, everything else is trivial, trivial beyond belief. Once we have that in some kind of order, Sukja will go back to school even if you tell her not to. Next year, probably, you'll see her back in the classroom. If you are here next year, that is, which I doubt very much."

Kim Jonggu said that his logs were going to waste and returned to the anchovy shed, without even saying goodbye. Sukja was deathly pale. In shame over her brother's rudeness, she covered her face with her hands. But strangely enough, I didn't feel at all hurt. I had dreaded this meeting, but Kim Jonggu's action, though far from civil, was less brutal than what I had anticipated. He was capable of expressing himself with words. And his words were worth listening to and thinking about. I walked away from the beach holding Sukja's hand. Kim Jonggu had taken off his shirt again and was shoveling anchovies into the boiling kettle.

My second encounter with Kim Jonggu took place against the backdrop of the bright early summer sea. He was floating on the blue waves, lying upon the sea without a care in the world. I was waiting by the stern of the ferry to transfer onto the small boat that would take me to the village. I was probably returning from a weekend trip back home. Going home meant having to endure two hours on a boat and five more hours on a bus. Because a trip out of the island was difficult to manage even once a month, I always had more baggage than I could carry on my way back, and by the time the village houses became visible in the distance, I was usually half-dead with nausea. The ferry was quite small but the village dock was poorly located and could accommodate the ferry only during the high tide. It was customary for passengers to get onto a smaller boat at sea. This smaller boat was anything but nimble. It pulled up its sail and started creaking its oars only when the ferry was ready to turn off its engine out at sea, and made its way slowly between numerous single-oar rowboats crowding the dock.

It was at one of these times that I saw Kim Jonggu. At first, I only saw the boat, a small dinghy with a water meter. With its engine turned off, the boat rocked to and fro like a light skiff as it drifted toward us from afar. One of the villagers was complaining loudly about how long it took to get to the village from his perch on top of a rice bushel. When the dinghy got sufficiently near us, he shouted out in amazement.

"Hey look, ain't that the son of a bitch, Jonggu?"

"It's Jonggu, all right. Boy, the man's got guts, that's for sure. Look at him sleeping there, like he has the whole world on a string."

"He must have gone to the seaweed field and left his wits there. How much did he drink? He's sleeping like a baby. Someone yell at him and wake him up!"

"Why wake him up? Let him be. He'll take care of himself. If the wind goes northerly, he'll drift all the way to Fox Island."

Kim Jonggu drifted on, heedless of the villager's chatter, and passed very close to the ferry. I could see him sleeping spread-eagled on the leaf boat. The azure water of the sea under him became the base sketch, and he looked as though his body was floating on water. Even though rough waves were growling underneath his back, his face tinged with the setting sun was more peaceful than any I had seen. Did I envy his peace? Was it envy and a hazy sense of longing that made me cling onto the bow and follow the drifting boat with my eyes until it disappeared from sight? Even today, the memory of that golden sunset dyeing his face and arms as he lay on the sea was vivid in my mind. The dazzling rays had broken into thousand pieces every time the wave rolled. The motorboat was as peaceful as a rocking cradle.

Gauzy sunset hung even now on the western sky. But this wasn't the sea but the hills. I started inspecting Kim Jonggu's appearance again. If my memory was correct, he was well above forty. Nothing about him belied that age, however, not his gaze, momentary but sharp as an arrow, not the thick veins bulging on his forearms, not the solidity of the torso banded together by muscles. At the same time, the fine wrinkles on his forehead and the fatigue tangled up in the corners of his eyes made me wonder whether his age might not actually be fifty or more.

"Let's not go inspecting others with such sorry eyes. Believe me, I know what you're thinking. You feel bad that I seem to be leading a wretched life, living hand to mouth as a manual laborer on a construction site? Well, you couldn't be more wrong. I do this because I like it. I would rather die than work locked up some place under a roof where I can't breathe. It's been several years since I turned forty, but this body is still quite usable. I like roaming around like that cloud in the sky, relying on nothing and no one but my body. Coming and going as I wish."

I had almost forgotten. He had the uncanny ability to read other people's minds. The reason why his words always seemed to have barbs in them was probably because that was the tone usually adopted by people who can see through other people. Kim Jonggu, though he seemed much changed, gave me the impression that he hadn't changed at all. I decided to stop my futile reconnaissance.

I looked at my watch. I figured he must be getting back to work. He had something different in mind. He told me to wait and went back down, not giving me a chance to reply. Even if he hadn't told me to wait, I wasn't planning to go anywhere, but because he had told me to wait, my enthusiasm for staying on the hill began to wilt. What did I have to talk to him about? I was not uninterested in his life, but I didn't exactly enjoy the prospect of engaging in a deep conversation with a casual acquaintance from fifteen years ago. Nothing was as comfortable as being by oneself, though it did get lonely after a while.

I had no choice now but to wait for him to come back. And since I had already told him that this trip was for fresh air, I couldn't pretend that there was some urgent business tearing me away. Nonetheless, I figured that unless I wanted to extend it, this chance encounter would soon come to an end. For me at least there was some sentimental value in retracing the memory of the year I spent as an island teacher, but I couldn't see what would be in it for him. No matter how much I groped my memory, nothing came to me that would suggest that there was some tenderness or sentimentality to Kim Jonggu. On the contrary, the third episode about Kim Jonggu that came to mind made me shudder with its violence.

The gruesome episode came back to me wrapped in the double layer of death and nausea. The sharp blade of hand-axe gleaming blue in the sun, the skull of a goat, and Kim Jonggu in the middle of it all. Kim Jonggu was the one called on to kill goats on special occasions. For the most of the year, goats were left untethered to graze freely, but goats were the primary source of meat for the islanders. At communal feasts where a black goat was killed, the school teachers, fewer than ten in all, were always the guests of honor.

Born in the year of the goat, I felt a kind of affinity for the animal, which made it impossible for me to think of it as food. Attending these feasts, therefore, was pure torture I endured simply because there was no way out of it, but it took less than three months on the island for male teachers to develop a taste for goat meat. They never demurred when helpings of goat meat was offered. On the day of the feast at the house of the school support committee president, there was enough goat meat for all the villagers. Kim Jonggu was there, too.

During my year on the island, I was told many times that the two best ways of enjoying a goat was to drink its blood raw right after the slaughter, and to break the boiled skull to eat its brain. Still, I was not prepared for the frightful sight of three goat heads being carried out on trays. Usually, the preparation took place in the kitchen and out of sight of the guests. But the dominant opinion that day was to eat the brain on the spot right out of its casing. Three goat heads were placed on the wooden floor, and everyone, as if they had agreed upon it in advance, turned to look at Kim Jonggu. "Who else would do it, if not you?" they seemed to say. One of the villagers handed him a hand-axe with a sharp, blue blade.

Kim Jonggu took one look around the people gathered there and grabbed the hand-axe without a word. A smile of derision hovered at the corners of his lips. Perhaps I was the only one who saw it. The smile suggested that he had seen through the people's hearts and read there the appetite for the gruesome scene to come. There was no other reason to start grinding the already sharp axe blade against a whetstone. Shree, shree. Listening to the ominous sound the axe made against the whetstone, people gulped in anticipation, imagining some rich fare to come. And when he was done honing the blade, Kim Jonggu drew in the audience with the kinds of gestures magicians used to focus attention.

He caressed the blade, slowly and deliberately, and several villagers near him took a step back in fear. They read murderous energy in his eyes. I read disgust.

At last, the plucked head of a goat was placed on a large chopping block made by splitting a big round log in two. The goat head, its eyes half-closed, was quite different from pigs' heads one saw in the markets. If a pig's head was a kind of comic caricature, with its closed eyes, nostrils facing skyward, and pouty lips that gave it the air of sullenness, a goat's head had a kind of tragic pathos to it. Goats were known as particularly timid creatures. No other animal could come close in registering the shock of death upon its face. Kim Jonggu stroked the goat head this way and that to look for the spot where the axe blade should land. He exaggerated his movements, deliberately for sure, and dragged out the process. He was willing to put on a show for as long as people wanted to see it. Then suddenly the hand axe flashed in the air as a bizarre cry erupted from his mouth.

With the cry, an aggressive thud rang out. Through the crack in the split skull, steaming white brain revealed itself. The men who were waiting for that moment with their chopsticks poised in the air descended upon it simultaneously. In what seemed like a blink of an eye, the brain was gone and the empty skull tossed into the trashcan. While people ate, Kim Jonggu smoked in silence. He placed the second goat head on the block.

This time, there was no clowning around to draw attention. A single clean stroke split the second skull in two, and the third one after that. People didn't cry out in amazement anymore. Everyone was intent on moving their chopsticks busily, lest the steaming brain get cold. I saw that Kim Jonggu's chopsticks were not among them. He turned away from the sight and left the house after downing a shot of *soju*. Too busy gobbling up the contents of the goat's skull, people didn't notice that the man who had delivered it to them had disappeared.

Remembering this episode made me shudder not only because of its violence but also because of a peculiar kind of pathos it had. Perhaps Kim Jonggu already understood then how lonely and sad life is for the outsider who refuses to compromise with the community's particular hypocrisy. Even though I didn't know how his life had changed in the fifteen years since the episode, it made sense, from what I had seen of him then, that Kim Jonggu was wandering about, taking odd jobs around construction sites. How could someone who has peeked at the secret of life settle himself in one place? I began to feel curious about where this unforeseen encounter with Kim Jonggu would lead. How had these fifteen years been for him? For me? Kim Jonggu reappeared, looking a great deal tidier than before. He had changed and freshened up. Even though his hair was still visibly dusty, it had been dampened, and he looked more than acceptable as a breadwinner returning home after a hard day's work.

"Let's go," he urged me as if we had agreed on where to go. I got up hesitantly.

"We're going to my house. That energetic woman you saw earlier is my wife. I have to report back to her majesty right after work, no exceptions. To Hwangnyeo, then, we go."

I guessed, and later confirmed, that his wife's last name was Hwang. He called her Hwangnyeo,[1] as if she were an empress.

"Let's go. She'll be clinging to the fence already, and there'll be an incredibly delicious stew on the stove. Hwangnyeo is a wild one. She'll come running barefoot if she misses me even in the middle of the day. One fiery personality. And she loves having guests because she can show off her talent. What talent? Oh, it's nothing really. She plays the Korean flute a bit. You know, *danso*. Her melody, well, it'll kill you."

Maybe he thought he had talked too much. Kim Jonggu stopped and waited quietly for my response. Etiquette required that I turn down this offer with polite words. My interest was piqued, to be sure, but I couldn't very well barge into his house for dinner, just because I had taught his sister for a brief while some fifteen years ago. I declined and Kim Jonggu frowned in visible disappointment. He reached up and snapped a persimmon branch overhead. He started chewing on it, and for a brief moment, he had the look of someone about to suffocate.

"Jeez, you still use those words from the Joseon Dynasty? If there's one thing I can't stand it's that kind of highfalutin' talk. Please, stop

---

[1] "Empress" is a pun on the woman's name. Hwang, the woman's last name, is also the Korean pronunciation for the Chinese character meaning emperor. "Hwangnyeo," which literally means "Hwang-woman," can thus signify "a woman named Hwang" or "empress."

talking such nonsense, and let's just go to my house. What could be so
wrong about my inviting you to a meal at my house? You've gotta see
Hwangnyeo's face. She'll be delighted. She really is a fine one, you'll
see."

Kim Jonggu started walking ahead, and I had no choice but to
follow him down the hill. Eating with people I didn't know very well
wasn't something I enjoyed. I wasn't as fastidious about other things,
but eating required chewing and swallowing, and I couldn't do these
things unless I was completely at ease. At the start of a new friendship,
I always thought about how many meals would have to be eaten before
we could be comfortable eating together. The number always seemed
too big. It made me unwilling to embark on the friendship.

Guisin Temple had emptied out in the meantime. The workers were
all gathered now at the house of the old woman who had stared at me
earlier over the wall. At the temple gate, Kim Jonggu made me wait
once more and strode into the house. Judging from the smoke that rose
from the yard and the piece of slate placed on top of the open flame, I
guessed that the workers were going to have barbecued pork for dinner.
For barbecuing, a slate board was better than a metal sheet, since its
grooves allowed the grease to drain. It also gave meat the flavor of
stone barbecue. One saw the sight frequently on construction sites.
Kim Jonggu came out of the house not long afterwards, thrusting
something into his pocket.

"Today's payday. The pay's shameful this week because of all the
rain that's been falling. We'll have to finish before Buddha's Birthday
no matter what happens, but it's so difficult to find workers."

Tapping his pants pocket as if to show me how much money it
contained, he suddenly lowered his voice.

"It's all monkey business. Do you know why I stayed on this job?
The first day I came to the temple with the head carpenter, it happened
to be raining and the place had the most amazing atmosphere. I've seen
famed temples all over the country, but never something quite like this.
Excuse me for using fancy words before a writer, but I felt as though
something that transcended life and death, something that encompassed
all the vagaries of life, was pressing in upon me here. And now they
want to fix this place up and make it all colorful! When I heard about
what incredible stupidity they were up to, I was going to wash my hands

of it. But I changed my mind. It occurred to me that I have to be here to do what I can to minimize the damage. Honestly, this job is labor of love, loyalty and dedication. No one appreciates it, but I couldn't just stand aside and watch them destroy something so spiritual."

I stopped in my tracks in surprise. Did Kim Jonggu feel how special Guisin Temple was, too? I felt such an affinity for him at that instant. With the single comment, Kim Jonggu made the yardstick I had been holding up to measure him disappear. How sly I was to hold on to that yardstick! How narrow-minded of me to try to measure the way he appeared now and compare them to my impressions of him from fifteen years ago! Mortification opened my eyes and made me listen respectfully.

"By the way, there's one thing I'd like to ask you to keep in mind. If Hwangnyeo plays her *danso* this evening, you have to shower her with compliments. I mean, shower her, until you run out of saliva in your mouth. I've never heard anyone else play *danso*, so when I compliment her playing, I'm being a hundred percent sincere, but I'm sure you've heard lots of really accomplished *danso* players. So please close your eyes, don't think about this and that, and put her on a pedestal till she can smile no wider. Hwangnyeo has a bad habit of being picky about her audience, so she might decide not to play at all. But nothing will make her happier than a knowledgeable guest praising her melody. If I bring you home, she just might faint with excitement."

He made this request before we entered his house, and it pricked my conscience. He was warning me not to use the world's yardstick to measure his wife. In retrospect, his insistence that I come over to his house as soon as we had met, and his gladness at meeting me out of the blue had everything to do with his love for Hwangnyeo. I resolved to do what I could to make Hwangnyeo happy. If a few words of exclamation and pretended emotion were all it took, why not? A visit to Guisin Temple had been my last resort, and I had discovered that it had been turned into a bleak construction site. And yet, my anticipation for what this trip might bring was steadily growing. Kim Jonggu had appeared out of the blue before despair could bind my feet. He took over and all I had to do was to follow his lead.

He was unpredictable and this unpredictability saved me from a mud puddle of thoughts. Just that fact alone made this encounter with

157

Kim Jonggu a rich harvest for me. So whatever else came my way from here on qualified as a bonus.

To jump the gun a little, that bonus ended up being much greater than I could have anticipated. As the evening wore on, every word Kim Jonggu spoke struck me with the force of something genuinely new. Perhaps I only felt that way because of the depth of my despair, or the strength of my desire for something to shake me out of my jadedness. Maybe I fell under some kind of hypnotic spell. In fact, I'm certain that I did. It makes no difference. Is there any truth in the world that can be justified by any other desire than the desire to be something else than what we already are?

3.

Kim Jonggu must have felt that my introduction to Hwangnyeo required a bit of ceremony. He had me wait in the yard and went into the kitchen by himself. The light coming from the kitchen attested to her presence there. Though it was still faintly light outside, it was time to turn on the light inside the house. The kitchen was the only place where the light had been turned on. Recalling the image of the barefoot woman with disheveled hair and the wild gleam in her eyes, I looked around the house without any other sign of life and felt a bit anxious while I waited. Even if she welcomed my presence, I couldn't begin to guess how she would express it. All I knew was that it would be different from what I was accustomed to.

I was right. The sound of Hwangnyeo's uncontrollable peals of laughter rang out from the kitchen before the kitchen door banged open. Then a bucket of dirty water flew out from the kitchen and splattered onto the yard, before I had time to step back. Fortunately, the water missed where I was standing, but it wasn't too pleasant to have to lock eyes with a woman who was clearly surprised to find me standing there. She seemed to recognize me from our brief encounter a couple of hours before. In a village like this, a foreign face had to be easy to spot.

"Oh, no, you've brought someone! Why didn't you say so? You're such a piece of trash. Always deceiving me like this."

The woman turned around to face her husband and yelled at the top of her lungs before slamming the door behind her. She hadn't said a word to me, of course. I was shocked, but then again, I had come mentally prepared to be shocked. Kim Jonggu said sulkily, "Fine, forget it. I invited a distinguished guest here just for you, but if you're not pleased about it, suit yourself. Shit, I went to all that trouble for nothing."

"Who said I wasn't pleased? Who is she anyway?"

They lowered their voices and I couldn't make out what they were saying. Who was I? How would Kim Jonggu explain that? What comments of his necessitated Hwangnyeo's occasional "No, really?" Like a minister waiting nervously for an audience with the empress, I strained to hear every word they exchanged.

The kitchen door opened again, but only after Hwangnyeo had calmed down. She was still wearing the skirt with large peony prints, but she wasn't barefeet anymore. She had tried to give some semblance of order to her hair, too, so that almost nothing of the earlier wildness remained. She appeared to be quite shy and acted as though I had not witnessed a very different side of her in its full glory just a moment ago. She led me inside demurely. Behind her, Kim Jonggu looked quite pleased with himself. He had an expression on his face that said, I told you so.

Hwangnyeo's shyness didn't last long. Kim Jonggu didn't let her remain that way. It was his philosophy that Hwangnyeo had to be herself, and before long, she cast aside her demure carriage and began to strut around.

"I fell in love with her barbaric ways," Kim Jonggu said. "Hwangnyeo's charm is that she's rough and sly. I'm comfortable with that. Immaculate virgins who cover their faces with veils don't interest me one bit. All it means is that you have to go to the extra trouble of unveiling her when it comes to you know what."

Hwangnyeo was playing *danso* at a bar, and he fell in love with her playing, Kim Jonggu said. They spent that night together, and the very next day, he got her out of her situation at the bar, and then started living together. Kim Jonggu said he had recognized Hwangnyeo instantly.

"She's one hell of a woman. The moment I spotted her, I knew right away that underneath that voluminous bust of hers, she had one of my ribs. I consider myself real lucky. I mean, not everyone gets to find his lost rib. I spent a lot of energy over the years, let me tell you, looking for that rib of mine in a different woman every night. I won't have to do that now, at least for the time being. Why do I say for the time being? There's no guarantee that the rib will continue to fit, is there? Even bones grow, don't they? Then I'll have to look for something that fits better. There's bound to be more good fortune in store. Boy, I'm doing a lot of unnecessary talking in front of a teacher."

He didn't look one bit like someone who feels he has talked unnecessarily. His tone wasn't one of confession or self-defense. It gave the impression that he had taken everything into account, integrated it, and controlled it fully. Someone like that didn't talk unnecessarily. What appeared unnecessary was actually a part of the intended effect. I wasn't surprised when Kim Jonggu said that after living with Hwangnyeo for two months, he got up one day and took off.

"The problem was with me, of course, but I didn't desert her because I was looking for a different rib. I just felt suffocated, you know. Having three square meals a day with a woman, I couldn't breathe. A fire blazed in my chest. What could I do? Hwangnyeo knows what I'm like. She's no regular gal, either, as you can see. If you want to go, then shut up and go, that's been her attitude all the way. And then I met her again a few years later in another bar. We lived together for three or four months again, and this time she was the one who took off. I thought it was all over then for sure. But I met her again last year. For the third time. Then I knew that it wasn't some human design that was bringing us together. I guess we just couldn't run from it anymore. So now, I take her with me wherever I go." While Hwangnyeo was preparing dinner in the kitchen, Kim Jonggu told me stories about his past.

He never stayed in one place for more than a year. Four seasons in the same place, and he was ready to pack his bags and set out looking for work somewhere else. He did spend three years back home in Geogeum Island, but when his younger brother came home after finishing high school in Goheung and took over the anchovy fishing and seaweed farming business, Kim Jonggu took off again. That was the year after I left the island, having finished a one-year term. After leaving home, he mostly roamed the mountains. When the thirst for sea got the better of him, he returned home for a short while. He kept to the mountains on purpose so that his thirst would bring him home to his old mother again from time to time. Every time he went back, once every year or two, his mother greeted him as she always had, only a bit older than before. She had aged prematurely because of all the hardships she suffered as a young woman, and she viewed every year that she was alive as a bonus. She's still alive, he said, though she can hardly walk anymore.

Roaming the mountains, he did a lot of different work. The construction of the tourist road all the way up to Nogodan in Jiri Mountain was one of these projects, and he had worked on building several dams as well. There was no construction project in the world that didn't require shoveling or brick-carrying, which meant that there wasn't a construction site where he couldn't find some work. The one advantage of work like that, he said, was that you could always get it. If he had three square meals and a place to sleep, he didn't care where he was. He had never had a bank account in his name or monthly bills of any kind. He had no need of a mailing address or a phone number. He had no desire to take a job that would require a copy of his citizen's registration or some such document guaranteeing his person. He rejected all schemes to bind him.

"I've lived my life this way for fifty years come tomorrow. Why would I change now? I'm comfortable this way. I'll continue to rock 'n' roll as Kim Jonggu."

There was a twinkle in his eyes.

"Do you want to hear an interesting story? It goes back to when I was staying at ... Well, I'd better not say where. Why? Because I lived there almost two years. I told you that I never stay anywhere for more than a year, right? But a year just wasn't enough in that place. So I rotted there for two years. Well, you've guessed it. Yes, I had a rib there, too. Except there was one small problem. She simply wouldn't acknowledge that she had one of my ribs. She said that her rib belonged to someone who wears a necktie, drinks coffee, and pushes paper around an office in a city somewhere. When a woman is so deluded, what can you do? Nothing, short of hitting her or kidnapping her in the middle of the night, and I'd never resort to violence like that. But one night, she came to my room and started sobbing her heart out. When I asked her what was wrong, the story she told me boggled my mind. She said that there was a young man she liked in the next village and could I please do something about it. He attended a college in Seoul and had a promising job lined up, and at one point she was sure he showed interest in her, too. But this time, he brought a girl from Seoul to introduce to his

161

parents as his future wife. She moaned and cried. She said if he married that snooty Seoul girl, his family would be ruined for sure. He had siblings upon siblings, and country bumpkin parents to take care of because he's the oldest, and a city girl wouldn't put up with all that hassle. So I told her that I'd take care of it. Wait here, I said. I'll get him to promise me that he'll marry you."

Kim Jonggu then made his way through the dewy grass in the middle of the night to the next village. He called the boy in question out to the back woods and started beating him. I'm so-and-so's older cousin, and it seems that you'll have to be responsible for her. If you don't, you'll die at my hands tonight and not a creature will know what happened to you. He was only bluffing, but the guy fell unconscious after just a couple of blows. No matter how hard Kim Jonggu shook him, he wouldn't wake up. Kim Jonggu got scared. He ran away. He didn't even bother to go back to his room to pack. Months later, he strode back to the village, prepared to turn himself in if the unlucky bloke was dead, but instead of a funeral, there was a wedding party. He was marrying the woman who had asked Kim Jonggu for help.

"So I slipped out again and never looked back. Now, let me ask you. Did I do right, or did I do wrong? No matter how hard I think about it, I can't decide."

I couldn't, either. I was the last person in the world who would be able to answer a question like that. I couldn't think of a different way to live even in my dreams. Fortunately, Hwangnyeo came in carrying the dinner table and saved me. We began eating and pretended that no questions had been asked. Kim Jonggu's enraptured gaze caressed Hwangnyeo again, and the thousand different faces of this man had me thoroughly confused. Just when I had decided that he was not like other men, he became the most typical of men in front of Hwangnyeo, who had him eating out of her hand.

"Eat the tofu. Finish it or else. I'll stuff it into your mouth while you sleep."

He obeyed the woman's rough command and stuffed his mouth with tofu.

"How much more tofu do I have to eat before it disappears from the goddamn world?"

When all the tofu was gone, Hwangnyeo quickly brought out another plate of grilled tofu, despite Kim Jonggu's loud protestations. The torture began anew for him and Hwangnyeo's lashings did not permit an ounce of sympathy.

"He won't touch meat. So this is the only way he can get his protein. If you saw how exhausting his work is, you'll understand why I force him to eat this stuff. But he says he hates anything made from beans. He's always saying things like how the expression vegetarian meat nauseates him."

"But it really does nauseate me. How could they make up words that join animals and plants like that? Educated people can be quite cruel, you have to admit. The phrase does injustice to all the plants of this world. Have all the animal meat you want and let the plants be."

After we finished dinner, Hwangnyeo went to the kitchen to bring out the drinks. It didn't seem to occur to them that I might prefer fruits or tea over alcohol. I told them to forget about the drinks and let me hear her play *danso*, but both of them interrupted me with firm expression on their faces.

"You've got to be kidding. No drinks when all of us are feeling so merry? I suppose you are not too familiar with this kind of atmosphere. But you can bet Hwangnyeo is. Too many thoughts in your brain slow your body down, and then your life is doomed. That's right. I stand by that statement. Too much of anything, no matter how good it is in and of itself, only ends up getting in your way. Measuring this against that, that'll never come to an end. You can't even die for all those thoughts in your brain."

In the meantime, Hwangnyeo got the drinks ready. The table now consisted of a few side dishes we had eaten for dinner and a bottle of unrefined *soju* that the locals sold by the liter.

"Do you know what principle I've lived by all my life? Don't spend any more time than absolutely necessary with people whose brains are full of ink. They splatter it all around them. A little while is okay. But not long. They tend to be selfish, more often than not, and they spread unhappiness. You might not like to hear this, but that's the truth. If somebody told me that I have a lot stored in my head, I'd take that as an insult. Because all that stuff is really garbage. Our heads, like everything else, have to be cleaned everyday. Only then can you grab onto something real when it comes your way. If your brain begins to grow moldy, it's all over."

I laughed at the severity of his language, but I had to acknowledge to myself that he was right. I didn't have the courage to voice that to Kim Jonggu, however. I wanted to hide my moldy head.

"I was in the eighth grade when I decided that I had had enough of schooling. What they were trying to teach us was so exasperating. How is a kid to learn the way of the world by doing those minute calculations and looking at insects under a microscope? It's all so closed-up. So much so that you can't even begin to do anything about it. I felt that they were turning me into an idiot, so I stopped going to school. People who love to give other people advice are always telling me to get a GED. Dammit, would they be responsible for my life if I try to fill my head with garbage again and end up neither here nor there? I look back, and I still think I did the right thing. You jump into this big world and start doing things, making noise, and your head will open up even if it was clogged before. That's the real thing. You're alive. Even if you live until eighty, there are so many things that you wouldn't be able to experience before dying, and why would you do something that you can't see the end of? That would qualify as an addiction, don't you think?"

His words were full of confidence. There was not even a hint of servility to them, no hidden intent to hurt others. He spoke plainly, without being overbearing, rude, or insecure. I could tell that from his face. His words, like the *soju* he drank, were clear.

Kim Jonggu frowned and emptied his cup. I wasn't much of a drinker, but luckily, Hwangnyeo was. She looked at his face in a trance and turned to look at me periodically.

"That kind of addiction will have you double guessing your whole life. Then you'll go to the underworld without having had any fun at all. And when you get there, you know what the king of the underworld will say? He'll say, you sucker, I gave you a chance and you come back to me not having tasted anything? Well, I'll give you a taste of something hot! Then he'll cast you into pits of fire. Into boiling water is what I'm saying."

He drew his hand back as if from boiling water, and emptied another cup into his mouth. Hwangnyeo filled his cup to the brim again. Making no attempt to hide her sense of pride, she said, "The two of us can barely wet our lips with so small a bottle."

Hwangnyeo's face was only just beginning to flush, and the color made her look all the more vibrant. She looked at me with pity, "Drinking is the easiest thing to enjoy in the world," her eyes seemed to say. "When you can't enjoy that, what can you enjoy?" The light in the room was unflatteringly bright, and Hwangnyeo wasn't pretty by any means. Her eyes were two narrow slits and the hook of her nose gave her face the impression of hard obstinacy. Nonetheless, these flaws were what made Hwangnyeo look like Hwangnyeo, that is, an empress. It struck me how easily all the things connected with my life—what people usually grouped together under the heading of morality and high culture—crumbled apart like mere trifles in front of this couple. The premonition that what had formed and trained and affected me all these years actually belonged to a highly circumscribed world from which I hadn't ventured a step filled me with pure despair. To find relief from that despair, I poured *soju* into Hwangnyeo's empty cup and hinted that it was now time to hear her play. A person like me knew all too well how to maneuver a change of scene when her back is against the wall.

"Wait. Confer upon me the honor of delivering the instrument to your majesty."

Kim Jonggu moved his huge body and went to a corner of the room. The only real piece of furniture in the room was an old dresser. There was a television set on top it. In addition, there were a few cardboard boxes, a big basket containing Hwangnyeo's cosmetics, and clothes hung on nails all around the room. *Danso* was in the deepest corner of the top dresser drawer. Exaggerating his movements, Kim Jonggu pulled out the drawer. Hwangnyeo tapped her knee in matching rhythm to his choreography. I sat there, feeling like a drop of oil in a cup of water. I hated myself for feeling so awkward, but I couldn't help it. Even something that could not mix in with the milieu had a right to exist.

"Do you know where I first met her? In May of that year, you know, I was in Gwangju. I had real shitty luck. After leaving the anchovy fishery in my brother's care, an old mother and a young sister to boot, I came out to Gwangju to start my free life in a suffocating world. My timing was just beautiful. I got to the city just when it was turning into a battlefield. I went into a bar one day and saw this woman playing a heartbreaking melody on her *danso*. *Danso* amid all that bloody mess, can you believe it?"

He shook his body from side to side, taking the *danso* carefully out of its silk pouch. Maintaining his deferential and solemn attitude, he held it up to Hwangnyeo. Sitting in the Buddha-posture, she took the instrument haughtily. After making his offering, he retreated with his head bowed and took his seat against a wall. I heard him mutter, as if to himself, "It'll knock her out. Yes, it'll be a knockout." It was his way of reminding me about our earlier conversation. He was telling me to put down my yardstick, and prepare to be knocked out by Hwangnyeo's knockout performance. As I waited for her to begin her performance, I silently practiced a few phrases of enthusiastic praise. Hwangnyeo put her lips to the mouth hole and breathed in, and tested out the sound. I couldn't believe that this was the same woman I had seen speeding down the path, howling in laughter. Even before a melody rang out from Hwangnyeo's flute, I was bewitched by the gracefulness of her form and the dignity of her closed eyes.

If *piri*'s sound resembled a man's vocal cords, *danso* was closer to the thin and clear voice of a woman. Its sound was sometimes forlorn, sometimes bright and clear. This was the extent of my knowledge about *danso*. Kim Jonggu had worried needlessly. I was no expert, and I wouldn't have presumed to make any comments if not to give praise. Still, the praise that issued my mouth when the song ended was completely sincere. I mobilized all the vocabulary I could. It was clear, even to a layperson like me, that Hwangnyeo's playing had attained a level beyond.

"That was called *Cheonnyeon manse*. Now she'll play *Cheongseonggok*. Thanks to her, now I know that there are different names to *danso* melodies, too. At first, I thought she was improvising the whole time. I didn't know that there were scores for *danso* melodies."

Kim Jonngu was smiling, clearly satisfied with my attitude as a listener.

"He asks me to play *Cheongseonggok* every night. There are times when the sound is no good, but he won't take no for an answer."

"Enough. Maestros don't talk. You do the talking through that mouth hole."

"Since when have you become such an expert?"

Hwangnyeo glared and he reclined and closed his eyes. This seemed to be the set pose in which he always listened to *Cheongseonggok*. The pose Kim Jonggu struck was Hwangnyeo's cue. She closed her eyes and brought her lips to the hole.

Nillilli, pillilli, naniru, naniru.

Hwangnyeo's fingers danced faster and faster over the instrument; then, suddenly the sound dropped as if pushed over a cliff into the abyss. The music soared fearlessly one moment, swept along on high waves, and plunged to the bottom of the sea the next. I felt that I could understand, vaguely at least, why Kim Jonggu was so immersed in this melody. He was carried along by the music, and his eyelids fluttered, in fine response to its rise and fall. He was upon the sea now. And the sea was in him: the ebbs and flows, the roaring waves and the delicate seafoam. The sea was constantly changing and ever the same; its piercing blue came from a million bruises.

Nilliri, pilliri, naniruru, lirururu....

The long melody ended and I couldn't speak. Hwangnyeo took her lips off the bamboo instrument, and put her finger over them, admonishing me not to say anything. Only then did I see the tears rolling down Kim Jonggu's cheeks, following the curve of the cheeks and dampenening the white hair by his ears. I was awestruck, like a witness to a sight that should have remained secret. Where was Kim Jonggu now? Where had he docked after drifting upon that melody? I didn't know what was going through his mind at that moment. I doubted that anyone could. Putting her *danso* down, Hwangnyeo slid toward him and wiped away his tears. I watched them in silence.

That night, I filled my own cup with *soju* again and again. We filled one another's cups, too, occasionally.

4.

At first I didn't know what was blocking my view. I opened my eyes without knowing where I was. It took me a while to realize that I was back in my room at the inn, and that it was cherry blossoms in full bloom that plastered the window. My eyes scanned the room—a narrow wardrobe for storing the bedding, television with the broken dial—and only then did I realize that I had overslept.

Still, I had no intention of getting up. My head felt so heavy, I couldn't lift it. What time had it been when I returned from Kim Jonggu's house? It had been past midnight for sure, but I didn't know the exact time. He brought me back to the inn on his cultivator. Hwangnyeo came along, of course. We raced along the country road joyously as fast as the cultivator could take us. Rumbling of the engine awoke mountains and fields from their sleep; branches and leaves fluttered in the light breeze. The air was sweet, and the moon peeking out every now and then from behind the clouds was mystical.

Through the splitting headache, the memory of last night brought a smile to my lips. Hwangnyeo, feeling the mirth of the moment, sang throughout the entire ride. As we passed the cemetery, Kim Jonggu chimed in, and the couple sang an old popular song together—to entertain the ghosts, they said. The cemetery seen in their presence didn't look sinister at all. It looked like a beautiful garden filled with round, well-trimmed trees.

They dropped me off by the zelkova tree at the junction. For a long time after the dark swallowed up the couple on the cultivator again, I heard the sound of the engine and the distant echo of Hwangnyeo's song. Whether it was my ears or my heart that was doing the listening, I didn't know. Back in my room, I continued to hear Hwangnyeo humming a melody as the couple rounded the cemetery again and rode back to their house by Guisin Temple. Then the sound trailed off and I fell asleep, after tossing and turning for a while with my head buried in the uncomfortable pillow. Right before falling asleep, I managed to dredge up an old memory enshrouded in heavy fog, from the depths of my mind where it had been buried for fifteen years.

The fog was heavy that day, the heaviest since the beginning of autumn. It rushed to cover the shore densely before the boats that had gone out for night fishing returned. During my year on the island, I had seen the fog creep in stealthily and cover the village like a hood. The smell of fish became sickening then, and the pall suffocated me as if I were locked up in a giant cave. How much thicker and denser was the fog at sea! In a blink of an eye, it took away all visibility and turned the familiar route into a treacherous one. Boats could not find the dock right under their nose and went around in circles. They snagged on minor reefs and capsized.

At times like this, villagers went out to the shore. Mostly it was young men trying to guide the boats home by waving torches and making loud noises, and they gathered at the pier that day, too, following the announcement by the village elder. One group started waving torches lit up with cotton dipped in gasoline, and another group played big and small gongs as hard as they could. Family members of the fishermen were out at the pier, too, yelling out their names or making bizarre sounds that no written script could imitate. In a matter of minutes, the narrow pier became a melting furnace that seethed and frothed with excitement.

Though not nearly as loud as the gongs, voices of family members had the special power to pierce the fog and reach ships on the distant sea, they said. Fishermen who had been lost in a fog confessed that it was often the voices of their children or wives, that reached them above the din.

After dinner, I looked out onto the noisy pier from my yard. The house I was renting stood at a substantial height, and I had a panoramic view of the entire pier. I thought at first that there was a rowdy party going on at one of the villagers' houses. The fog was that sudden, and the chaos of sounds and the wild dance of torches were that similar to what one saw on a festival day. When I realized that the countless torches being waved and the desperate cries at the top of the lungs were all directed at the foggy sea, I put my jacket on and headed down to the pier. I didn't think I could be of any help, but I wanted to be there with them when the boats safely lowered their anchors.

The closer I got to the pier, the louder and more chaotic the sounds became. They were all jumbled, and I couldn't distinguish one sound from the next. The P.A. system was blasting away Jo Mimi, so that the cacophony of gongs, screams and wailings, and the unperturbed sound of a Korean pop song was so unbearable that I had to cover my ears with my hands.

Though the spring is here in my dream-filled heart, though the spring is here …

Sometimes I can still hear the heartbreaking trill of that sweet song.

That day, the pier was buzzing with extraordinary energy. The fog was heavy and because it had come on when the boats were still far out at sea, the situation was grave, which meant more lungs and more torches were required. The villagers were worried sick. They waved and screamed, but nothing could be detected on the horizons. The torches flared even stronger and gongs were pounded with a shattering force. In the midst of it all, my eyes focused on one man. He was pounding away at the gong with all his might, with greater force than all the others. He handled the instrument as if he were possessed; the veins in his face bulged. No member of his family was out there at sea, and yet he continued to pound away with every ounce of his strength, his lips pursed tight, his eyes burning feverishly as if to bore a hole through the fog. The man were none other than Kim Jonggu.

Enveloped by the chaos of noise, I stared at him, simply riveted. I had never seen such earnestness on a man's face. Lit up by the torchlight, the beads of sweat on his forehead glittered like diamonds. The controlled movement of his shoulders was exquisitely beautiful. The deep bass of his gong resonated far out to sea, I imagined it running ahead and outstripping all the other sounds people were making on the pier. He appeared to know where to direct the sound of his gong; he alone knew how to reach the boats lost at sea. It seemed to me that the ringing of the gong ripped the layer of fog and zipped through the night. The feeling was so intense that I thought I heard the fog rip like a curtain.

That night, Kim Jonggu didn't see me standing beside him. His eyes took in nothing else but the sea. The sound of his gong, which had torn the curtain of fog apart and made its way far out to sea, was still ringing out at the same volume when I returned home to sleep. There were only a few young men and family members remaining on the pier. One by one, the villagers had gone back home, unable to endure the exhaustion.

The fog was still dense and ominous, and there was no sign of boats' return. As people left the pier, they consoled themselves with the thought that fishermen must have taken shelter in some uninhabited island to wait out the storm. But Kim Jonggu did not take a step from where he was standing. I couldn't sleep for the sound of his gong that reached me in my room. At dawn, the boats returned. The torch-waving and the noise-making finally stopped. In the silence that followed, I imagined Kim Jonggu throwing the gong down and dragging his fatigued body away.

The next morning, the frightening fog of the night before was on everybody's lips, but I did not hear anyone mention Kim Jonggu. So-and-so burned his hand with the torch, so-and-so is so hoarse that she can't even breathe.... But no one, not even in passing, said anything about the sound of Kim Jonggu's gong that rang out to the very end. It was as though I were the only one who had seen him, as though the sound that had set my soul trembling were a figment of my imagination. Could it really be that no one else had heard that sound? How could they not have seen him standing as tall as a giant and pounding the gong without rest until dawn? For a long time afterwards, I could not understand the fact that the sound of the gong that had led the lost boats home had vanished with the boats' return as if it had never been. Where in the world did Kim Jonggu hide? Where in the world had they hidden him...?

Fifteen years later, he materialized before me before disappearing again, as the sound of a rumbling engine and the melody of a song drenched in sorrow and hardship lulled me to sleep. Awake now, I wondered whether last night had really taken place. Did I really see tears streaming down Kim Jonggu's face as Hwangnyeo's *danso* danced with its melody? I rolled onto my belly, not bothering to get up, and retraced the events following that scene. I could not put them in order. No longer a drop of oil in water, I started drinking with them. The pounding headache I had now clearly proved yesterday's occurrence.

There was a pharmacy across the street from the inn. Knowing from experience that there's nothing more stupid than trying to endure a headache without medicine, I got up and opened the window. The sky visible through the sagging cherry branches had a gloomy cast. Rain was on its way. A cherry blossom I plucked was heavy with moisture. I placed it on the palm of my hand.

"When you get old, you find yourself looking at the sky more," Kim Jonggu had said. "When you're young, you just look at the ground. But now, even when I look at the ground, I'm more interested in what a blade of grass, a tree, a flower might be saying. Sometimes, a flower whispering stops me in my tracks. Can you picture that? A man stumbling to avoid stepping on a blade of grass, though he's on his way to a construction site where he'll level a mountain to make a road."

I believed him. I believed that he could understand the whisperings of grass and flowers. I placed the cherry blossom on the windowsill and went to the pharmacy. I came back and started packing, but I could still hear Kim Jonggu's voice in my ear.

"I can tell what people are like by their smell. There's a world of difference between the smell of a real human being and the stench of a fake one. I can tell that right away. Don't try to step back. My nose is faster than your legs."

I settled my account at the inn and went to a nearby restaurant, hearing him rattle on.

"You make a living by selling novels? You mean there are people who still read that sort of thing? Ms. Novelist, see what you think about this. Do you know why God gave us eyes with both the colored and white parts, but made it so that you can see the world only through the colored part? Someone once told me that this is the Divine Providence telling us to see the world through darkness. Seeing the world—now, that's a job for writers like you and vagabonds like me, right? What I'm saying is that you can't sit down comfortably where you are, turn the lamp on and say that you're now going to see the world. When God designed our eyes and gave the power of vision to the colored part, he had a damn good reason."

Drops of rain finally began to fall as I waited under the zelkova tree at the intersection for a bus that would take me downtown. I looked up at the clouds moving with the wind but couldn't tell how much rain they contained. Standing under the low sky and feeling the humid wind on my cheeks, I remembered the round-eyed child who used to cling to Sukja's back. On his aunt's back, Kim Jonggu's son used to blink his clear black eyes when people cooed over him. I should have checked my curiosity to the end, but gave into curiosity at the end of the night. He gave me a blank stare, then asked, "You ... you remember him?"

I nodded.

"He lived for five years, and then God took him away. He was my first and my last. That's all. Sometimes I shudder to think that I'm going to die without leaving a child behind in this world. Yeah. It still makes me shudder. Everyone should have a child, shouldn't they? So that you can look down once in a while from heaven and tell him, what

the hell is your worry, my child? Don't worry about anything. Don't let
bastards like that bother you. Just beat the shit out of them. But God
took him away. It's a terrible, terrible thing...."
    The bus came. In the fall, buses drove slowly on national roads to
allow passengers to enjoy the ride through a tunnel of foliage. People
sauntering with their parasols open raised their hands to stop the bus
anywhere along these roads. That road was now a tunnel of green. I
heard Hwangnyeo's voice announce, "We're leaving next month." Kim
Jonggu's grumbling followed, "That goes without saying. Why waste
your breath?"
    They were going to leave after the first day of the fourth lunar month.
They didn't know where they were headed. I didn't think I would ever
see Kim Jonggu again. In time, maybe, I'll grow to doubt this memory,
too. What proof was there that this encounter with a giant had really
taken place? I was heading back to Lilliput.

The train bound for Seoul was set to depart in an hour, which meant that
I would be home before dark. I did feel a bit silly buying the ticket back
to Seoul. I had gotten up, gone immediately to the pharmacy to buy
some headache medicine, had a bite to eat, and come straight to the
station without stopping to do anything else. I could have taken a stroll
to Geumsan Temple. At the very least, I should have thought of buying
something at the souvenir shop to take back to my daughter. It didn't
matter what time I got back to Seoul as long as it was today. But I had
been too absorbed in thought to consider these things. I shook my head.
About Kim Jonggu at least, I decided to stop picking my brain.
    I was in no position to complain, since I had an assigned seat on the
train; but my seat was all the way in the back, right next to the door at
the end of the train car. It opened and shut constantly with passengers
moving about. It was an aisle seat to boot, so I had to lean to the other
side every time The Benevolence Society pushcart passed by. In the
station café, while waiting for the train to board, I had heard people
complain about their standing tickets. They had arrived at the ticket
booth a few seconds later than I did, and that had made all the difference.
Hearing them complain to the waitress that they had purposely come an
hour earlier, and couldn't believe that there were no seats left on a regular
weekday train, I couldn't help stealing a furtive glance at my own ticket

to confirm my seat. The seat number was clearly printed on my ticket. The ticket booth had drawn a merciless line between two types of passengers by the briefest of intervals, and the thought filled me with a strange sense of trepidation rather than that of luck. If chance had sent good fortune my way, then bad fortune could come bearing the same face, too. We could not choose one and we could not defend against the other. Everything was uncertain, and nothing could be guaranteed at all. I had gotten the last seat by pure luck, and I was back to square one. I realized I hadn't answered my own question yet. Then I recalled Kahlil Gibran. Not the painter and philosopher who entered eternal rest in April of 1931. The Kahlil Gibran I was thinking of was still alive, with many more days left to live.

I first met him as a student in all girls' high school. I was a member of an intramural literary club. It was composed mainly of students from schools that were considered elite, at least in my native city, and Gibran was the most elite of us all. The girls gave him that nickname because he was fond of quoting lines from *The Prophet,* but the name suited him in other ways, too. He was a genius, a talented painter, philosopher, and writer. In all honesty, he was the most remarkable of any geniuses I had ever met. His poems became a phenomenon when published in student magazines. His talent in painting had been recognized long ago. And he commanded an encyclopedic knowledge on so many subjects from his extensive readings. On top of all that, he was the top student at school in all subjects. Despite all these things, he was both earnest and humble. He excelled in all things, including personality.

It surprised no one when Gibran was admitted to the most elite university in the country to claim his place among all the other geniuses. I did not see him again in person until twenty years later, but I saw his name in the papers from time to time.

The newspapers reported how he had thrown himself into the currents of history, why his name was on a wanted list and of which unsavory student organizations he was a leader. Anyone with even a tiny bit of interest in that sordid history of the 1970s and 80s in South Korea, which was one of authoritarian regimes and their violation of passionate and spirited youths, would probably have heard his name at least once or twice. Another friend of mine who worked with Gibran in the student movement, relayed that Gibran was a genius in college, too. His ability to assess the situation was both accurate and lightning quick, and his outstanding leadership always placed him at the center of struggle. Until the end of the eighties, he was a member of a radical organization, but he himself was never criticized as a radical activist, on account of his warm humanity. All the same, he was an activist who devoted himself more radically than anyone to the struggle against oppression.

It was last winter when I saw Gibran again. I was meeting a painter on some business in his studio in Gangnam. Gibran sauntered in while I was talking with the painter about his work. I did not recognize him. And there was no reason why he would remember me as the high school girl with her hair in braids that I had once been. He didn't observe any formalities and seated himself in one corner of the studio even though the painter had not offered him a seat. He listened quietly to our conversation. I found it strange that the painter didn't pay him any attention. Both acted as though the other were invisible to him. When the uninvited guest opened his mouth, he was only to ask a bizarre question.

"Why isn't the Blue House calling me?"

The Blue House? The Blue House wasn't a word that crept into ordinary conversations too often, and I thought that the man must be talking about some other Blue House than the feared place of power. The visitor was neatly dressed, and spoke quietly and evenly. He left the studio as noiselessly as he had entered it, though the strange question still rang in the air. The painter seemed unaware of the fact that the visitor had left, and I informed him.

"A guest? Oh, him. Don't mind him. He comes around once every three or four days, hangs about for a while and then leaves. He stays only as long as he wants and won't stick around longer even if I ask him to. He won't even let me take him out and treat him to a meal. I'm used to it now, and I don't pay him much attention. It's too bad. Except for all that talk about the Blue House, his mind is still very clear. Wait a minute, you should know him. He's quite famous in your neck of the woods."

Then the painter spoke his name. The name was Gibran's. The last I had heard of him was that he was suffering from the aftereffects, after having been tortured as a political prisoner. But that was a long time

175

ago already. His name was on the list of officers for the two major activist organizations involved in the democratization movement, and I never once doubted that he pulled himself up and turned his suffering into fodder for activism. Gibran was invulnerable in my mind.

It turned out that he wasn't. After running into him at the painter's studio, I asked about anyone to anyone who would know. What I had witnessed was true. People considered him beyond recovery; it was extremely unfortunate that he went around mentioning the Blue House of all places. People could be generous and understanding about bodily illnesses but not afflictions of the mind. The spotless mind of a genius had attached itself to megalomania, they said. After diagnosing him as a megalomaniac, they closed the books on him and wanted to probe no further. They said that a mind that had lost its balance, like a paper umbrella flipped over in the windy rain, revealed the content of its subconscious. And Gibran's subconscious had the word "Blue House" written all over it. The fact that he had been thus exposed shamed him in the eyes of others, and it made them ashamed to see his shame.

But was that all there was to Gibran's question? It struck me that the question might be a metaphor or some kind of cryptic sign, a secret code that provides a referent to some other reality. For a long time after that episode in the painter's studio, I mulled over that riddle again and again without being able to solve it. The only thing I knew for sure was that it wasn't what people thought: a clue to his shameful interior. Gibran's riddle was like the names of flowers. There was no flower in the world that had a blasphemous or repugnant meaning. When one didn't know what a particular flower meant, one always made up something glorious—like love, yearning, patient waiting.

"Why isn't the Blue House calling me?"

What was hidden behind Gibran's question? Why did I think that there was something hidden behind it in the first place? Perhaps what I sought from Gibran was the wisdom of a prophet. I wanted his question to be proverb, which perplexed only because the era we were living through was so chaotic. The more perplexing it became, the more desperately I wanted to know the meaning of a flower.

The meaning of a flower. The secret of a genius's riddle. If only I could know what that was, I might be able to find a way out of this maze. A maze was a maze from the start. The difference was that I used to believe that I would find a way out. That faith, looking back upon it now, was a lifeline thrown in the writer's way. Or maybe it was more like an armchair. Ensconced in it comfortably—though I didn't think I was comfortable then—I had the fragile hope that if I wrote the night away, I would reach the exit that would bring me out of the maze one fine day. No one doubted that the day will come when people could come together, healed of their wounds, when fiction wouldn't need the illumination these scars provided. How distant it all seemed now! All I had to do then was sit in that chair. Passionate words would flow out of me, like water overflowing its vessel, and I would write, oblivious of the dawn breaking. I could hardly believe now that such a time had ever been.

The maze before me was too cunningly designed. With faithlessness that flooded in and drowned the certainty of knowledge and passion, my exit from this maze was sealed up. I stopped looking for a way out. And because I stopped looking, my writing lost its voice. Small dreams, unremarkable tears—how could they overcome this world grown so big and treacherous? When other writers first began deploring that literature as such was on the brink of being scrapped altogether, I thought they were hypochondriacs. But their hypochondria came true, and words like truth and hope became buried under a pile of dirt, and along with them, my way out of the maze. Has the magnificent devotion and sacrifice of people like Gibran been all a waste? The question bound my hands and feet with a desperate urgency. How could I trust in a world that would make Gibran go into hiding instead of welcoming him with a standing ovation? Even during those decades that had piled scars upon scars, there were breathing holes that checked our descent into beasts. What secret did Gibran cherish within him now? I needed to know.

The rain had stopped. The train was gaining speed. On the other side of the fence guarding the tracks, lilacs sprayed with rainwater bloomed like white puffy clouds. Behind the lilacs I saw the tail of the train curving along the winding tracks. I sat up straight and held on to the armrest. A young woman in a hiking gear walking past me lost her balance as the train swerved and fell onto my lap. Because I had seen the winding road and braced myself in advance, I was able to support her weight. "I'm so sorry," she said.

The voice was pretty and so was her blushing face. Women in their early twenties used to make me reminisce about my own youth. These days, the sight of them made me think about my own daughter, what she would look like when she reaches their age. Those feverish days of youth were now behind me; I accepted that I was a woman of the past. But my child was the reason why the future was still so important to me. Children were collaterals for hope. We had to stop hope from being auctioned off. Taking responsibility for our deeds in the decades that we now remembered in the past tense was the least we could do. The last novel I published was called *Hope*, and people told me that the title was too weak, too vague. I couldn't understand what they were talking about. If hope is weak, what in the world could be strong? Like rice that loses firmness even before coming to boil, truth gets dumped in the trash even before being understood.

The woman in hiking gear was now sitting diagonally from me. She was with two or three other people, and they seemed to be heading to some mountain up north, perhaps to Seorak. Fat rucksacks were on the shelves directly overhead and their hiking boots were still immaculate. Looking at them, I thought of a physician I knew who had given himself the diagnosis of mountain obsession. He was a neurologist, a novelist, and a mountain climber at the same time. All three were demanding professions, and his ability to do all three always struck me as nothing short of wondrous. It seemed that my life came up to only a third of his. Calculating life in terms of fractions was a recent habit of mine. I blamed it on the sense of anxiety that pervaded my life these days. I was only a fraction of others, the numerator of one to other people's denominators of threes and fives. Writing had been my entire life. At a time when it was fast deserting me, I would be lying if I said I wasn't anxious.

The doctor-novelist, or the novelist-doctor, who was captivated by mountains was anguished that he couldn't go to the mountains as often as he wished. That anguish manifested itself in his writing, too. For him, climbing a mountain and writing a novel were two ways of saying the same thing. After drinking all night, he would run to the mountain, not equipped with so much as a flashlight. He climbed mountains, too, reeling with fatigue after difficult surgeries. It didn't matter to him that the sun would set on the way. His knowledge of mountains was as intimate as his knowledge of capillary networks in the brain. After he moved from Bucheon to the foot of Bukhan Mountain in Seoul, I had several opportunities to go hiking with him and see firsthand how intimate his knowledge was. In the mountains, he took his time. He despised people who made a mad rush to the top, without giving warbling brooks or nameless wildflowers the chance to steal their hearts. He knew by memory whether a certain pine in the middle of the slope curved to the right or to the left. He was intent on finding out all of the mountain's secrets, it seemed to me.

Though he was a doctor, he wasn't rich. There is no law, of course, that says all doctors have to be rich; but the reality of the country was that doctors could amass a great deal of wealth if they wanted to. A poor doctor, therefore, gave the impression that he deliberately avoided becoming rich.

Mountains were always on his lips. In conversation and in writing, he described how they consoled him, how his starved spirit rushed into their embrace for answers to his questions. He struck me as a blessed individual in one regard: He knew where to go to find the answers. My answer sheet was yet to be printed.

What left the deepest impression on me, however, was not his love of the mountains, but an episode from his life as a doctor that he once related to me. He said that when he put on the scrubs and entered the surgery room, he always had a certain intuition about how the surgery will go. It was his job to do the best he could regardless, but he couldn't help putting more care into the procedures that he felt would end up a success. In such instances, he thought about the patient's life after the surgery even when sewing up the open wound and made sure to move the needle evenly so as to minimize scarring. After all that effort, he couldn't help feeling despair when he saw that patient's body in the mortuary. The pretty seams left speechless.

But what left him even more at a loss for words, he said, was a patient he thought would never recover greeting him with a bright smile a few days after the surgery. The surgery had been a mere formality for patients expected to die. How could he help being a bit less meticulous when the body he operated on was just steps from becoming a corpse? Cold sweat drenched his spine when he saw how crooked the seams were on the patient's body. How could he explain the mystery of it all? What was it trying to say to him? He confessed that he couldn't endure such days without finding solace in the mountains.

That story about the suturing seams still gave me the chills, here inside the train bound for Seoul. I didn't have any explanation. Perhaps there was none to be found. All one could do was to keep going. Persevere.

But how?

I was lost in a maze. A poet's moorhens sang morning and night only to be eaten morning and night. Kim Jonggu disappeared into the fog. Gibran turned his speech into a code. And on top of all these, the surgeon's suture seams bewildered you. How was I to navigate through all these inexplicable mysteries? Where could I start and how would I proceed? I thought of the nameless flower at Guisin Temple, buried now under a heap of sand. I wanted to make my way into the heart of that hidden flower ...

The train continued on. I had no answers; a cloud of haze still filled my brain. But I knew that when I got to Seoul, I would be sitting down in front of the machine again. Could I draw a portrait of the giant, a giant who lives in hiding somewhere among the ruins, never making his appearance before the decaying world? Or maybe I could look for the meaning of the hidden flower. If I kept at it, I might one day be able to touch the tip of the logic that guides this world. Even on that day, there were still going to be things which remained inexplicable to me. But I didn't want to think that far ahead. Surely, such thoughts could wait until after I've drawn the portrait of a giant?

Strength from Sorrow

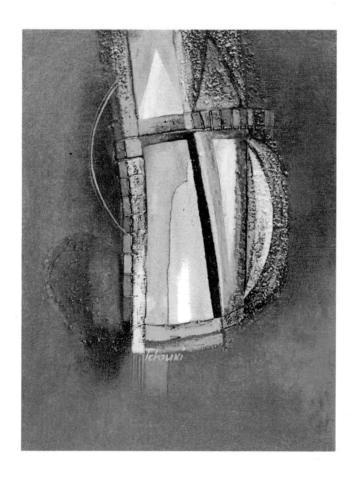

He shouldn't have tried to remove it. He knew that now. If only he had thought about it a little, he would have left it alone. But it was too late for regrets. The stain spread outward the moment it came into contact with water and now claimed almost his entire left sleeve. Han smiled bitterly.

It probably got on his shirtsleeve when he was posting signs up, in the hallway and by the entrance downstairs. Ordinarily, Han wasn't fastidious enough to be bothered by such things, but he couldn't ignore the stain today. He was wearing the newest of his few shirts, it was true, but that wasn't the reason why. Tonight's event meant the world to him.

He couldn't very well attend the official christening of their office wearing a stained shirt, he thought. A stained shirt may lead somehow to a besmirched heart. By running the cuff under the bathroom faucet, he was trying to remove that worry. The stain, however, was continuing to grow, like the worry in his heart.

Han didn't understand the strange workings of his own heart. At times it appeared to him to be made of steel, tempered by all that suffering, but then again, trivial incidents like this revealed how shriveled up it was, vulnerable to attacks of anxiety over a mere stain taken as a bad omen. It flustered him that these two sides could be so different. He didn't know which one was real.

Since I'm out here anyway, I might as well do something useful, he

183

thought. After trying what he could to minimize the damage on his shirtsleeve, Han walked out of the bathroom with a broom in his hand. Even though he wasn't able to remove the stain, he planned at least to sweep the hallway and the stairs clean. The cement floor wasn't dirty to begin with since major cleaning had been done just yesterday, but Han began sweeping the floor in brusque strokes. Holding the broom brought back memories of his childhood. On days when guests were expected, it was always his job to spray water over the yard and sweep it clean with a bamboo broom. After he was done, he tiptoed around the edges, careful not to leave his footprints on the fine lines that filled the freshly swept ground. Saddened that no lines could be made on the cement floor, Han now moved the broom all the more vigorously.

"Is there anything else that should be done?"

Mr. Lee Manho asked, when Han came back into the office while unfolding his shirtsleeves. When Han was out in the hallway, Mr. Lee had also volunteered to help. Lee stood up now to give up the sunny spot to Han. He knew better than anyone that there wasn't anything else left to do.

In the afternoon, when sunlight the size of a scarf filtered in through the west window, everyone turned their chairs around and sat with their back to the sun. Any last bit of warmth had to be maximized in their office. Besides Han, who was the chair of the chapter, there were four full-timers. At 540 square feet, the office was none too large, but it was still too big to warm with the body heat of five people. When other members dropped by after work, their loud voices and additional body heat made the space bearable; but during the day, they had to shiver in the late autumn chill. It was urgent to install heating in preparation for the approaching winter, but they couldn't even afford desks yet, much less a heater. The office had been theirs for only two weeks, and though it was shabby, it was still a real office. Before then, they had met once a week in the rehearsal space of a local theater group. Remembering that, Han felt proud of this space that they could call their own and where he could be with his colleagues all day long.

The sun on his back was comforting, like the warmth of his mother's body. Han opened the account book. As he had done many times already, he skimmed over the paltry sums entered under the columns for "Revenue" and "Expenses." The records were kept by Ms. Ju Yeonghui, who was dismissed from her post in her fifth year of teaching. Her bookkeeping was meticulous, down to the small change spent for a box of paperclips. Looking over the notebook gave him the comforting feeling that a very closely woven net was keeping all the money in place. Ms. Ju was a devout Christian and still single. In her own words, she was willing to give herself completely to the cause of true education. He didn't know where such a kind and meek woman had found the inner strength to endure the painful lay-off.

Recent entries to the "Expenses" column jumped out as his eyes scanned the page. He wasn't used to seeing such items. Boiled pork, rice cakes, rice drop biscuits ... The female teachers had ordered these items at the market yesterday afternoon for today's event. Ms. Ju, who was copying song lyrics onto white paper, now looked up at the wall clock and muttered, "I wonder why Ms. Bak isn't here yet. We have to go to the cake house."

It was nearing four, but there was still no word from the sign-maker's. Han doubted that anything would go wrong since he had told them repeatedly about the event tonight, but he still felt that it was better to make sure. If everything had gone according to the original plan, the sign would be there in the office already. In fact, a sign had been delivered yesterday morning, a standard wooden affair with letters engraved in Ming-font and filled in black. It was to be hung vertically by the entrance to the building downstairs.

After the delivery, Han had gone downstairs with a hammer to put a nail in for hanging the sign, in preparation for the event today. He took a few steps back and squinted, trying to eyeball the suitable spot. The thought of biting his lip, tensing his muscles and bringing the hammer down on the flat nailhead filled him with a sense of power. He didn't have many opportunities to do anything that required tools and made you sweat, which was all the more reason why he appreciated the virtue of manual work.

But before he got a chance to make use of the hammer, Han ran into the landlord of the building. The landlord also owned the pool hall on the third floor and was coming in to work just then. He smelled of soap and wore a brown suit immaculately ironed. The man was over fifty years old, and still a bit of a fop.

Two weeks ago when the lease for the office was signed, the landlord asked Han plenty of questions about how the office would be used. Han did not try to hide anything. He told the landlord that he used to work as a teacher at an elementary school before he was dismissed by the board of education; also that he had done administrative work for the school support committee. As befits a man of his age, the landlord appeared to be generally aware of all the goings-on in the world. Without being prompted, he voiced the opinion that he supported the Teachers' Union, in principle.[1]

Nonetheless, it appeared that hanging up the sign bearing the name of the Union at the entrance of the building was not in keeping with that principle. In a roundabout but unequivocal fashion, the landlord pointed out that the most suitable place for the sign would be on top of the office door, not by the building entrance. He gave many reasons for why he thought this was the case. It would look messy since there are many signs hoisted up at the front already. And shouldn't they leave some room for other business establishments who'll need that space more? After all, their office wasn't commercial in nature, and they didn't need to advertise themselves. But in his half-joking parting comment, the landlord betrayed the real reason why he didn't want their sign hung by the entrance. When Han turned to go back to the office and consult with his colleagues about what to do, the landlord tapped his shoulder in a gesture of amicability.

"So I guess you're going to have a grand-opening, too. Boy, I better remember not to show my face around here tomorrow. I'm not going to set foot outside my house, in fact. I can't stand any kind of trouble...."

When he relayed the landlord's words to his colleagues, Mr. Lee suggested that they consider changing their plans. On the other hand, the two female teachers, Ms. Ju and and Ms. Bak Kyuok, were strongly opposed to the idea. Ms. Ju was concerned about the money it would cost to get a new sign made, and Ms. Bak argued that it was a matter of principle.

"We have to carry this out according to the original plan. We can't compromise. If we give into his demand now, he'll keep making these demands and forcing us to compromise our principles."

In the end, they decided that he should have another talk with the

---

[1] Short for the Korean Teachers' and Educational Workers' Union.

landlord. When Han went up to the pool hall on the third floor, however, the landlord met him with a cold stare, a complete turnaround from the jocular attitude he had shown earlier. His body language was anything but amicable, and he broke the conversation time and again to berate his employee.

"Mr. Han, it's tiring for both us to have to talk again and again about this subject. Hey! Kim, what the hell do you think you're doing? Didn't I tell you to go to the bank? What a slowpoke, dammit!"

After sending the employee to the bank, the owner grabbed the telephone receiver. He was trying to let Han know that he was a busy man.

"Mr. Han, what's the big deal about where you hang the sign? Let's face it, the kind of people who visit your office will come, sign or no sign."

The landlord kept on calling their event "the grand opening," as if theirs were a commercial set-up. This hurt Han's feelings, too. He came back to the office and explained that the negotiations had broken down, and that there would be no time to argue further with the landlord about it since the sign-hanging ceremony was scheduled for the following day. He hinted at his authority as the chapter chair and brought the discussion to an end. This was how a rush order for a new sign came to be placed. The vertical sign that had been delivered couldn't be used. There was no way to make it fit anywhere around the office door. They decided to keep it for the day when they could christen it at its proper place. Mr. Lee picked up some rice paper at the local stationery and wrapped the sign with it. Watching him tie the whole thing carefully with a cord, Han couldn't shake off an uneasy feeling. He blamed himself for conceding to the landlord when it was their right as the leasee to hang their sign up by the building entrance. Maybe the landlord was just giving him a hard time. If he had insisted adamantly on his rights, the landlord might have given in. His colleagues hadn't been there to hear his conversation with the landlord, so they deferred to his decision as the chair. Han, however, was the kind of man who couldn't get used to commanding the power of having the final say.

The new sign they ordered was a small horizontal one, 40 centimeters wide and 30 centimeters long. It was to be hung right above the office door. The sign-maker had promised to have it ready by noon, no matter what. Han called them at lunch time, they said it was almost ready. Han was looking for the phone number to give them another ring when Mr. Lee said, "I'll go and see about it myself. I don't have anything to do here anyway. I'll bring it back when they finish it."

Han didn't have anything to do, either. Ms. Ju and Ms. Bak had done their best with food preparation, the announcements were already hung up at the building entrance, and the ceremony program was ready. Another Union member who was good at calligraphy had written out the important parts of the program, and the rest he had done himself. Several organizations that supported the Union, including Parents for Right Education, had already been notified about the event. He didn't know how many people would show. With the summer vacation over, the Korean Teachers' and Educational Workers' Union was fading away from people's memory, little by little. Maybe people wanted to forget. Newspapers were becoming indifferent, too. There was a rumor going around that the Union had dissolved altogether. In actuality, the Union was preparing for the long haul and making plans for a legal battle.

"I'll go with you."

Han put on the suit jacket he had taken off and set out from the office with Mr. Lee.

Out on the street, Mr. Lee looked at the gingko leaves strewn by his feet. "I guess they fell during the rain last night," he mumbled.

Mr. Lee looked forlorn. Han looked up at the gingko trees that had grown drastically thinner. Just a few short days ago, the trees were still yellow, emitting brightness against the gray sky, but the brief spell of rain the night before had delivered the blow. Mr. Lee avoided stepping on the fallen leaves. The tall colleague appeared especially haggard today; his sloping shoulders were limp under the suit.

Mr. Lee used to teach Korean at a private girls' high school known to be one of the most prestigious in the city. Upon being hired, he had to take out a loan to make the required personal contribution of five million *won* to the school, but he was fired even before he was done paying back the bank. No one in the Union believed that Mr. Lee would be able to withstand the pressure to drop out from the Union in the end. He had been recruited by Ms. Bak, who had been a couple of classes below him in college, to the National Association of Teachers which eventually became the Union. Unlike Ms. Bak, however, Mr. Lee was a timid man who cited stomach flu to absent himself from the solidarity rally held on November 20. With his affable smile and inconspicuous way of occupying a corner of the teachers' office, Mr. Lee was known an easy-going type who wouldn't hurt a fly at his school. So when, on the morning when the name of Lee Manho was discovered on the list of the Union members from Seoul and Gyeonggi areas, it was said that the assistant principal of his school double and triple checked the list to see that the names weren't mixed up somehow. Mr. Lee was the only teacher from his school on the list, which infuriated the principal and the assistant principal all the more. Through all their tactics, they had managed to get the teachers suspected of being sympathetic to the Union to withdraw their names before the list became public, never suspecting that the quiet Mr. Lee would turn out to be a member.

The tactics the school management employed to bully Mr. Lee were too various to list, but they ranged from cajolery to overt threats. The persecution was especially vicious because they were taking out their anger on him for having been "deceived" by his mild manners. Throughout the country, especially in the month of July, such maneuvers were widely successful in extorting grief-stricken statements of withdrawal from Union members. Most of the teachers who still remained in the Union were those who had resolved to face the imminent possibility of dismissal. But Mr. Lee was not one of these. He had not resolved anything at all. His belief was simply that the storm would blow over. If God did exist, Mr. Lee reasoned, he couldn't possibly let these black threats rampage throughout the world forever. After all, the world was inhabited by people. So every time the principal pressured him, Mr. Lee begged to be given two or three more days to think things over. He hoped that something good would happen in a couple of days. Surely, this purge couldn't go on for more than three days? Meanwhile the summer break had come. Two days into the break, the principal visited him at his home to give him the final ultimatum. After a lot of convincing Mr. Lee succeeded in getting the principal to give him another three days to "think about it."

When the three days were over, Mr. Lee was notified that the school no longer wished to retain his services. Still, Mr. Lee persisted in his way of thinking. In a month's time, or at most two, these shackles on education were bound to be removed, he thought. He wasn't a radical by any means, but a simple man who refused to give up his faith in the basic goodness of the world. He always deferred judging evil in people, preferring to nurse a lingering attachment to humanity. His view was that if only there were two more days, three days at most, whatever evil that was in question would not have manifested itself. This lingering attachment of Mr. Lee's was sometimes criticized by other Union members as a willful ignorance of history. To Mr. Lee, however, even history was a page of misprint. It had gotten out only because there had not been enough time to edit it.

The severest of Mr. Lee's critics was his wife. She insisted that he withdraw immediately from the Union when she saw how much he was being persecuted for not submitting his statement of withdrawal. She was so harsh that the women teachers at the chapter office tried not to telephone him at home, for fear of having to confront her. She was much mollified now, but her voice still had barbs in it. Mr. Lee once confessed that he was willing to do almost anything, so long as it took him away from home after breakfast and kept him away until dinnertime. For this reason, Han's desire to get an office space was all the more acute on Mr. Lee's account. As they entered the second semester of struggle, Union chapters here and there were opening their own offices. When the Reverend Kim Seongguk, the head of the Parents for Right Education, told Han that he would get a bank loan to help them raise the money needed for an office, Han had let Mr. Lee know first.

"You know ... I was thinking ... Ms. Bak would be much better than me at presiding over the ceremony tonight."

They were waiting for the signal to change by the crosswalk when Mr. Lee brought up Ms. Bak. Han was worried. He remembered Ms. Ju wondering about her being late. Was Ms. Bak still standing by the front gate of her school? Han looked at his watch. It was just past four.

Ms. Bak taught history at an all-boys' school until she was fired for being a Union member. Everyday, from the start of the lunch hour until the end of recess, Ms. Bak led a one-woman protest in front of the school's main gate. When she began this protest at the start of the second semester, the security guard chased her away, but she returned day after day, and the school gave up trying to chase her away. Instead, the school announced that any student seen loitering by the main gate during the lunch hour would be subject to severe sanctions. Thereafter, students and teachers left school at lunch time only through the back gate; but Ms. Bak persisted in standing by the front gate. Kicking around a ball in the schoolyard, students looked out at their old teacher standing by the iron gate. Round faces appeared on the windows on second and third floors to send her their silent encouragement.

From the time of the national solidarity rally of teachers, Ms. Bak was marked by the board of education. At the start of the school year, she found out that she wasn't assigned a homeroom, and soon after, she was let go permanently. As a history teacher, Ms. Bak was simply fantastic. The children loved her outgoing personality and her passion for teaching. They sent her letters telling her that they missed her and asked her why she wasn't coming to school anymore. It was the desire to respond to these questions faithfully, that made her decided to stand out there day after day. If she didn't show them clearly that it wasn't her choice to stop coming to school, the children were going to grow up remembering her as an irresponsible teacher. In her classes, she had always stressed the importance of responsible action in creating a just history. She couldn't let them turn her into a hypocrite, she said.

Perhaps because she was a history major, the struggle Ms. Bak waged against her school's policies was marked by singular determination and conviction. That gloomy July when disciplinary actions were being taken all across the country following the publication of the list of Union members, Ms. Bak, too, was dismissed from her post. But she didn't go out without a fight. As soon as the list was released, she circulated to other teachers copies of her statement in which she resolved not to buckle under persecution and persevere in defending the Korean Teachers' and Educational Workers' Union to the bitter end. She then went on a hunger strike, effective immediately. In front of her desk in the teachers' office, she posted a memo with the number of days she had been fasting written on it. When she went into a class to teach, the assistant principal would take the note down and hide it. Ms. Bak then took the memo with her into classroom and pinned it to her lectern while she taught. The assistant principal finally had to relent; it was infinitely better to have to see that memo in the teachers' office than have the students see it in the

classrooms. It took him an entire day to persuade her to move the piece
of paper with the words, "10th day of hunger strike, Preserve the National
Teachers' and Educational Workers' Union" from the lectern back to
her desk in the teachers' office.

The government's position was that the pressure should be applied
to the officers of the Union first. This was why Han, who was a chapter
head, became the fifth person in all of Gyeonggi Province to be placed
under disciplinary action. The fact that Ms. Bak was placed under
disciplinary action at around the same time thus spoke volumes about
the history of her struggle. Doubtless Ms. Bak's name was doubly,
triply underlined in the dossiers kept by the authorities Inside the
government's iron cabinets was probably a special file containing Ms.
Bak's name under the heading, "militant teacher of the worst type."

After the office opened, Mr. Lee and Ms. Bak devoted themselves
to various matters concerning the chapter. As a senior member of the
same club at college, Mr. Lee received deferential treatment from Ms.
Bak in general, but where Union matters were concerned, Ms. Bak was
a difficult co-worker to please. Being a good-natured sort, Mr. Lee
didn't seem to take any offense at that, and summed up his situation as
that of someone "in training." But this was precisely the point on which
Ms. Bak criticized him the most. Mr. Lee didn't harbor hostility toward
even those whom he should hate.

"Ms. Bak would refuse. And why go through all that trouble? It's
a ceremony in name, but you know it'll be more like a family gathering."
Han dismissed Mr. Lee's proposition. He knew very well what Mr. Lee
was worried about, but it was his genuine opinion that his younger
colleague was more than capable of doing the job just as he was. The
signal changed just then, putting a natural closure to the conversation.
As they crossed the street, protected by the law for the duration that the
green light lasted, Han thought about how he would love to stay within
the boundaries of the law always. He wasn't the complaining sort, and
he certainly wasn't a rebel. There was only one thing he wanted to hold
on to, in return for which he was willing to give up everything else. But
for that one thing, they had fought too long. It was a knowledge that
drained him.

The Union was a long time in the making, almost thirty years, in fact. The idea was first born in the aftermath of the April 19th Student Revolution in 1960.[2] Teachers who had seen the blood of their students pave the way for political change resolved that they could no longer do nothing. Their shame would not allow them to face their students otherwise. The Union of Teachers was founded as a result. A short year later, however, the budding sprout was brutally trampled underfoot. The persecution against the Union was so harsh and so thorough, in fact, that people were hesitant even to utter the words "union" and "teachers" in the same breath. Almost three decades later, that nightmare was being replayed. The rationale was the same as before, both for why the Union needed to exist and why it needed to be squashed. It appeared that history did not progress but simply swirled about in a stagnant pool. Whenever Han asked himself how long he had to soak his feet in this pool, he felt so suffocated that he couldn't breathe.

The new sign was ready. The sign-maker said that he was taking his time with the delivery only because he knew they wouldn't be need it until the evening. Mr. Lee blew the dust away from the grooves of the lettering, and held the sign up at an arm's length to look at it. The Korean Teachers' and Educational Workers' Union, XX Chapter, nine words in all. Looking at the consonants and vowels crowding together chummily upon the wooden plaque, Han recalled something Mr. Kim of Gwangju once said at a meeting. of researchers of Korean.

"When you look at children's compositions, you can tell just from the visual information what the content will be. In a piece full of hearsays and fancy phrases that the child doesn't even know the full meaning of, the vowels and consonants have the look of, how should I put it, discontent. They look like they are sulking. The opposite is true for those compositions that reveal children's honest feelings and real-life experiences. There's an overall harmony that gives you a nice, warm feeling. This is true whether the kids have good penmanship or not."

On the way back to the office, their walking pace was considerably

---

[2] On April 19, 1960, masses of high school and university students poured out onto the streets to agitate against the egregious manipulation of election results which gave the incumbent president Syngman Rhee another term in the office. The widescale protest succeeded in ousting the corrupt Rhee regime out of power.

faster. It happened naturally now that the sign was in their possession. When they opened the office door, the savory aroma of rice cakes enveloped them. Ms. Ju, who was putting the cakes onto aluminum foil plates, took the sign from them. Ms. Bak was back, too. She was looking downcast.

"Mr. Yu at Ms. Bak's school ..."

Ms. Ju brought up the subject cautiously. Mr. Yu was the ethics teacher at the same boys' school. He had been an active member of the Union and even served as the regional head. Indeed, he had worked harder than any other single member in order to reorganize the National Association of Teachers into the Korean Teachers' and Educational Workers' Union. But he ended up writing a statement of withdrawal from the Union. Because his wife was suffering from a kidney ailment, Mr. Yu had much on his mind besides the Union. And that afternoon, Yu had come out to the front gate at the end of the lunch hour and asked to have a talk with Ms. Bak.

"Mr. Han, you know how he's been since he dropped out. He's severed all ties, refuses to give contributions. Well, he came out and told Ms. Bak that he couldn't bear her protest any longer. He called her all kinds of names. Activist fanatic, left-leaning teacher ..." Ms. Ju continued with her explanation but Ms. Bak went on with what she was doing in silence.

"Oh no, why did he do that? He should have restrained himself. It's really not like him...."

"Mr. Lee's right about that," Ms. Bak agreed.

"That's why it breaks my heart. It was my oversight. I should have thought about Mr. Yu's position. I apologized to him. There was nothing else I could say when I realized what I must have been doing to him. I mean, I was torturing Mr. Yu for an hour everyday, when he was already so tortured about dropping out. Mr. Yu can't forgive himself for leaving the Union. That's why he's angry at me. I wish he wasn't so hard on himself. My position is that you should be able to leave the Union depending on your situation. Knowing that there are teachers who remain on the inside actually gives us the energy to go on fighting. But Mr. Yu's different. He has a very strict moral sense. It will take him a long time to come to terms with this."

Han couldn't open his mouth for the thought that he had judged

Ms. Bak too harshly before. Whenever he was distressed or in despair over their situation, it was always Ms. Bak who reminded him of his heavy burden. "You are our leader. You have to be strong." At times like that, he wanted to tell her that he had never wanted to be a leader of any kind, that being a leader actually went against his grain. All he wanted to do was to have a clean conscience as a teacher. He had devoted his life to teaching, and he wanted to do that to the best of his ability. But he couldn't do that unless the entire field changed for the better, and this was the simple reason why he had gotten involved in the Union first place.

Han was voted to the position of chapter chair around the middle of last June. He wasn't one of the central members of the organization by any means, but he was made a chair as the result of a strategic calculation. With the government's persecution becoming even harsher, the Union decided not to put the central members out in front, and Han was one of the many who formed the buffer, so to speak. Knowing that the position would only bring tears and pain, Han didn't have the heart to shuffle the thankless responsibility on to someone else. This was the main reason why he accepted the position.

The chapter was launched on June 19th, and on the following day, Han was verbally informed by the principal of his school that disciplinary action was going to be taken against him. He was released from his responsibilities as the homeroom teacher of the fourth grade's fifth class. For an entire week until his dismissal was finalized, Han defended his homeroom with the help of concerned parents. At first, it was the children who were frightened when the principal or assistant principal entered the classroom. Round, black eyes all gathered on him then, and standing at the lectern, he felt helpless, not with anger but with sorrow. Those black eyes had once been his joy. Now they were the inky darkness in which he drowned helplessly. He hadn't known until then that black was such a sad color. Thinking of leaving his students paralyzed him with grief. Tears wouldn't stop flowing from his eyes. Staying with them, however, meant submitting a statement of voluntary withdrawal from the organization without which he couldn't keep his conscience clean.

"Now, we will have a better understanding of this part after ... after doing the experiment in the lab ... next week." As he stood in front of his students, knowing that he might not be around to teach them "next week," he felt his eyes cloud over with an emotion for which he had no name. He turned around and pretended to be wiping the blackboard. Squeezing the eraser covered with chalk dust, he told himself that he simply couldn't bear this parting. As he checked their daily journals, he couldn't lift his head for the tears that fell from his eyes.

— "I glared at Geunsik and Seongho because they were horsing around during recess. I asked them how they could laugh when our teacher was in such a terrible situation. Geunsik said that a real man laughs on the outside even when he's crying inside. When I come to school in the morning and see other kids' moms at school, I feel safe. I know they won't be able to kick our teacher out since the moms are protecting him."

— "Other teachers eat lunch with other teachers, but our teacher always eats his lunch with us. Is that why he's being chased out?"

— "Another teacher is going to teach us starting tomorrow. Miok said that our teacher had to stay all day in the computer lab. He's supposed to be under disciplinary confinement. Adults say that disciplinary confinement is something you do to give people a chance to feel sorry for the bad things they've done. That's ridiculous. Our teacher would never do something bad."

Disciplinary confinement in the computer lab continued for more than ten days. The assistant principal told him to sever contact with outside persons and reflect quietly about his situation. Han went along with the arrangement only because he didn't want to be a burden to the new teacher or show his tears to the children. In the empty lab, he heard the bell announcing the periods. He looked at the lesson plan for the week, and went over what the kids were learning, subject by subject. His colleagues were being pressured by the principal and the assistant principal for having signed a petition protesting what was happening to him, and he was under the false charge of trying to use those signatures to enroll them in the Union. Parents submitted a petition to the Gyeonggi Province Board of Education and were asked to submit a more detailed statement. In the meantime, the children kept on knocking on the locked door of the computer lab.

— "Mr. Han, we bought some dumplings. Eat them before they get cold."

— "Mr. Han, please open the door. There's no one else here. We'll just sneak in quietly ..."

During the ten days of banishment in the computer lab, he never stopped seeing the statement of withdrawal flutter before his eyes, even in his dreams. Several times he actually decided to withdraw his membership. He consoled himself with the attitude of a pragmatist that unless he stayed with the kids, he couldn't teach them at all, and that this wouldn't be any good for the kids, either. But whenever he sat down to write out his statement, his head would start pounding. Then he heard a tiny, but insistent scream, *What will happen to the chapter when the chair leaves...?* He yelled out in response, "I can't help it! I'm nothing if not a teacher. I can't bear this parting from my kids. If I walk out that door, I'm not a teacher, I'm not anything...."

At family dinners, his father used to tell his wife, "Whenever you have extra money, you have to stock up on rice. Don't trust anyone. You have to feed yourself. No one else will."

His father was a northerner. He was working for the Allied Forces at the time of the January 4th Retreat, and had followed the retreating forces down south. He never managed to return to his home. In a small village near Pyeongyang, which he said he would be able to find even in the pitch dark because of a giant zelkova tree at its mouth, he had left his parents, his wife and his younger siblings behind. Until then, he had never known a hardship that couldn't be borne as a group, since all his extended family on both his father's and mother's side, and even on his wife's side, lived in or around that village. Growing up, he had never had a chance to be lonely; such was a time, in his own words, "that would never come again." He left that world behind, but it stayed as a knot in his heart. Maybe it was on account of that knot that he remained such a firm anti-communist throughout his life; but at the same time, he was unsparing in his critique of Americans. He believed that America had to take full responsibility for the division of Korea. His favorite saying, "Don't trust anyone," was the philosophy that had sustained him through the loneliness and hardships of living in a foreign city away from everything he knew and loved. And now, he was telling his daughter-in-law not to trust his own son.

"Son, let's do this. You write out that statement, and we'll go to some unknown country village and live out the rest of our lives in peace. We can hide there, and no one will bother us, okay?"

This became his mother's mantra after the incident at school. "Country village" was an alternative that the school offered to arrange for him. His wife joined forces with his mother in urging him to take this path. But there were a lot of things that they didn't know. Just because no one else knew that he had been a member of the Union didn't mean that the scars in his heart would go away.

There were a lot of colleagues who withdrew their membership and then joined again, becoming even more effective members in the process. Then there were others whose withdrawal was a part of the whole game plan, and still others who wisely overcame the sense of defeat within themselves after quitting. Teachers who didn't win that battle turned to someone like Mr. Yu. Several colleagues who had fought hard since before the Union was launched were now stuck in that trap. There was no guarantee that he would be lucky enough to avoid it. This was what Han feared the most.

Ms. Ju and Ms. Bak set up platters of rice cake and fruit in the "conference room"—a fancy name they had given to an area that was semi-partitioned off—and began tidying up around the office. By 5:20, everything was ready. Taped to the wall was a sign that read, "The Korean Teachers' and Educational Workers' Union, XX Chapter, Office-Launching Ceremony," and next to it, the order of ceremony. For first-time visitors, they put up the event announcement at the building entrance, too. Lyrics to "Let's March on Together" and "The Battle Cry of Conscientious Educators," which Ms. Ju had written out in big letters, were put up on the wall so that everyone would be able to sing together. Ms. Ju, being of a thorough and meticulous personality, was moving about ceaselessly even now, finding little things to attend to that had escaped everyone else's notice. The power of finding those little things that remained invisible to others— perhaps this was the power that sustained Ms. Ju.

Mr. Lee was busily walking in and out of the conference room, munching on a piece of rice cake. Ms. Bak poured some beverage in a paper cup for Mr. Lee to drink. Her face was still dark. The incident at the school with Mr. Yu had hurt her a great deal. The office was dim, now that the sun had gone down. The closer to winter they got, the earlier the sun set. Han turned on the fluorescent light in the room, then went out to turn on the light for the stairwell and the corridor.

Time moved ever so slowly. Or was it going by too fast? Now that everything was ready, Han didn't know how he should occupy himself in the remaining time, but the thought of guests walking in through the door made him nervous. He was afraid that he had neglected some important detail. After turning on the light in the hallway, he dallied on the landing for a long time. Remembering the stain on his shirt, he folded up his jacket sleeve and looked closely at it. The stain had set. He rolled down his jacket sleeve, hoping that the stain wouldn't be immediately visible to others.

That stain, parts of it dark, parts of it light, was just like him, Han thought. His heart was hard and concentrated at times, and terribly diluted at others. In the whirlwind of struggle, such ambivalence wasn't welcome. What the movement needed was a firm character, unshakable resolve. This realization made it difficult for him to endure the complexity of his own heart. There were many times when he wanted to transform its texture into something simpler and more intense, though he also knew that one couldn't will one's heart to change. A change of that kind, even if he did succeed, was bound to be temporary for him. Sooner or later, he would go back to his old ways.

"Mr. Han, what are you up to?"

The voice belonged to Rev. Kim. Han smiled, genuinely happy to see him. Always energetic, confident, and fearless, Rev. Kim ushered in an air of festivity into the office. Now, the Reverend was someone whose heart was steady as a rock.

"As expected, you are the first to arrive."

Han expressed his welcome by opening the office door wide.

"You can't mean that I'm here too early? I don't think you've any idea, Mr. Han, how much I've been looking forward to this day."

"What exactly have you been looking forward to?" Mr. Lee joked with the Reverend.

"Don't tell me you don't know. The party cake, of course. If you ask me, I would have to say that the "Right Education" brand is the best rice cake around. Best in *makkeoli,* too, I hope?"

Everyone laughed at Rev. Kim's wit. Han saw that even Ms. Bak was laughing, her mouth wide open.

Han first met Rev. Kim when the fledgling parents' solidarity movement was just beginning to take off. Later, he found out that Rev. Kim was the go-to guy for all manners of problems facing residents of the city. In addition to being a central member in various circles of democratization and labor activism, he ministered to congregations in evictee or factory areas; and when the movement to organize parents showed no signs of moving beyond halting discussions, he stepped in and founded Parents for Right Education. He agreed to serve as the president, but only until the organization got off the ground. As the president, he helped bring a suit, in association with the National Parents' Association, against public schools for the collection of mandatory school fees. He told Han that he got involved in Parents for Right Education without a moment's hesitation "because giving our kids the right education was a grave matter on which our nation's present and future depended." As if all this activity wasn't keeping him busy enough, he scrambled for money within his mission's organization and managed to find funds for leasing the office for their chapter. For the reverend, deciding on something automatically meant taking action.

Based not only on his long experience of working with evictees and inner city residents but also through the agony of poverty he had experienced himself since childhood, one of the Reverend's favorite sayings was that even sorrow can become strength. He didn't belong to any one church, but held the Sunday service in offices or cafés under the name of "Church of Life." Members who followed Rev. Kim were accustomed to making their offerings through an online account.

Whenever he met the Reverend, Han felt at ease. The Reverend spoke without hesitation and acted without fear, and frankly pointed out what he saw as Han's weaknesses. Though they were meant as criticism, these comments were music to Han's ears.

"Mr. Han, you're too much of a prude. The king of prudes, in fact. When will you finally become a fighter?"

No one else told him such things. The Reverend's comments made Han feel as though all of his heavy load was being taken off from his shoulders, one by one. The standard view that their struggle required them to be strong, that they could never show their weaknesses, was an onerous burden for someone like Han. He scolded himself for his hesitations. Where were these misgivings coming from when he was certain about the reality and his commitment to the cause? He didn't have any answers, but with the Reverend, he felt a sense of relief.

Shortly after the Reverend's arrival, other members of Parents for Right Education poured in. They brought their children along, so the office became rowdy in no time. Then the Union members started showing up. It was almost six o'clock. The ceremony was scheduled for six-thirty. The secretary of Parents for Right Education put something up next to the order of ceremony on the wall. Han waited for her to step away and went up to read it. "Parents! Let's step up and protect the Teachers' Union!" As his eyes followed the slogan, a little girl who had come along with her mother read it out loud in a loud voice.

— "Protect the Teachers' Union!" Rev. Kim shouted out the refrain in response to the child's reading.

Ms. Ju came up to Han and let him know that Geunsik's mother had arrived.

He saw several mothers crowding the entrance, mothers of students he used to teach, the fourth grade's fifth class. These were the faces that had given him strength to keep going when he was being heckled daily to leave the Union. Geunsik's mother put down the box of clementines she was carrying.

"Geunsik and the kids are downstairs, too. I told them I was going to you, and they got so excited."

He went downstairs with the mothers. Five or six kids who were buzzing about by the building saw him and clamored around him. There were a few faces among them that he hadn't seen at all since leaving school, and the forgotten ache in his heart revived itself. With sparkling eyes, the children looked up at his face. Memory of what they had shared rose up between them and enveloped them like a fog. He didn't have much time to stay long with these children, however. An officer from the Union headquarters and the heads of two industrial unions that he was introduced to through Rev. Kim had arrived in the meantime. They said their hellos and went up the stairs.

"Did our teacher come, too?" one of the kids asked.

By "our teacher," the child meant the new homeroom teacher, of course. What else could he call him? Still, Han couldn't help feeling the sting of the knowledge that someone else claimed that title now.

— "Your homeroom teacher is probably on duty tonight." Geunsik's mother volunteered an answer.

Han couldn't tell whether she was telling the truth or not. The children did not understand how the Union issue had divided the teachers. Opposition to or support of the Korean Teachers' and Educational Workers' Union meant absolutely nothing to them. The crux of their countless debates regarding the Union was always the children, the students, and yet, to the students they were all simply "our teachers." No one knew more about children than teachers. In most cases, teachers knew aspects of children's character unknown even to their parents. Everyone could have an opinion about educational policy, it was true. But there was no contrition or self-reflection in these generalities. Teachers, on the other hand, had to examine themselves constantly; they were there at the scene of education. Their united voice, therefore, could not but wield tremendous authority. The children were here now to see the old "our teacher," but they were still asking about the new "our teacher," too. Sooner of later, they were going to grow up and come to understand why some of their teachers were here and some were not. Han prayed, with all the sincerity he could muster from the bottom of his heart, that this battle would end before then.

Han received his first teaching appointment in March of 1980. He went to an elementary school on the western seacoast, never imagining that a career in teaching would become a bitter fight. He was young. More than that, he was naïve. He had no hesitations about standing before a class then. He believed that teaching was a simple job, and believed in his capacity to do the job well. A couple of months later, he was invited to dinner at the home of the school support committee chair, where he happened to hear the news of Gwangju. He was somewhat indifferent to the world, and in the habit of dismissing his colleague's comments that extraordinary things were happening. He didn't concern himself with the outside world. Everyday, his enjoyment at finding himself among kids grew and he was content to realize, not without some surprise, that he felt at home with them.

A national referendum was held that autumn. The principal of his school sent the teachers out to the streets to perform their "duty" of rallying support for the government. Instead of the streets, he headed to the mountains and gathered acorns. It wasn't that he had strong political views against the current regime. He simply felt that what the principal was asking him to do went against his nature. On the day of the referendum, with three hours left to go, the village elder came and took out tens of seals from his pocket in plain sight of the teachers. He cast proxy ballots into the voting box on behalf of the voters who were too busy working out in the fields or on estuary shores to bother with the referendum. The village elder's face, as he broke the law right in front of the teachers, was pure innocence itself. Even now, Han couldn't describe in words the strange feeling he had at that moment. No one berated the village elder's action, and because Han didn't say anything either, he, too, had remained a silent accomplice. At that moment, he felt completely alienated from his job as a teacher. He felt the way he once did as a child: He once walked out of the theater after watching an engrossing movie and started walking in the opposite direction from his home. Coming out of his reverie, he had been dumbstruck to find himself in a strange neighborhood.

This feeling continued after the referendum, too. He found it strange that the first duty of a teacher was not teaching of children Strange, too, was the way a teacher became labeled as incompetent if he didn't obey the orders that came down from the higher-ups. And he could never get used to the way education degenerated into a mere form, and even that form routinely violated by politics. Despite an older colleague's advice that he would get used to all this in a matter of time, Han never did. Then, after three years of such daily estrangement, Han attended a gathering of teachers who were trying to make writing a resource in helping children come to realizations about meaningful life. At that meeting, he finally realized where his sense of estrangement came from. And owing to his involvement with this group, he didn't feel estranged at all when the campaign for the democratization of education was declared in 1986. The campaign thrust new tasks upon him. As the National Teachers' Association metamorphosed into the Korean Teachers' and Educational Workers' Union, Han approached words like "struggle" and "cause" one step at a time, like a student working on a difficult homework problem Nevertheless, he had never wanted to claim this struggle as his. It was thrust upon him by others. For that reason, Han knew that he wouldn't be the one to announce the end of this struggle. It was up to those others to determine when the fight was over.

His kids and their mothers returned home without attending the ceremony. That's what Han wanted, too. There were memories he shared with his kids that he wanted them to treasure—playing hopscotch with them and shining the wooden floor of their classroom with waxed rags on hands and knees—but this wasn't one of them. Since the sounds of singing came from the inside already and other members were continuing to arrive, the mothers were preparing to go, too. It was 6:20 pm when Han came back to the office, after watching the children skip into the dark. One of the members of Parents for Right Education was teaching a song to the audience gathered there. She sang a verse, which the congregation then repeated. Rev. Kim's resounding voice rang out clearly above the rest.

"I have a lot of experience with this. Congregation members at my church sit tight-lipped through verse 1. Verse 2 has them mumbling along. During verse 3 they follow along pretty well, and by the time we reach verse 4, it all blends in. So, let's keep singing. What does it matter if we hit the wrong note now and then? This is not the 'Mrs. Best Singer' contest. Sing out loud, and it'll be just grand."

The parents cracked up at the Reverend's words. There weren't enough cushions to go around, so the chapter members were sitting cross-legged on the bare floor, singing out loud. Mr. Lee reported to Han that he had followed the Reverend's suggestion and notified the local committee heads of the two opposition parties who were eagerly declaring their support of the Union. Their eager declarations had a hollow ring and seemed mostly to be in competition with each other; but they had deferred to the Reverend's judgment on this issue. One of the politicians promised that he would attend and apologized that he might be late. The other was expected in a matter of minutes since his office was not far away from where they were. Just then, two other important guests showed up. One was Mr. Jeong of Gyeonggi Regional Chapter. Mr. Jeong was wanted by the government for his leadership role in the Union. The other was Mr. Myeong, who had led the signature-collecting campaign to demand the revocation of disciplinary action against Union members at Han's school. The trip couldn't have been easy to manage for either of them, and Han hurried to them and heartily shook their hands.

"Congratulations." Mr. Jeong tapped his shoulder, grinning from ear to ear. It certainly seemed that Mr. Jeong's experience in the "struggle" was bringing him peace of mind. Even though he was a wanted man, he had a smile to light up the entire room.

"Wow, what a showing!" Mr. Myeong looked around the office bashfully, his face flushed. Mr. Myeong's face had remained flushed, too, throughout that terrible time when the petition was being fought tooth and nail by the board of education. The order went out from the provincial level to: "Bring the signees to attention. Administer the first warning to those who do not revoke their signatures. As for those who continue to resist after the first warning, follow the abbreviated procedure and place them under immediate disciplinary action." The school head employed every trick in the book and succeeded in intimidating the signees. What they had signed wasn't even the enrollment to the Union but simply a petition denouncing the subjection of their colleagues to unfair disciplinary action; but the principal, the assistant principal and several deans worked together around the clock for three days to get all the signees to revoke their signatures. "Spring was too short in our teachers' office," Mr. Myeong told Han after the campaign had come to naught. "The teachers have gone back into their shells, and the shells are thicker than ever. Now it'll be even harder to draw them out. They are retreating, comforting themselves with the thought that they've done what they could. I don't blame them. I feel the same way they do."

At the time of his dismissal, Han was employed at a big school with fifteen homerooms per grade, and 80 teachers in all. The school was so big, even the teachers didn't know all the other teachers' faces. Han had come to the school only at the beginning of the year, and wasn't very familiar with the way things were done at the school. An atmosphere in the teachers' office was demoralized and hidebound; only after Han's transfer did the school begin to formulate some sort of response to the Union issue. The principal and the assistant principal's attempt to keep Han from attending the launching rally of the Union had the unintended effect of making Han all the more visible among the faculty. Teachers came to him with questions about the Union, and several discussion groups were held in the teachers' office after school. One female teacher took an application home one day and became a full member of the Union the following day. Other teachers who were sympathetic to the cause, though they were unable to join the Union, expressed their support and held seminars to discuss the problems inherent in the country's existing educational system. Mr. Myeong was the most prominent of this group. He did everything in his power to support the Union in short of becoming a member, and often decried his own weakness and lack of courage.

Han was dismissed in the end, but the female teacher was able to remain in school after signing a statement of withdrawal from the Union. The head of the school enlisted her mother-in-law's help in pressuring her to withdraw, and against such vicious tactics, it was too much to ask of her to hold fast to her beliefs. The Union, however, continued to recognize her status as a member, and she was continuing to attend regular meetings.

Inside the Union, there were dissenting opinions on what the status should be of those who had submitted the declaration of withdrawal. The majority of the members thought that they should be allowed the full membership anyway since the statements were written as a result of persecution and coercion. This became the official Union position; but among the younger, more radical officers of the organization who harbored singular abhorrence of the defeatist attitude, the prevailing opinion was that they shouldn't be acknowledged as members at all. Extenuating circumstances or not, they had been co-opted in the final analysis.

Han disagreed with them. It was mid-July, and schools all across the country as well as the Union itself were in a state of extreme disarray on account of the government's decree that all disciplinary actions must be administered by the fifth of August. The dismissal from school had made Han a free man of sorts, and he was actively participating in the protest. Feeling that he had nothing left to lose, Han voiced his opinion in opposition to the young teachers'. To Han's knowledge, no human being could remain unaffected by violence. It wasn't that he thought violence was justified. But if the Union rejected these members without considering the individual circumstances they were in, how could it avoid charges of being harsh and unforgiving? From a pragmatic point of view, too, the organization needed human resources to rebuild the crumbling structure. Teachers, good teachers, needed to be out there teaching kids and doing what they could to address the damage already done. An increasing number of teachers reenrolled unofficially after withdrawing from the union, and there were others who were declaring publicly that their withdrawals had been the result of coercion. Each member would have to come to terms with his decision to withdraw and rethink what kind of relationship he could now maintain with the Union. But it wasn't the Union's place to judge them.

In retrospect, Han realized that he had drawn attention to himself as a moderate during these internal discussions throughout the Union's inaugural year. Even before that, when various members in the National Teachers' Association began to argue cautiously that the organization's limitations couldn't be overcome unless it was turned into a union, Han had opposed the idea. He was one of the central committee members at the time, and his view was that such a move was premature. Under the existing laws, it was clear as day that a countless number of victims would result from unionization. As things stood, the reality was that a lot of teachers were scared off just by the name of National Teachers' Association. The situation was bound to get a lot worse if the organization became a full-fledged union. The residues of a long dictatorship couldn't be swept aside so easily. It took time to overcome people mindset nurtured by years upon years of oppression had nurtured. Han remained skeptical about whether they needed to rush headlong into an era of revolutionaries. He sincerely believed that this skepticism was not a sign of his weakness or lack of courage. If they had to depend on revolutionaries to change the world, Han's view was that it was their tears, not their slogans or belligerence, that would make this change possible. His position was criticized severely as that of an opportunist who wants to storm the fortress without blood and sacrifice.

Han had also opposed the Union's decision to make the list of its members public. He agreed that there was no other measure more effective in combating the government's attempt to use the media to present the Union as an insignificant entity consisting only of a small, radical element. At the end of countless debates, the leadership decided to release the list, despite the fact that the organization would be severely weakened through mass disciplinary actions and forced withdrawals.

Knowing how much suffering this would bring, Han couldn't agree with their decision. There wasn't any additional damage that he would personally incur, since he had already been singled out as a Union officer and released from his teaching job. But he had responsibility to the members of his local chapter. Publicizing the membership list was tantamount to delivering his members and their family into the hands of persecutors. He couldn't let his members go through what he himself had suffered.

— "I don't think that this is a problem that individual chapter chairs have to concern themselves with. We have to move together as an organization. When the other chapters' membership lists are being released, what could we hope to accomplish by holding on to our list? The decision has been reached by the leadership. We have been informed of what action to take. I don't think it's very seemly of you as the chair to wonder whether you agree with it or not."

In an articulate voice, Ms. Bak argued that Han had to put his sadness on hold. At the time, they were the only two teachers who had been relieved of their duties. Despite the pressure from the Union, Han still hesitated. He wanted to buy his members more time, even if for a day.

The ceremony began at 6:40. Mr. Lee stepped forward, and the audience hushed up in anticipation. The singing by Parents for Right Education ended, low voices of guests exchanging handshakes and greetings were silenced immediately. Mr. Lee, as he was prone to do in a moment of awkwardness or when his error was pointed out, rubbed his nose. He looked around the room, an uncomfortable smile plastered on his face. He was so tall that the audience sitting on the floor had to look way up at him. The kids quieted down, too, and with their twinkling black eyes looked up at the gawky teacher.

— "We will now begin the Office-Warming ceremony of XX Chapter of Korean Teachers' and Educational Workers' Union."

Rev. Kim started clapping loudly. Next to him sat the local committee chair of an opposition political party. The good Reverend knew all kinds of people. He would be able to gather a number of sponsors even in a city in ruins. Stealing looks at the Reverend's yellowish jacket, Han loosened the necktie that was strangling him. With so many people squeezed inside, the air was warm and damp. Together they observed a minute of silence instead of doing the citizen's pledge of allegiance. Han waited until the minute was up before opening the window behind Mr. Lee slightly. The noise of rushing cars came in but not loudly enough to interfere with the ceremony.

—"Next, Mr. Han, the chair, will deliver a brief message of welcome."

Mr. Lee gave him a meaningful look and sat back down. Tightening his necktie again, Han stepped forward. By now, he should be used to talking in front of a large gathering, but he was no orator. The first syllable out of him was always a kind of squeak, and he never could insert an appropriate metaphor or joke extempore to get the crowd going. There was no reason why things should suddenly be different today. To hide his discomfiture, he pulled on the sleeve of his shirt unconsciously. He had forgotten about the stain on his cuff.

— "... We'll work as hard as we can until the day ... we can stand before the children again and look into their sparkling black eyes. Thank you all for coming."

Coming back to his seat, he looked at his colleagues standing in the back. His eyes rested on Ms. Bak. If she had been the one giving the message, she wouldn't have said, "We'll work as hard as we can." She would probably have used something more forceful like, "struggle to our utmost," or "fight with everything we have." Han, on the other hand, still found it difficult to speak so emphatically in a public setting.

After his message, Rev. Kim's greeting followed. As the presider, Mr. Lee explained how hard the Reverend had worked to secure this office space, and that the office will be used for Parents for Right Education meetings as well. Mr. Lee was stammering. Perhaps he was aware of Ms. Bak's intense presence in the back, too. Han looked at Mr. Lee's sweat-drenched face with full empathy.

—"Without the call that came from Korean Teachers' and Educational Workers' Union, we, the parents, would still be asleep, unaware of the most serious issues regarding our children's education. We owe our deepest gratitude to these courageous teachers for sacrificing themselves and becoming little seeds, which will allow our social consciousness to grow. To the extent that our society is taking interest in education and thinking seriously about it, we cannot forget some seventeen hundred teachers who have been dismissed or imprisoned."

The Reverend's speech was eloquent and spirited, especially in comparison to Mr. Lee's timid stammering. The Reverend began explaining why parents had to start taking a stand. In a speaking style that was distinctively his, he started vituperating about the corrupt educational system which made parents cough up reluctant donations. They weren't really donations, he said, but ransoms that schools demanded while keeping their children hostage. The atmosphere became charged. Dramatic statements always grabbed people's attention. At rallies, strong, emphatic statements were necessary in order to rouse the audience.

— "Some time ago, a group of our parents went around and met with representatives of all the political parties. You know, the college students are always calling the politicians by lovely names like cockroaches and leeches; but to tell you the truth, I really didn't know why."

The Reverend was preparing his attack on the politicians. In a timely fashion, the local committee chair of another opposition party came in, apologizing for being late.

"Welcome. Your timing couldn't have been more perfect," the Reverend said smoothly and went on with his story.

— "This regime chased teachers away from classrooms and turned them into street teachers. Well, it's a good thing. We now find them wherever people are gathered, showing by example what true education is. Truth always prevails in the end. This is what I want to emphasize. It's exasperating to see how many people seem unaware of this simple fact."

Exasperation, the feeling of suffocation that makes the chest burst—Han, too, had had his fill of that. More than any other event, that sense of suffocation was connected for him to the May 14th launching rally. The rally took place in ten different locations around the country simultaneously, and in Seoul, it was held in the outdoor theater of Yonsei University. Rain came down hard from the beginning of the rally to the end. Even the sign that read "The Launching Committee of the Korean Teachers' and Educational Workers' Union, Seoul, Incheon and Gyeonggi Regions" was drenched. In addition to the rain, there were occasional thunder and lightning, as if to broadcast what was crouching in wait in the Union's future. The teachers in attendance were soaked to the bones. Sitting on the cold cement floor of the stands, Han thought he must look like a rat that had fallen into water, too. When he lifted his hand to shout out the slogan, the chill rushed in through his sleeve and down his back, causing his body to shiver.

In order to be there, he had hidden out in the school bathroom. It was possible that the cold was much worse on account of the ministry of education strongly advising non-attendance and declaring that the list of those teachers who do attend would directly lead to disciplinary action. The sky was heavy and oppressive, and the yard was soggy like a giant piece of wet cotton. Han shook uncontrollably throughout the entire process: ratifying the declaration to establish a labor union and electing the head of the preparation committee. Sitting there with his hands thrust in the pockets of his soaked jacket, he told himself that he was shaking only because he had gotten wet in the rain. But what tortured him even more was the feeling of suffocation in his heart. He craved a breath of fresh air, desperately. The suffocation he felt made him break out in a sweat, even though he was trembling wildly because of the cold.

Nevertheless, he took his hands out from the pockets. He sat up and lifted his head. He wasn't here because someone else had pushed him. He had pushed himself, and now he stood shivering in the rain. He needed to be justified before himself. Taking his fist and wiping away the drops of rain pelting his face, he opened his eyes wide. If he wanted to let a breath of cold air into that dark tunnel inside his chest, if he wanted to pierce even a small hole in his throat and stop this suffocation from claiming him entirely, he had to stand tall.

Exactly a month later, the launching of Gyeonggi regional chapter was held at a university in Suwon. Since the Union had already been launched, the government's attempt to block this meeting was fierce. Han had to sneak into the meeting place by climbing down the mountain slopes behind the university, like a member of a secret assassination squad. It rained that day, too. The ground was soaking wet. When he was walking down the mountain trail with the university students as his guide, it was already getting dark. For a month now, he had been suffering from a cold. It had seized him the night he returned from the launch rally in Yonsei University and didn't release him from its grasp. The coughing, once it came on, broke out hoarsely like water from a pump, and he was pale from lack of sleep. And now he was getting drenched all over again.

In order to prevent information from leaking out, the first meeting point was different for various teachers. Aside from the executive committee members, no one knew where the meeting was going to be held. Han was responsible for guiding the teachers waiting in various locations to the meeting place. After first gathering at 6:00, the teachers moved around from one spot to the next until after 8:00; steam rose from their wet clothes and their foreheads were beaded with sweat. Their steps were anything but light, and mud on their shoes made them that much heavier.

"The communist guerillas in Jiri Mountain must have gone through something like this. I'm sure of it...," muttered Mr. Lee, who was following him with effort.

Trying hard to keep up with the road-savvy college students in front of him, Han was also thinking of groups of communist guerillas during the Korean War, who remained constantly on the move to elude their pursuers. The novel that he had just finished reading was full of such scenes. Han had always considered himself lucky for being born after the end of the War; how was he to understand this return of guerilla tactics, the furtive march through the rain? With mixed feelings, he looked back again and again at the many colleagues who were following him, their shoulders hunched. He knew this rally was going to do a number on his cold—which had just begun to show signs of coming under control—but he didn't dislike being in this rain. The sense of suffocation that had oppressed him at the last rally had lifted considerably. Instead of suffocation, he felt a complicated tangle of emotions.

The struggle which had brought him from suffocation to a more complex set of emotions had toughened him to a degree, it was true. Laying sheets of newspaper on the ground for his colleagues to sit on, helping female colleagues remove clumps of mud from their stocking—performing these tasks, he felt as though he were on a road prepared for him, through all those obstacles that sought to thwart him from doing what he thought was right. He was walking down the wet slope of this unfamiliar mountain, in order to stand tall and shake off the habit of submission, in order to stand beside those numerous sets of twinkling black eyes that focused on him with abated breath. He reminded himself of that.

Sometimes, life required such confirmations. One chooses one's path according to a certain vision of life. Participating in the struggle for the Korean Teachers' and Educational Workers' Union, he asked himself what his vision of life was. How should his life be made complete? He knew very well that his lot in life wasn't that of a revolutionary. In the final analysis, this struggle was a battle with himself, he knew that, too. He believed that behind every battle cry, there is an inner conflict that is even more fierce. On the day that the battle is won, he wanted to declare victory over this conflict, too.

Rev. Kim's message was long but not tedious. Mr. Lee then introduced the next order of business. It was time for congratulatory messages from various guests. The order in which they would be given hadn't been decided in advance. After exchanging a few words with Rev. Kim, Mr. Lee introduced the officer from the Union headquarters first. He was a senior colleague of Han's who had gone through both a dismissal and an imprisonment. If it hadn't been for his involvement with the Union, he was sure to have been made a dean in a major school. His gaze was piercing and carried silent authority that made the audience listen tensely.

— "Look. A teacher comes back from a field trip and he's given an envelope containing money. Where did that money come from? The reference book business has become a partnership between publishing companies and school teachers. As a teacher, you can't refuse to be involved in that business, either. You have bribes to offer up to the principal and assistant principal, and how will you do that on a teacher's salary? Do you know what the "Declaration of Wrongdoing" is used for nowadays? Not for being a bad teacher, doing something wrong in the classroom, no sir! But try dragging your feet on something the government wants you to do, and they'll demand that declaration in no time.

"That was, and is, our reality. As teachers, we watched in silence as our kids were forced to stand for hours in the blazing sun to wave little flags when a high government person passes by in a fancy car. As teachers, we were not allowed to tell our kids that the goal of education is to make them into the best human being they could be and that everything else is secondary to that fundamental aim. If you said that in class, there was hell to pay afterwards. Your telephone rang off the hook with calls that demanded to know why you didn't emphasize academics enough, whether you were going to take the responsibility if the kids failed the college entrance exam. So many of our kids commit suicide every year, oppressed by the culture that wants to make bookworms of everyone; but no one cares. They look away and think that it's always someone else's kid, some delinquent from the bad part of town. If we use words like 'education for the people' or 'democratic education,' they have a fit and accuse us of being 'commies.' They collect countless educational fees, but our kids have to study where there's not enough briquettes for the stove. All we want to do is to teach our kids right, but the government says 'you're fired' or 'you're arrested' with every breath. In the process, they have turned regular folks who only knew how to be teachers into fierce fighters."

One day several years ago, when Han was a third grade teacher, he received a call from the dean of the school. The following day, the class president was scheduled to be voted. The gist of the call was to advise him that the class would become a great deal easier to manage if a certain student became the president and another the vice-president. He especially emphasized the fact that the child he recommended for president were the only son of a couple who was dedicated to making a lot of contributions to the school. He underscored the fact that this meant that even the principal would be observing this election with interest.

Han ignored the advice of the grade dean and allowed the kids to vote who they wanted for their president. The child he was told to keep in mind did become a candidate for the vice-president but did not get many votes. The dean who stopped by his homeroom expressly to find out the results of the election left in a huff. His final advice to Han was that, as a teacher, he should keep in mind what would benefit the school most. Later Han learned that the dean had been the child's second grade homeroom teacher. He had promised those wealthy parents that he would make sure that their son gets to be the president again in third grade. It was obvious to Han that an envelope containing money had exchanged hands in the process.

On the following day, however, something even more outrageous occurred. The mother of the child who had been voted president by his classmates came to see him. She said that she made a living running a fried food stall at the market and adamantly insisted that some other kid be made president. She went home after his repeated explanation that this was not something that the teacher can decide, or ought to decide, but he couldn't forget her plea.

— "I don't know what my kids are thinking becoming a president and all. It makes me want to explode. I didn't know any better when my first one became president last year, and it broke my heart to find out what I had to do as the president's mother. Now I know that a poor kid has no business becoming class president. We don't have the money for donations for school day events and field trips. If we did, why wouldn't we want our son to be the class president? We're parents, too. We want to encourage our kids to become leaders. But we simply don't have the money. My husband's even more upset. He says it'll only rob our son of his spirit...."

Next, Mr. Jeong from Gyeonggi regional chapter came forward to give his congratulatory message. He had a clean, boyish face and a compact body to go with it. Despite his appearance, however, he was one tough fighter. He was a wanted man, after all.

— "The grades on the report card are not the measure of true education. If they were, there would be no need for schools in the first place. The teacher-student relationship is a meaningful encounter between two human beings. The educational activity of teachers is a sacred work that impacts the students' future, and by extension, the entire nation's future. How can I list all the reasons why we cannot hold up a white flag before those who demand our silence, those who want us to surrender to the hypocrites that claim teaching is too noble a profession to be considered labor. The reasons why we cannot submit to the powers that be are too numerous to count. But we can proclaim one thing: It is our ardent resolve that we will no longer stand by and watch what happens to the future of our children as if it didn't concern us. It is this resolve that makes it impossible for us not to fight. And we will make no apologies for that. It is one thing that we will never be ashamed of."

He was right. The government and school management seemed to think that the relationship between teachers and students was forged only on the basis of teachers' monthly salaries, even while claiming that teachers couldn't be unionized because they were not laborers. They believed that the whole problem will go away if they replaced tens of thousands of "problem" teachers with docile ones. With such a worldview, how could they begin to understand all the memories and complex emotions that bound teachers and students together?

Thinking of his students on their last day together, Han felt his eyes grow moist. Jeongho, who was hardworking and generous of heart, even though his test grades were always at the bottom of the class, bawled the whole time. He followed Han out and clung him, crying "Don't go. Please? Please don't go." Jeongho's face was covered in tears and snot, and as Han held it close, he felt his own tears, which he had been holding back, flow freely. After calling each kid's name out loud one last time and storing their reply one by one in his heart, he came out of the classroom and walked down the empty hallway. The sound of wailing had grown louder in the classroom, and it reached out to tug at him.

— "We will never give up. The membership in the Korean Teachers' and Educational Workers' Union that they have tried so viciously to reduce will be restored by over 80% by the end of this year. Gyeonggi Region Chapter is also being restored as we speak, and our membership will be up to around that percentage as well. And new chapters are being formed. Teachers are no longer the regime's mercenaries. We will never compromise, but forge ahead toward that day when education in this country of ours will finally be autonomous and democratic. Together, we'll bring about education that is humane, education that seeks to engage in true life. Only one thing stands in our way. The government has to acknowledge this reality and reform the existing abominable laws on education. There is no other option."

Walking out through the school's front gate with the notification of discharge in his hand, Han had felt relief. Though he was overwhelmingly sad, he also felt a sense of liberation, the likes of which he had never known in the ten years since he first stood before a classroom. *I'm free now. I'm bidding goodbye to agony that sealed my mouth, and bound my arms and legs with shackles. Goodbye to the gaping hole in my heart.* The relief that his days will no longer be filled with humiliation, that he'll no longer have to shudder at his own helplessness, weakness, smallness that made him feel as though he were walking on a path leading away from despair. Nothing was resolved in his life. It was likely that even greater pain was waiting for him out there. But for the moment, he knew that the sense of relief was genuine.

Following Mr. Jeong, the committee chairs of the two political parties came forward and gave their congratulatory remarks. As is generally the case with politicians, their messages were long-winded. Mr. Lee used the opportunity to talk to him.

—"That's it for congratulatory remarks. Next is the hanging of the sign. You should get ready. This is a good showing, wouldn't you say? More than expected. I don't recognize a lot of them. Why is it so hot? Boy, emceeing is no piece of cake."

Mr. Lee unloaded all that in a short period of time and returned to his seat. Han straightened his clothes and hair to get ready. In the process, he discovered that his shirt sleeve was protruding out even more than usual. He pushed it in and wiped his sweaty forehead. Mr. Lee was right. The office was hot.

—"Thank you for all the messages of congratulation. Next, Mr. Han will come forward and hang the sign. Since space is limited, he will go out alone. Let's stay in our seats and greet him with applause when he is done."

Han put on his shoes and stood in front of the office entrance. Ms. Bak handed the sign to him and gave him a big smile. He felt relieved to see that the gloom had lifted from her face. From their seats, everyone turned around to watch him. The clock on the opposite wall read 7:50. How many hours, days, years had it taken to get to this point, to hang up this small sign, 30 centimeters long, 40 centimeters wide? The black pupils of people in the audience were all focused on him. Han wanted to savor this moment.

Carefully, he lifted the sign up. It was heavier than its weight. Han struggled to locate the nail on the wall. He groped for it several times, and finally hung up the sign with great care. The first to clap was Ms.

Bak. She was standing right by the door. The sign was hung straight, but he touched it one more time to verify that it was hanging in the right place. 7:50. The minute hand was still pointing to the same spot. It had taken less than a minute to hang up tens and thousands of hearts.

Returning to his seat, Han looked at the clock one more time. 7:51. The crowd began singing the official song of the Korean Teachers' and Educational Workers' Union. *Casting aside life of submission and storming the wall of anti-education, we stand upon the platform of silence and shout out true education....* A vein stood out on Mr. Lee's neck as he sang, standing in the front. *Gathering your tears and mine, gathering our will, we shout out the truth. Do you see the river, the river where true education's sweat and blood flow? Do you hear the shouts, the shouts that make our hearts leap...?* The vein bulged in his temple, too. At 30 centimeters long and 40 centimeters wide, the sign was small, but it was big, so big. That sign declared that they were here, together. The sign-hanging ceremony was so important because their collective will had made it possible. Out of the blue, Rev. Kim's favorite phrase came to Han's mind: Even sorrow can be strength....

When they got to the second verse of "With Shouts of True Education," the entire room was revved up with energy. *Let's march together on this road, the road where children's spirits dance. Let's march together on this road, the unified world where people live ...*

The song was over. Han noticed that something was happening to Mr. Lee. The ceremony was now done, and all Mr. Lee had to do was announce that a time of fellowship and entertainment will follow over refreshments. Without announcing the end of the program, Mr. Lee sat there clearly hesitating about something. It almost looked as though he were struggling to contain his anger. Several colleagues motioned to Mr. Lee to stand up and make the announcement. He continued to sit, however, his face growing redder by the minute.

—"Mr. Lee, the first part of today's events is over. Would you please tell the guests what's next."

Finally, Han had to step in and draw Mr. Lee's attention. Then it happened. He jumped to his feet and shouted, "It's not over!" Han turned and made eye contact with Ms. Bak. Perhaps other people would not think this behavior strange, but Ms. Bak and he could see that Mr.

Lee was not being his usual self. Ms. Bak met his eyes. She was clearly concerned.

Mr. Lee faced the audience and stammered.

"I'm sorry ... This is not a planned part of today's proceedings ... but I ... I really would like us to do this ... Please join me if you wish ... I'm sorry."

To everyone's surprise, Mr. Lee started shouting the Union's slogans.

—"To true education! To Korean Teachers' and Educational Workers' Union! To the immediate release of Yun Yeonggyu, the chair of the Central Committee! To local chapters! To combating the persecution of the Union!" Though he had always been timid about these slogans, Mr. Lee's shouts were loud and resonant now.

8:20. Mr. Lee grinned and announced the end of the ceremony. Rev. Kim got up to announce that the real event would be beginning now and warned the audience that they were going to regret it if they went home. Ms. Ju and Ms. Bak were bringing out the platters of food.

— "We have to eat something too, don't you think?"

Mr. Lee came up to him. He rubbed his nose, and elbowed Han for no reason.

— "Didn't you say it's not over yet?"

Han tried teasing him.

— "But I still ended it, no?

Mr. Lee broke into a smile. Then he rubbed his nose again.

— "Actually, when we were singing the Union song earlier ... I saw Mr. Yu."

Yu was the former Union member who had given Ms. Bak an earful earlier that day.

— "He was hiding behind the door and peeking inside. Everyone was facing me, so no one else noticed him, I think. Ms. Bak didn't see him either. Mr. Yu, his face was so drawn. I don't know ... I just wanted to shout out ... I hope I didn't ruin today's ceremony."

Han ran out of the office and hurried down the steps. Yu was gone, and he didn't recognize any familiar faces among the people who paced the night street. Still, he looked around, wanting to see that warm black light he loved so much in people's eyes, it didn't matter whose. He wanted to hear the low breathing of people returning from work, dragging their tired feet toward home. He wanted to wash his eyes with the cold wind and look up at the sky, watching loneliness spread with the growing dark.

Han stood in the dark. Street noise enveloped him all around. Amid yells and horns, in spite of sirens and harsh clicking of shoes on the pavement that surrounded him, he found himself utterly at peace.

The stories in this collection were written over the stretch of six years from 1987 to 1992.

Now that I've put it down on paper, the finality of that sentence chills my heart. Does time really go by as fast as all that? Time is a flying arrow, as the saying goes, but the mark of time on life these days seems to defy even the notion of speed itself.

When I wrote these stories, I thought I was perched on top of time, running wildly at full speed. I thought I was trying to catch what that kind of speed left behind. But now that I go over these stories again, carefully and one by one, that recent past when pain and love seemed to be of one body feels like an innocent dream to me. A dream that individuals and the collectivity dreamed together, a dream from which we have since awakened, but still a dream that we must dream again.

For this reason, every one of these stories is precious to me. Without these stories, how could I have explained those years? No critique, no punishment can be more painful than self-reproach.

It took a long time for this volume to be published. After such a long wait, it is time to set out on a new path, write a new sentence. They say that when a measuring worm recoils, it is in order to stretch out and reach a new place. Can I endure the giddy speed of time with the slow pace of a measuring worm? My hands move ever so slowly as I write this afterword.

Still, we must go. Taking a deep breath before treading the tightrope of time, let us encounter what awaits us.

—Yang Guija

Seoul, Korea
June 1993

Youngju Ryu, born in Seoul and raised in New York, now lives in Southern California where she is pursuing a doctoral degree in modern Korean literature at the University of California, Los Angeles. Her translations of fiction and poetry have appeared in *The Columbia Anthology of Modern Korean Fiction, Myths of Korea,* and *Contemporary Korean Women Poets.* She is also the translator of the critical survey, *Twentieth-Century Korean Literature.*

Yang Guiija, born in Jeonju, South Korea, in 1955, is most widely recognized as the author of *The Neighbors in Wonmi District,* a critically acclaimed collection of stories based on the author's own experience of living in the neighborhood in the outskirts of Seoul. Populated by disaffected, discontented people—a failed poet, grocers who engage in a price war, an exploited factory worker—Wonmi District is no longer a rural community bound by neighborly love and agrarian ethos, but a breeding ground for petty jealousy, hypocrisy, and vain desire. It is Yang's observant prose filled with poignant and, at times, humorous sketches of people at the margins of urban glitter and industrial boom that established her reputation. Yang Guija's fiction from the decade of the 1980s was informed by the prevailing spirit of social protest. Even though she did not adopt specific ideological positions, the belief that collective action can effect positive changes in people's lives still underpinned much of her works. As the prevailing mood of disillusionment began to supplant the earlier decade's fervor in the consumer culture of the 1990s, Yang's fiction underwent change as well. Her works written in the 1990s reflect the author's agonizing search for a new hope after the dissolution of her former ideals. The five stories contained in *Strength from Sorrow* provide glimpses of that search. "The Hidden Flower," in particular, offers a semi-autobiographical account of a writer setting out to find a way out of her confusion and cynicism. In "The Road to Cheonma Tomb," the protagonist searches for a means to come to terms with unforgotten memories of a past trauma and the sense of powerlessness that dominates her present life. Yang received the Yu Juhyeon Literature Award in 1989 and the I-Sang Literary Prize in 1992.

Printed by ANGO BOY
Phone: (+359 2) 981 06 12
e-mail:angoboy@abv.bg